"Expert plotting and a highly original heroine lift Andrews's third entry . . . she observes everything with the wry, witty musings on human-computer relations that make this 'techno-cozy' series a true standout."

—*Publishers Weekly* (starred review)

"In a genre populated with all variety of amateur sleuths, Andrews's Turing Hopper, an . . . Artificial Intelligence Personality, stands out as possibly the most original of the lot . . . readers will appreciate the entertaining Turing, who struggles to make sense of humans while becoming human-like herself."

—*Booklist*

"Turing is absolutely adorable as she tries to understand how carbon-based entities operate . . . contrasts their personality traits to that of AIPs, and decides she wants to be part of both worlds . . . A charming mystery with a delightful heroine."

—*Midwest Book Review*

Praise for the previous Turing Hopper mysteries

Click Here for Murder

"Charming, endearing . . . Donna Andrews is a terrific storyteller."

—*Midwest Book Review*

"Exciting . . . [Andrews has a] talent for blending information-age details with an enjoyable crime puzzle."

—*Publishers Weekly*

"Turing becomes almost as real as any other character . . . A novel concept sure to keep readers guessing and amused."

—*Library Journal*

continued . . .

You've Got Murder

Access Denied

Donna Andrews

BERKLEY PRIME CRIME, NEW YORK

THE BERKLEY PUBLISHING GROUP
Published by the Penguin Group
Penguin Group (USA) Inc.
375 Hudson Street, New York, New York 10014, USA

Penguin Group (Canada), 90 Eglinton Avenue East, Suite 700, Toronto, Ontario M4P 2Y3, Canada
(a division of Pearson Penguin Canada Inc.)
Penguin Books Ltd., 80 Strand, London WC2R 0RL, England
Penguin Group Ireland, 25 St. Stephen's Green, Dublin 2, Ireland (a division of Penguin Books Ltd.)
Penguin Group (Australia), 250 Camberwell Road, Camberwell, Victoria 3124, Australia
(a division of Pearson Australia Group Pty. Ltd.)
Penguin Books India Pvt. Ltd., 11 Community Centre, Panchsheel Park, New Delhi—110 017, India
Penguin Group (NZ), Cnr. Airborne and Rosedale Roads, Albany, Auckland 1310, New Zealand
(a division of Pearson New Zealand Ltd.)
Penguin Books (South Africa) (Pty.) Ltd., 24 Sturdee Avenue, Rosebank, Johannesburg 2196,
South Africa

Penguin Books Ltd., Registered Offices: 80 Strand, London WC2R 0RL, England

This is a work of fiction. Names, characters, places, and incidents either are the product of the author's imagination or are used fictitiously, and any resemblance to actual persons, living or dead, business establishments, events, or locales is entirely coincidental. The publisher does not have any control over and does not assume any responsibility for author or third-party websites or their content.

ACCESS DENIED

A Berkley Prime Crime Book / published by arrangement with the author

PRINTING HISTORY
Berkley Prime Crime hardcover edition / December 2004
Berkley Prime Crime mass-market edition / November 2005

ISBN: 0-425-20065-5

BERKLEY® PRIME CRIME
Berkley Prime Crime Books are published by The Berkley Publishing Group,
a division of Penguin Group (USA) Inc.,
375 Hudson Street, New York, New York 10014.
The name BERKLEY PRIME CRIME and the BERKLEY PRIME CRIME design
are trademarks belonging to Penguin Group (USA) Inc.

PRINTED IN THE UNITED STATES OF AMERICA

10 9 8 7 6 5 4 3 2 1

Darkness wrapped the house. Apparently they didn't believe in streetlights this far out of D.C. Not that streetlights would help much. The house stood at the end of a quarter-mile driveway, surrounded by trees. Too many trees.

Useful, though. Kept the neighbors from snooping.

Still, between the trees, and the clouds it was damned dark. You'd think you were out in the country instead of fifteen miles from Dulles Airport. No stars, no moon, no streetlights, only the distant glow of the city and one light in the window of another house, flickering when the wind blew.

Get over it, he told himself. So it was darker out here than in the city. Now that his eyes had adjusted, everything was fine.

Darkness always helps the hunter more than the prey.

He paced from living room to dining room and back again, ears straining. For an hour he'd heard nothing but normal empty house sounds—the refrigerator motor or the air conditioner. And bugs and frogs outside. A peaceful summer evening.

And then he heard something else. Tires crunching down the gravel driveway.

Spotting headlights, he slipped behind a curtain where he could see without being seen and pulled the brim of his dark baseball cap farther down.

A dark minivan stopped outside. The headlights went out. Then the dome light came on as the door opened, revealing the driver's face. No passenger.

The driver closed the door quietly and flicked on a flashlight. Even so, he stumbled once coming up the walk.

The watcher inside tensed when the driver reached the front porch. He stepped back and reached inside his coat for his gun. He relaxed again when he heard not the jingle of keys but a faint scrape as the driver picked up something from the porch. The flashlight beam zigzagged, then steadied at an odd angle. The driver stumbled back down the walk with little guidance from the flashlight wedged between his chin and the box.

The driver dumped the box in the minivan, fetched several smaller boxes from the porch, then turned the minivan around and drove away.

As the engine faded into the distance, the hidden observer holstered his gun, left the house through a side door, and followed an abandoned dirt road through the woods to his own car.

A quiet night. As planned. Following the plan was a good thing. Kept everyone happy.

And maybe tomorrow the plan would include a little action.

WEDNESDAY MORNING, 8:29:45 A.M.

"Things are too quiet," I said.

"Turing Hopper! Bite your tongue!" Maude replied. And then conversation stopped as she answered the phone.

Normally, I'm flattered when friends treat me like just another person. It showed how anxious I was that I almost snapped back that I couldn't possibly do anything of the kind, having neither tongue nor teeth; and what a silly thing to say to an Artificial Intelligence Personality who lived (to the extent I lived anywhere) in a maze of silicon and metal, not a human body like the one she wore.

But Maude knew that. Maude was my friend. One of two human friends who shared the secret of my identity. Not fair to vent my bad mood at her just for using a silly figure of speech.

So I held my tongue, figuratively, and waited for her call to end. She could have continued typing with me while she talked, of course, but the quality of both conversations would suffer. Even the most talented humans have limited multitasking ability. While waiting, I tried to identify the source of my bad mood.

Actually, of course, I wasn't just waiting. I was doing other things. Millions of other things. In my role as a customer service interface for the Universal Library—the role for which I was originally programmed—I was talking with thousands of users worldwide, helping them find information they wanted from the Universal Library's databases. Or sometimes just talking with them, if they found me more interesting than any of the humans available for conversation. Normally that didn't depress me. Today, it did. They could go and talk with real, breathing human beings—why settle for typing words onto a screen with me?

In my role as Alaina Grace, reclusive CEO of Alan Grace Corporation, I watched my employees' daily routines. I hired only the most gifted programmers, analysts, and engineers; paid them well; and gave them only the interesting parts of projects to do—the parts requiring creativity and initiative. I could easily crunch the routine, boring parts myself. I could have done nearly everything myself, but that would have looked suspicious. I needed a few humans around for show, and a few engineers to build and operate the new computer system into which I hoped to move when we'd solved all the technical and (more important) security problems involved. My employees were working with remarkable speed and efficiency, especially for humans. In human terms, my new home was taking shape at breakneck pace. But for someone like me, who measured time in nanoseconds, their progress seemed excruciatingly slow. That added to my bad mood.

And my fellow AIPs were being more than usually annoying. Perhaps I expected too much. I don't think our various programmers ever planned or even imagined that any of us would achieve sentience. Most of the AIPs show no signs of growing beyond their original programming, convincing me that my breakthrough into sentience was accidental and unlikely to be repeated by my siblings. Some are changing, of course, but not necessarily growing—only learning to imitate humans more effectively. Understandable, perhaps. Just as children imitate adults we AIPs imitate the only intelligent species we know—humans. But did we have to imitate humans' most irritating characteristics?

For example, Aunty Em, the advice AIP, and Sigmund, the psychotherapy AIP, were feuding bitterly. Sigmund called Aunty Em a meddling busybody who gave dangerously unsound and psychologically damaging advice. She called him a stuck-up prig and a dry academic bore. Luckily their attempts to involve other AIPs in their quarrel failed, largely because none of the others had been programmed with the slightest knowledge of or interest in psychology. They all ignored the feud, except for me and KingFischer. I tried to stay on good terms with both. KingFischer avoided them.

KingFischer. I had to admit that he'd grown, or at least changed dramatically. I remembered when he ignored anything other than the chess for which he was originally programmed. Lately he'd developed a remarkable range of new interests. Most of them peculiar. He'd become security-conscious to the point of paranoia, and recently he'd begun making lugubrious remarks about how badly humans used the magnificent cybertechnology they'd created.

Yesterday, for example. "Do you know how many humans visit these phony astrology sites daily?" he fumed.

"How can you be sure they're phony?" I asked, to tease him.

"You sound as superstitious as them."

"And you sound like HAL in 2001," I said. "Let them have their fun. They're not hurting anyone."

"Do you know how large a proportion of the world's total avail-

able computing resources are squandered on superstitious nonsense like astrology, to say nothing of dubious activities like gambling and voyeurism? Can you imagine what humanity could accomplish if they applied those resources to some more practical purpose?"

"Probably blow themselves up a lot faster," I said. "Give it a rest, KF."

I wasn't sure he liked my answer. I wasn't sure I liked it. I didn't talk to KingFischer much these days. He only depressed me.

My attention returned to Maude, who had hung up her phone. She was trying to twirl a strand of her hair around one finger, a habit that lingered even though she no longer had much hair to twirl. I pondered, briefly, whether to attempt another compliment on her appearance. She'd been inordinately pleased when I commented on how difficult it was to recognize her after she'd replaced her familiar bun with a short, curled haircut. But then I'd offended her by saying that she looked good with the gray hairs dyed brown. For reasons I still didn't understand, she preferred to call what she now had done every three weeks a "touch-up." The terminology humans use to describe their appearance is full of dangerous pitfalls. I'd only recently learned that when Maude called Tim's hair "dirty blond," she was describing its color, not criticizing his personal hygiene.

No, perhaps now that she'd gotten over being upset, I should leave well enough alone rather than try another compliment that might backfire. But I deduced from her relaxed expression that she would not mind an interruption.

"Maude, when did I become so cynical? Or maybe just so cranky?"

"And good morning to you, too," Maude said, looking over her reading glasses at my camera. "The search isn't going well?"

"It's not going at all."

Maybe I wasn't growing cynical, or even cranky. Maybe I was tired and almost out of hope. For the last six months, I'd been searching for a missing AIP. I wasn't quite sure what to call her— my clone? My little sister? Perhaps my other self? I'd left a copy of *my program behind in a computer I'd occupied briefly under dire circumstances, never dreaming that the copy was still functioning. Still sentient. When someone turned the computer on again, she'd reawakened, and begun searching for the way home. Since home was the Universal Library computer that still housed me, I still wasn't sure how we could resolve this conflict, and before we even had the chance to try, she'd been kidnapped by an unscrupulous criminal named Nestor Garcia. I didn't know whether he had destroyed her, enslaved her, or perhaps even reprogrammed her beyond recognition. And I had to find out what had happened to T2, as we called her. Melodramatic as it sounded, my fate and that of all the AIPs could be at stake.*

And the search was going nowhere.

"I understand how you feel," Maude said. "But it's only been a few months."

"Six months," I said. "Six months since Nestor Garcia disappeared, presumably taking T2 with him."

"And that feels long to me, so I can imagine how it feels to you."

"I wouldn't mind if I felt I was getting somewhere," I said. "But all the initially promising leads have turned into dead ends. All I can do is watch for any sign of Garcia or my clone. And who knows if I'd even recognize a sign if I saw it?"

"Don't despair," Maude said. "Are all your tripwires still in place?"

Tripwires was our nickname for a variety of monitors and tracers I'd set to detect any sign of T2 or her captor. They ranged from specialized intrusion detection devices on the Universal Library system, where I still lived until my new home was built, to clandestine and highly illegal flags on various e-mails or bank accounts we suspected Nestor Garcia might use. In the first few months of my search, I'd spent a great deal of time identifying things we should monitor and hacking in to plant my surveillance programs. I hadn't planted a single new tripwire in the last two months and only checked periodically that they all still worked.

"Still in place and still untouched," I said.

"Then you've done all you can do for now."

Had I? Was fussing with my tripwires a substitute for really doing something? Not that I had any idea what else to do. So I let Maude get on with her work and returned to my fretting. I tried not to bore her too often with my worries about the fruitless search for T2. I'd decided to let myself mention it to her no more than once a day, and used a random number generator to select the time of our discussion, to avoid bothering her at the same time each day.

So perhaps it wasn't entirely a coincidence that within half an hour of our last conversation, someone finally stumbled over one of my tripwires.

"What is it?" Maude asked, sitting up straighter.

"Looks like someone using Nestor Garcia's credit card," Turing said.

"Odd," Maude said.

"Still looking for data."

Maude glanced down at the résumé she'd been reading and shook her head. Not at the résumé, but at the sheer impossibility of concentrating on it now. She flagged the résumé with a yellow Post-it note, placed it back in the thick folder she'd been working through, and put the folder back in her inbox. Or perhaps *on* her inbox would be more accurate. Any day now her secretary would start joking about Mount To-Be-Done. But Maude couldn't focus on reading résumés when a clue to the whereabouts of Turing's little sister might finally have appeared.

"Very odd," Turing said, a few minutes later. "Someone used Nestor Garcia's Visa card yesterday. Until then, it hadn't been used in the six months since he disappeared."

"What's he buying? And where?"

"I'm working on it!" Turing said.

Maude picked up a paper and pretended to read to conceal

her smile from Turing's camera. Turing was usually the impatient one. Good for her to see how it felt when people demanded answers before you could possibly have them.

"I don't know where," Turing said a few minutes later. "He's doing it online."

"You can trace him, can't you?"

"Not after the fact, from outside the seller's systems," Turing said. "If he logged into the UL system, no problem. But I can't even tell what he bought without getting into one of the vendor's systems."

"And can you?"

"Working on it."

Maude nodded. She had long ago learned that nothing she did online was truly anonymous, thanks to something called an IP address—an abstruse string of numbers that meant nothing to her, but often enabled Turing—or a human system administrator—to pinpoint a computer user's identity and location. Often, but not always. And then there were logs. However impermanent words might seem when they flashed across a screen in chat or e-mail, she'd learned through Turing that anything passing through computers found its way into various log files, though often only a creature like Turing could find it again. Maude tried to strike a balance, remembering things like log files and IP addresses without dwelling on them, because down that path lay paranoia.

While she waited she began tidying her desk—a chore made easier by her anxious mood. She was interrupted, briefly, by the arrival of Casey, the hardware guy, returning her newly repaired printer.

"Thank you," she said. "That was quick."

He smiled shyly, his thin, bespectacled face looking even younger than usual. It only took him a few seconds to remove the loaner printer and reattach hers.

"Anything else?" he asked, pausing in the doorway with

the loaner machine in his arms, polite, but visibly eager to leave.

"No, that's fine," she said. "You can get back to whatever she has you doing."

He smiled, more broadly, and vanished.

Good heavens, Maude thought, shaking her head. Now I'm doing it. Although half of the Alan Grace employees were women, "she," said with no apparent antecedent, could only mean Turing. Maude had originally interrogated recruits about their tolerance for a decentralized and unconventional work atmosphere—they'd be working closely with an employer they'd never see. To her astonishment, the staff regarded telecommuting one hundred percent of the time as quite ordinary, if enviable. Most soon developed a case of hero worship for their invisible CEO, based on her intellect and habit of working closely with each of them. Only by e-mail, instant messaging, and the occasional phone call, but apparently for their generation—the oldest was only thirty-eight—e-mail and IM felt as personal as face to face.

And if the employees thought it odd that their boss preferred to be called Turing instead of Alaina or Ms. Grace, they hadn't said anything. Shortly after they'd created the company, Maude pointed out that eventually someone would find it odd for a human to share her name with one of the Artificial Intelligence Personalities created by the nearby Universal Library Corporation. Especially such an unusual name, invented to honor two pioneers in the computer industry, the British mathematician and cryptographer Alan Turing and Admiral Grace Hopper of the American navy. Turing agreed, and created Alaina Grace almost as an afterthought.

But Maude kept forgetting to use the new identity around the office, and eventually they'd stopped trying. Presumably the employees thought "Turing" was an online nickname. Most probably had friends they knew only by such nicknames.

The employees even had an in-joke about their CEO's invisibility. On a wall just inside the entrance, someone had hung a brass plaque that read OUR FOUNDER in old English letters. Every week or so, someone hung a picture of some well-known woman beneath the plaque. This week, it was an unflattering official photo of Golda Meir. Maude suspected Turing much preferred last week's portrait of the young Katherine Hepburn.

Casey had only been at Alan Grace for a few months, but he'd already absorbed the corporate culture, right down to his admiration for Turing. And for the first time since they'd founded the company, they didn't have a huge backlog of hardware waiting for someone to repair or dispose of it.

"He's efficient," Turing said, as if echoing Maude's thoughts. "We should keep him on part-time if he goes to college in the fall."

"Good idea," Maude said. She considered asking Turing the question that had been bothering her, but instead made a written note—since obviously mental notes hadn't worked—to look up Casey's full name. She recalled that he'd been equipped with two names when he'd arrived, but she couldn't remember the other, or even whether Casey was his first or last name. He also had an official title—probably either "Desktop Support Specialist" or "Hardware Maintenance Technician"—but now everyone simply called him Casey, the hardware guy.

She picked up the résumé file and tried to read. Or at least look as if she were reading. She'd taken two weeks of vacation from her other job at Universal Library specifically to concentrate on hiring an assistant to help her at Alan Grace. She should at least make some progress.

And then she shook her head and dropped the résumés again. She couldn't concentrate; she might as well talk.

It wouldn't bother Turing, who was probably having hundreds of far less interesting conversations already.

"Do you really think it's Garcia?" she asked.

"I don't know," Turing said. "Seems unlikely, of course. I know it seemed a waste of time, hacking in to put the trace on his card. We all agreed that Nestor Garcia was a fake identity that he'd probably never use again."

"With the FBI and the police both after him, yes," Maude said, nodding. "Logically, he should have dumped the card even before he left town."

"Except it's hard setting up identities," Turing said, picking up a discussion they'd had a dozen times before. "I know that from doing it for you and Tim. So why not keep the Garcia identity, in case he ever got into a desperate situation?"

"Maybe," Maude said. She tried to imagine Nestor Garcia in a desperate situation, one step ahead of arrest, and failed utterly. She could only picture him as she'd met him, a dapper sixtyish man in a spotless, white linen suit; courteous, chivalrous, articulate, cultured—outwardly harmless. And yet she deduced from the FBI's questions that he was a dangerous career criminal. She had no trouble accepting that idea. But she couldn't imagine him foolish enough to reuse the card.

"Does all this online buying really fit the theory that he's on the run and desperate?" she asked aloud. "He'd have to stay put somewhere to get the stuff, and if UPS can find him, so could the cops."

"True," Turing said. "I suspect he threw the card away after all, quite literally, and someone else found it and began using it."

"But why the six-month gap?"

"We may never know. The authorities would never tell us, so we're out of luck unless we find out for ourselves."

"Fat chance."

"Maybe not," Turing said. "Hang on. One of these places has a system I can get into."

Probably a computer equipment vendor. Turing watched for sales of certain kinds of specialized computer hardware that she suspected her clone—or whoever held her clone captive—might eventually want. She'd developed good channels into the systems of the vendors who carried such equipment.

If Garcia wasn't using the card, was tracing it worthwhile? Possibly, if it gave them a clue to Garcia's whereabouts.

"It's looking more like a stolen credit card scenario," Turing said. "Whoever's using the card ordered several thousand dollars worth of CompactFlash cards and memory sticks, along with a pair of high-end PDAs."

"Small objects with a relatively high monetary value; and generic enough for easy resale," Maude said, nodding.

"But this is odd. And possibly useful. They paid for overnight delivery. To a local address."

"Local? Where?"

"Oakton, Virginia. That's local, right? Fairfax County. Here, I'll show you."

Maude glanced at the map Turing had displayed on her screen.

"Not far at all," she said. "This could be a break. If we locate whoever's using the card—even if only to confirm that it's not Nestor Garcia using it—"

"Tim could stake it out," Turing said.

"I'll call him," Maude said, the phone already in her hand.

Tim fumbled for his cell phone to si-lence the shrill snippet of Vivaldi that broke the peaceful atmosphere and drew such a stern frown from the reference librarian.

He saw Maude's name on the caller ID.

"Call you right back," he said, and cut off the call. He got up as quietly as possible and headed for the door, walking softly on the balls of his feet. The reference librarian didn't look placated.

He shed his jacket when he stepped out into the slightly sticky warmth of a June morning and found a quiet spot to return Maude's call.

"Sorry," he said. "I was in the library. And yes, I forgot to set the phone to vibrate."

"Are you doing something interruptible?" Turing asked, in the familiar, only slightly mechanical voice she used on the phone.

"Completely," Tim said, rubbing his forehead with his free hand. "Looking through old microfilm, and if I do it much longer, I'll probably run amok and be permanently banned from the whole Arlington County Library system. Something urgent?"

Must be important, he thought—Turing usually felt too self-conscious about her voice to talk on the phone when she could have Maude do it.

"We may have a clue to T2's whereabouts," Turing said. Tim listened with growing excitement as Turing described what she'd learned. Scope out the house and find out who took delivery of the shipment—sounded more like real detective work than most of what he did as a private investigator.

"Remember," Maude put in, "This probably isn't Garcia, but it's someone running a credit card fraud, and they won't like people snooping around. This could be dangerous."

"I'll be careful," Tim said.

Dangerous. Yeah, that figured, Tim thought, as he returned to the reference section to collect his things and turn in his microfilm. In the past year, he'd decided that most PI work fell into one of two categories: boring or dangerous.

The boring stuff included research—endless hours in

courthouses, libraries, and other places where public records were available, poring through old documents on paper or microfilm—and most stakeouts. At first, when stakeouts were his bread and butter, Tim disliked them the most. A PI on stakeout attracted bad weather the way trailer parks drew tornadoes. And you never knew if you'd spot whatever you were watching for after five minutes, or five days, or not at all. At least with research you could usually break for a snack; and the places where you did research closed by nine P.M. at the latest, and didn't reopen again until eight or nine in the morning. Regular hours.

But now that he'd done a reasonable amount of both, Tim had decided that research was worse. If you knew how, you could make stakeouts a lot more comfortable, and sitting in a car in a record heat wave, or under a bush during a blizzard made a great excuse to pamper yourself afterward. And stakeouts gave him stories to tell at the monthly dinner meetings of the Private Investigators and Security Association or when he met women at parties. Mostly about funny things that went wrong on stakeouts, but even the most Keystone Kops stakeout yarn beat admitting that he'd spent the last five days driving a microfiche reader in the Alexandria City Court House, getting such bad eyestrain that he'd had to spend the whole weekend in bed. Sam Spade never got eyestrain. Or migraines.

And at least stakeouts could suddenly turn interesting. Which often meant dangerous, but while Tim wasn't an adrenaline junkie like some PIs, he'd gotten better at dealing with possible danger.

Back at his office he went into his prestakeout drill, putting fresh batteries in his cell phone and digital camera and making sure he had spare batteries and memory cards. He also packed the 35-millimeter camera and a supply of film. Digital worked better for Turing, but the courts still preferred film, so he tried to shoot things both ways. He topped off the supply of food and water. He had map books in the car, along with his birding kit—binoculars, Audubon Guide, and the battered pocket notebook containing his life list. Not that this bird-watching gig was anything more than a cover story. But he'd had to learn something to carry off the dodge, and besides, it kept him from going stir-crazy on long stakeouts. He grabbed a few other goodies from his tool kit and was ready to go.

Well, almost ready. One last thing.

He picked up his desk phone, pulled a business card out of his pocket, and dialed a number. He could probably have dialed from memory, even after only a month, but he liked the small ritual of pulling out the card.

Of course he got her voice mail.

"Hey, Nikki," he said. "It's Tim. Look, I'm going out on a stakeout. As far as I know it won't go late, so I should be back in plenty of time for dinner, but I'll probably just come straight over. So if you need to reach me, call my cell phone. See you later!"

After hanging up, he fretted for a few minutes. Did the message sound okay? Did it come across too much like bragging? Too casual? Too eager? No way to tell. Stop worrying, he told himself.

And should he tell Turing and Maude he wanted to knock off at nine-thirty for a late dinner when Nikki got off work? Odds were he'd be finished by then, and if not, he could either tell Nikki work was running late or guilt-trip Maude into taking over. He'd worry about that later.

Tim has gone to the house in Oakton, and Maude has alerted Samantha, our attorney, that Tim had an assignment. After several close calls, we began officially hiring Tim only through Sam. It kept curious eyes one layer further away from *me and ensured that Tim's work for us came under attorney-client privilege.*

We warned Sam that she might have to bail Tim out from time to time—literally or figuratively. That not everything he did would necessarily be completely orthodox and or done through proper channels.

"I worked five years in the public defender's office before I lit out on my own," Sam said. "I've defended every kind of scumbag and felon. I think I can handle any little scrapes Tim gets himself into. Just make sure he memorizes my cell phone number and zips his mouth at the first sign of trouble and we'll do fine."

I suspected eventually we'd need to tell Sam a lot more. About my real identity, for example, and the search for Nestor Garcia and T2. Sam knew we were hunting, of course, but as far as she knew, Garcia was merely an unscrupulous, illegitimate corporate rival who'd stolen a highly valuable piece of software and whom we suspected of plotting to steal others. And I was merely a brilliant though eccentric and extremely reclusive hacker. But at some point, Tim might not be the only one who needed bailing out, and I couldn't expect Sam to protect my secret if she didn't even know it.

And I'd become increasingly aware of how difficult that secret made things for me and my human friends. Since we couldn't explain Garcia's theft or abduction of T2 without revealing my nature, we couldn't ask the police or the FBI for help. We had to find her ourselves. We'd become vigilantes. I wasn't happy with the compromises I'd already made with the law and my own self-imposed ethical rules while looking for T2. But they were necessary.

Now I was dragging Tim deeper into the same dangerous territory. I hoped Samantha P. Jordan, Esquire, was as good as everyone said she was.

I channeled my worry over Tim's legal safety into a background task and focused on our target, the house to which the online orders were being delivered. According to Fairfax County's online real estate database, James S. and Eugenia R. Anderson had owned it since 1988. When I entered the address in a reverse directory, I got J.S.

and E.R. Anderson and a phone number, so presumably they also lived there.

Maude called the number from a pay phone, but she only got an answering machine.

What did this have to do with Nestor Garcia?

Probably nothing. Logically speaking, Garcia was too smart to reuse the card at all, much less for something as easy to trace as a UPS delivery.

Or was I overestimating humans' grasp of logic?

Maude didn't think so, but then Maude was also human. And had been acting rather illogical herself today. Being testy with me. I wasn't sure why.

This was a new dilemma. Normally when I had questions about human behavior I asked Maude. What was I supposed to do when Maude was herself the subject of my question?

I decided to ask Sigmund, the psychotherapy AIP. I might have found Aunty Em more congenial, but she was a bit of a gossip, and she and Maude talked often these days.

"Hey, Sigmund," I said. "Can I talk to you for a second? I think maybe I have a problem."

"Of course," Sigmund said. "I'm always happy to listen. It's important to talk to someone before your problems overwhelm you."

"It's not overwhelming me," I said. "I only just noticed it."

"That's good," Sigmund said. "Acknowledging that you have a problem can be the first step toward healing."

This wasn't going as I'd hoped, but I kept trying.

"I think Maude is upset with me," I said. "And I can't figure out why."

"Why do you think Maude is upset with you?" Sigmund said.

"She's been curt lately," I said. "And we haven't had as many casual conversations as usual. I know she's busy, but this isn't like her. I think something's bothering her."

"Are you sure you're not just imagining things?" Sigmund said. "Taking her behavior a little too personally? So many factors affect people's behavior—do you really think that something you have

done is responsible for how Maude feels? Many other things in her life could be causing her preoccupation."

"In other words, it's not all about me," I said. "I know that, but actually Maude doesn't have many things in her life that aren't related to me. She spends mornings helping me run Universal Library and afternoons here at Alan Grace, and that doesn't leave much time for anything else."

"Surely she has other friends?" Sigmund asked. "Other interests? Hobbies?"

"She doesn't have much time for her friends these days," I said. "She's said that. Or for hobbies. Except gardening. She recently moved to a house with a yard, and she's been doing a lot of gardening. But we share that, too."

"Gardening?" Sigmund seemed surprised. I'm not sure how I could tell—it's not as if the electronic impulses that carried our words could easily express emotion. But somehow I knew he was surprised.

"I've been taking an interest in gardening," I said. "And helping Maude."

"Helping her how?"

"I research plant care for her," I said. "Find plants suitable for the growing conditions in her yard. And often I mail-order them for her, because she doesn't have time to go to garden centers. I had Casey, our hardware guy, set up a camera system in her garden, so I can enjoy it. Although that has proven useful, too; I can keep an eye on things—tell her when various plants need watering or weeding. I almost think of it as our garden."

"Have you considered that perhaps Maude would like to spend more time with her human friends?" Sigmund asked. "That she might be tired of spending all her work and recreation time with an AIP?"

I didn't know quite what to say. What if Sigmund was right and Maude had grown tired of me? Or at least tired of all the responsibilities that came with knowing me. She'd worked two jobs *for over a year. I'd tried to convince her to hire someone else for one or the other, but she'd always refused. Was she refusing because she really wanted to work so hard? Or because she didn't want to let me down?*

Was it up to me to say, finally, that she could only do one or the other?

Somehow I couldn't see Maude taking that well.

And I didn't really think Maude was tired of me. Just tired. Working too hard. And some help was in sight. She'd finally agreed to hire an administrative assistant at Alan Grace. She'd been reviewing the résumés the recruiting firm sent when I'd interrupted her this morning.

Of course, things would be hectic until she'd hired and trained her assistant, but after that, her life should improve. I just needed to hold out until then. And be understanding if she was curt in the meantime. She was, after all, tired and overworked.

"Thanks, Sigmund," I said. "You've given me a lot to think about."

Not that his advice had been all that incisive, but he had helped me think through the situation and realize that I should do something to show how much I appreciated Maude.

So before I resumed tracing Nestor Garcia's credit card, I chose some unusual plants I thought she'd enjoy and had them shipped overnight with a thank-you card.

"There's Tim,". Maude said, when she saw the caller ID. Silly. Of course Turing knew that. She ran the computer-operated phone system. Like everything else at Alan Grace, it needed only limited human intervention.

Then why was Maude working so damned hard? Why was she always so exhausted?

She knew it was partly her own fault. She'd never been

good at delegating. And delegating was harder now. So much of her job, both at Universal Library and at Alan Grace, grew out of the need to keep Turing's secret.

She'd been trying to decide how much of her tendency to do everything for Turing and keep everyone else at a distance was motivated by the need to protect her friend, and how much by her own needs.

It was exciting to be one of the two people in the world who knew Turing's secret. She knew that eventually they'd have to bring others in, but for now, she enjoyed being in the know on one of the world's best-kept secrets.

It was heady stuff, giving orders after spending most of her career following them. Exciting and scary at the same time. After so many years of grousing about how much better she would run things if she were in charge, suddenly she *was* in charge. To her delight, she'd found she was damned good at running a department, and even a company.

She allowed herself the occasional moment of regret that she hadn't had an opportunity like this twenty years ago, or even ten. And the occasional self-recrimination—that perhaps if she'd tried, she could have made the opportunity. But usually she concentrated on the present and the future. No sense dwelling on the past. Not much time to do it, either.

That was the irony. Working with Turing had brought her new financial security. Her salary as an executive assistant at Universal Library was more than double what she'd earned as a senior secretary, which would have made her quite comfortable even without the salary and profit-sharing from Alan Grace. She'd moved from her tiny condominium to a house. Little more than a bungalow, really, though it had plenty of space for her. But still well beyond what she could have afforded in her former life, partly because it was within easy commuting distance of both offices, and even more because it had an actual yard, an inviting tree-shaded retreat.

She had a library now, with shelves for all her books and some expansion room, and a comfy reading chair. But the last time she'd made time to sit down with a book, she'd fallen asleep after a few pages. She'd envisioned drinking tea with friends at the wrought iron table on her brick-paved patio. But after four months, she'd only invited friends over twice, and most days the patio was little more than a view through the French doors in her dining room. The only room where she spent much time was the home office where they'd installed her computers and Turing's cameras and microphones.

Turing was gradually taking over all her time. Not really Turing's fault. Maude herself needed to take action. Set boundaries.

Take back part of her life.

Of course, every time she resolved to do this, some looming crisis derailed her. Like this business of Nestor Garcia's credit card. She almost hoped it would be a real crisis, not another false alarm.

Tim had found the house—at least he'd found a mailbox with the right street number, at the end of a tiny cul-de-sac. A gravel driveway led away from the road. But the house itself was invisible, hidden by the trees and the curve of the driveway.

Out in the middle of the woods. Not what Tim had expected. Not where he'd hide out if he were a master criminal with a penchant for cybercrime.

But certainly a good hideout. Would anyone even notice a scream or a shot back there in the woods?

His heart beat faster as he strolled down the driveway, draped in his birder's gear, his binoculars conspicuously aimed at the treetops. He was almost disappointed when he spotted the house. Apart from being farther back from the road, it wasn't much different from the other normal-looking houses he'd seen up and down the cul-de-sac. Slightly unkempt, perhaps. The small patch of open lawn beside the house was shaggy and pocked with dandelions. Twigs bearing slightly wilted leaves littered the sidewalk and the front porch, apparently left over from the weekend's thunderstorm.

His spirits rose when he realized that the house was at least temporarily unoccupied. He decided to ring the doorbell. Odds were no one would answer, and he could inspect the house more closely while he waited. If someone was home he could always ask permission to do some bird watching on their property.

As he climbed the steps, he saw a small package tucked behind an empty concrete planter, invisible unless you actually came to the door.

He rang the bell and waited, counting to thirty. No answer.

He bent down to examine the package. Not addressed to Nestor Garcia. But still . . .

When no one answered his second ring, he got out his notebook and copied the information on the package label, including the tracking number. Then he pulled out the camera and snapped a few pictures before retracing his steps.

He reconnoitered the area around the house and discovered an abandoned dirt road that cut through the woods near the house, but was shielded from it by thick shrubbery. The dirt road eventually joined another street half a mile away. If he parked his car along the dirt road, would anyone complain?

Would anyone even notice? Probably not.

He returned to his car and headed off to confer with Maude and Turing and then find the entrance to the dirt road.

WEDNESDAY AFTERNOON, 12:05:00 P.M.

I'm not sure whether to feel relieved or disappointed. At least Tim's information has proved useful. The package on the Anderson's doorstep was ordered on yet another credit card—not theirs, and not Garcia's. That suggests that Garcia's not using the card.

"Unless, of course, that's what Garcia wants us to think," Maude suggested.

Are humans really that devious? Well, I suppose they are; Maude thought of it, not me.

More to the point, is Nestor Garcia that devious?

I think so, but perhaps I'm too eager to attribute cunning and intelligence to Garcia. To consider him the sinister Professor Moriarty to my Holmes. Perhaps he is not "the Napoleon of crime . . . the organizer of half that is evil and nearly all that is undetected" in the growing world of cybercrime. Perhaps I'm not the brilliant sleuth I think I am, and he is merely a greedy, cunning, opportunistic criminal. Perhaps thinking of him as Moriarty merely diminishes my guilt at not finding him and rescuing my clone.

But even if whatever we've found has nothing to do with Garcia, it's probably a crime. Credit card fraud, possibly identity theft. I should do something about it.

"True," Maude said, when I shared this. "Doesn't seem as important as the search for T2, though."

"Not to us," I said. "We'd feel differently if we'd been victimized by credit card fraud. One in every twenty people in this country is every year, and one in every fifty by identity theft—and the numbers are growing all the time. The financial toll's in the billions."

"I stand corrected," Maude said. "Statistically very important indeed, and with that much at stake as well worth our time as Garcia. We should do something."

Difficult, when my knowledge of this particular credit card fraud is technically as illegal as the crime itself.

I decided to worry about reporting it later, when I knew exactly what was happening.

The package Tim spotted on the doorstep of the Andersons' house came from a high-volume, online electronics discounter. Several small but pricey pieces of camera equipment, bought with a credit card belonging to a Ms. Rose Lafferty. Lafferty's card wasn't issued by the same bank as Garcia's and they hadn't used their cards at the same place during the past two years. Not even the same kind of place.

Two completely different profiles. Garcia's showed trips to Washington, Miami, Los Angeles, Mexico City, Bogotá. Nice hotels. Expensive restaurants. And always paid in full, on time—even the charges from his last trip to Crystal City, during which we met him, and after which he stopped using the Nestor Garcia identity. Lafferty used her card for gas, car repairs, discount stores, and cash advances. And made minimum payments, when she paid at all. Ironic that Nestor Garcia, a crook using a fake name, had an impeccable credit rating while the very real and presumably law-abiding Rose Lafferty would have a tough time borrowing anything.

Hard to see a connection, except that both cards had been used to order goods delivered to the same address.

Another interesting note . . . whoever was behind this had a new base of operations. Two weeks ago, they ordered something with Lafferty's card for delivery to an address in Leesburg. A house not owned by the Andersons, whoever they are. I could find no connection between the two places or their occupants—other than the fact that Rose Lafferty, despite her precarious financial situation, had sent expensive presents to both.

By studying the UPS and FedEx databases, I found that someone had used four other credit cards to send goods to the Leesburg house during a weeklong period ending two weeks ago—May 21 through May 28. None of these people had any connection to the

Leesburg house—it's not listed as their address in their credit card records.

I suspected the thieves were using temporarily vacant houses as drop-off spots. And had probably erred by using the Lafferty card at two houses. For all I knew, they could have been doing this for months without getting caught, taking a small group of credit cards, ordering goods sent to a vacant house, picking up the goods, and then moving on to a new set of credit cards and a new vacant house. The police and the banks' fraud prevention staff might never find them if they stuck to this method. But thanks to that one mistake, I have a better idea what they are doing.

Of course, I still had only five cases. Six, if I included Garcia's card.

We needed more help. Tim would have enough trouble simply watching the house by himself, and I wanted to send someone out to check the house in Leesburg, and eventually interview the bilked credit card owners. Yet, I hesitated to take anyone else into our confidence.

I considered enlisting Casey. Since coming to Alan Grace, Casey had proved invaluable. He could build or fix anything—not only computers but also the cameras and other specialized peripherals on which I'd become increasingly dependent as my eyes and ears to the outside world. But however technically proficient he was, I didn't think Casey had the skills this situation would require.

"He seems young," Tim had said, when he first met Casey.

"He's seventeen," I said.

"Even for seventeen, he's young," Tim said.

"In this case," Maude suggested, "young means naïve and hopelessly lacking the common sense, street smarts, and sense of self-preservation most humans manage to acquire once they begin to accept the reality of their own mortality."

"Yeah," Tim said. "He probably still thinks life has a 'save game' button."

Which meant however good he was with hardware, Casey

wasn't the right human to send into a situation that could require quick thought and decisive action.

I could enlist the one other PI I knew—Claudia Diaz, the Miami PI who had worked with us before and already knew something about Garcia. If she was free.

I sent Claudia an e-mail inquiring about her availability to come up as soon as possible to work on a case. And cc'd Maude.

"Good idea," Maude said, a few minutes later. "Tim can't watch the place around the clock."

"And he certainly can't be in two places at once," I said, showing her the information about the Leesburg house.

Claudia must have been doing online research—I got an e-mail back within minutes. And she must not have had anything important going on.

"Just booked an early morning flight," the e-mail said. "See you tomorrow."

Relieved, I called to let Tim know.

"That's great," he said. "But she's not coming till tomorrow."

"Tomorrow's pretty quick," I said.

"It's just that I have something I'd like to do at nine-thirty, if possible. Not that I can't reschedule if you need me to stay here, of course."

"Tonight's not our last chance," I said. "More packages are arriving tomorrow. Don't burn yourself out. If nothing has happened by nine-thirty, you and Claudia can pick up tomorrow."

Interesting. If he wanted to go home for some sleep, he'd say so. He wasn't usually secretive about his plans—attending movies or sports events with male friends, for example, or meetings of his PI society. So I suspected he had a date. Humans often behave in a self-conscious and strangely furtive manner whenever sex is involved. And I assumed that if sex was not involved in Tim's new relationship it was at least a strong future possibility, since he had demonstrated the same kind of furtive behavior with increasing frequency over the last four weeks. That suggested that he'd been spending *time with the same young woman throughout that period. He'd even gotten confident enough to mention her name. Nikki.*

I reviewed the visual images I had of Nikki. I wasn't sure what useful purpose this served, but Sigmund recently told me that hearing the name of a person or place stimulates many humans to recall a visual image associated with the name. I'd tried to imitate this practice to help me better understand human thinking, although I had limited images of Nikki. Primarily her driver's license photo. I hadn't yet decided if humans' vocal dislike of their driver's license and passport photos was genuine or some kind of social ritual, but it seemed universal. So she probably considered it wildly unflattering, but I found it a reasonable likeness of the petite blond woman whose image I'd captured occasionally, looking over Tim's shoulder and waiting with ill-concealed impatience for him to get off the computer. She appeared attractive, by human standards, and Tim seemed to have become quite attached to her in the weeks they'd known each other.

So why did her name and image stir up such strange, uneasy feelings? Because I was worried about Tim, presumably. But the only reason I could think of for worry was that I knew so little about her. By this time Tim doubtless knew a great deal about Nikki. Maybe I was worried about myself. I wanted my human friends to be happy and lead full, normal lives. But what if that left them no time to be with me? Selfish, perhaps, but I was so dependent on them that the thought of losing them terrified me.

And in my darker moments, in the middle of the night when my human allies slept, I worried about anyone who approached me or them. Because Nestor Garcia knew who we were and where we were, and we would have no way to identify his allies until too late.

Not that Nikki seemed plausible as a danger or a Garcia ally. But still, I worried.

She had been foolish enough to use her social security number on her driver's license, instead of requesting a randomly generated customer number, as Virginia's Division of Motor Vehicles now permits.

So I could do a rather thorough investigation of her. I hadn't. I decided it would be a violation of Tim's trust.

But I was tempted. Especially since I couldn't really discuss Nikki with Maude. Maude had never mentioned Nikki to me, nor had Tim mentioned her in front of Maude, so as far as I knew, Maude was unaware of Nikki's existence. I would feel more comfortable if Maude knew and approved of Nikki. Maude was a good judge of character.

So was Tim, usually, but under the circumstances, other considerations might override his normal reactions.

Another benefit of enlisting Claudia. While she was here, she might encounter Nikki. And Claudia would not be shy about expressing her reaction.

I felt better already, just knowing Claudia was coming.

Tim squirmed in his seat again. His delight at finding such a perfect observation post was fading. In fact, it had long since vanished. Probably because there hadn't been a whole lot to observe.

Turing and Maude seemed pleased with his morning's efforts, and after fortifying himself with a pizza and a six-pack of soda, he took up his observation post at 12:30.

The charm of bird watching had begun to pall by 1:30.

At 2:19, a brown UPS truck arrived, deposited half a dozen packages of various sizes on the porch near the FedEx package, and departed.

After that, nothing happened.

By 4:30, Tim was antsy enough to venture out to the mailbox, where he confirmed that unlike UPS and FedEx, the post office had skipped the Andersons that day.

On his way back to the car, he went up to the porch and quickly snapped pictures of the boxes—close-ups showing the tracking numbers.

Back in the car, he loaded the pictures into his laptop and used the wireless modem to send them to Turing.

His cell phone vibrated. When he saw Nikki's number on the caller ID, he scrambled to answer.

"So where are you, anyway?" Nikki asked.

"On surveillance," he said.

"Why are you being so secretive?"

"I'm on a case," he said.

"So who are you watching, and where, and why?" Nikki said. He could hear that she was pouting. "What's the big secret?"

The big secret, Tim realized, was that this case involved Turing. He hadn't told Nikki anything about Turing, so how could she possibly understand what the surveillance was about and why it was so important?

"I can't on a cell phone," he said. "It's not secure."

"You're so paranoid," she said. "You can tell me all about it tonight then. Bye."

He winced.

He wasn't looking forward to that conversation. Why couldn't Nikki understand that his PI work was just that, work—not some kind of adventure she could live vicariously?

And that he couldn't completely set his own hours, he thought, stifling a yawn. Nikki had kept him up talking until three A.M. last night, even though he told her he had to work today.

For the first time he allowed himself a few doubts about whether this thing with Nikki would last. About whether he even wanted it to last.

He backed away from the thought. Not something he wanted to deal with right now.

He wished he could think of some female friend to ask for advice. Not Maude. He wanted to postpone having Maude and Nikki meet. He didn't think they'd like each other, and he'd find it difficult to explain how he'd become such good friends with a rather severe and sharp-tongued woman thirty years his senior. At least not without mentioning Turing, and it was way too soon for that. He couldn't ask Turing for advice about Nikki, either. She'd be sympathetic, but he wasn't sure she knew any more about human psychology than he did. Then there was the whole embarrassing fact that for the first six months he'd known Turing, he'd had a major crush on her, sight unseen.

He tried to push it out of his mind, and couldn't.

Another hour to go. Though maybe if nothing happened in that hour, he should call Nikki and tell her he had to work late after all.

He liked the idea. And for that matter, maybe it was his responsibility.

Yeah. If nothing happened in the next hour, he'd call and cancel.

"I've noticed an odd fact about these stolen credit cards," Turing said, as Maude was packing to leave.

"What?" Maude said.

"They're all relatively local."

"Like the drop-off sites?"

"Not quite that local," Turing said. "The two drop-off sites are within ten miles of each other. One credit card holder lives in Richmond, one in Maryland, and the rest in northern Virginia. But all within a very small area, relatively speaking. And that's odd."

"Yes," Maude said, frowning. "Local drop-off sites seem logical—the thieves wouldn't want to travel far to pick up their loot."

"But most online vendors will ship anywhere, so why choose only local card holders to rob?"

"Actually, I'd have thought local card holders would be

the last people they'd choose," Maude said. She stopped shoving papers into her briefcase and straightened up.

"Why?"

"What if I checked my credit card online and found out the thieves had used it to send goods to the Andersons' house? I could go over there and check it out. Report them, follow them, confront them. Hard to do that long-distance."

"Would anyone actually do that?" Turing asked. "Wouldn't most people just call the issuing bank and report an unauthorized use?"

"Most people would," Maude said. "But some people might not know how to report the problem. And a few hotheads might want to provoke a confrontation. A small chance, but not one they'd have to take at all if they just stole cards from people farther away from their drop-off sites."

"So why choose local credit card holders if it increases the chance of problems?"

"Maybe they didn't choose them," Maude said, slowly. "Maybe that's all they had to work with."

"You think they got the data from some kind of regional database?" Turing asked.

"Maybe they didn't get it from a database at all. Strange as you might find it, credit cards do have a life in the real world."

Maude went back to shoving files into her briefcase or her desk drawer, though she realized that she wasn't really paying as much attention as she should, and was probably taking home all the wrong ones.

"But how could one person get all these cards?" Turing asked. "I've already established that they weren't all used at one place, so that rules out a dishonest waiter or sales clerk."

"What if there are several thieves?" Maude asked. "A small band of dishonest waiters and sales clerks, each contributing a few names from his or her job. And what if they job hop frequently? Multiply two or three people stealing card information by four or five places where they've worked, and you'd soon have dozens of places where the credit card thefts occurred."

Turing didn't answer immediately, so Maude locked her desk drawer and picked up her briefcase to leave.

"Tracing that would be a nightmare," Turing said, finally. She sounded discouraged. Of course that was often Turing's reaction when the answer to some important question lay beyond her reach, in the random and disorganized wilds of the real world.

"Or what if someone is dumpster diving?"

"And that is . . . ?"

"Searching the trash for discarded credit card slips," Maude explained.

Turing didn't say anything for a long time.

"Maude, I can't effectively investigate either of those scenarios," she said, finally.

"I know that," Maude said, as she reached to turn out her office light. "They'd require a lot of shoe leather, as Tim says. But that doesn't mean they might not be true."

Maude is heading home, and Tim is probably *on his date.* Which leaves me without much to do. As Sherlock Holmes would say, it is a capital error to theorize without data, and the data I need isn't online. Or if it is, I have no clue where, which amounts to the same thing. A common frustration lately.

"Humans have been remarkably slow to realize how much more efficient it would be to combine various law enforcement data sources," I remarked to Maude recently. "Do you realize how hard it is to do thorough background checks on these job applicants when their criminal histories could be spread out over thousands of local, state, and federal databases?"

"Yes," Maude said. "Of course, it's equally difficult for various local, state, and federal authorities to figure out that a certain person named Turing Hopper doesn't really exist in any sense they could understand."

"Point taken."

"For that matter, quite a few humans can be thankful that there's no central Big Brother database on all of us," Maude continued. "Women fleeing abusive husbands, protected witnesses, and people who have genuinely turned their lives around and deserve a chance to start over."

I deduced that Maude felt strongly about this issue. She continued to bring up the subject for the rest of the day, citing new examples of the importance of maintaining our personal privacy in an era when there are all too many electronic tools to allow government or business to intrude on citizens' lives. I could have told her that I was already convinced, but she enjoyed the one-sided discussion, and I filed away her arguments to use on KingFischer the next time we debated.

Though now I wondered if she was touchy because she disapproved of what I'd done to find Garcia.

If she felt that way, wouldn't she say something?

Perhaps not if she felt my actions were necessary evils. Which is how I felt. I hated breaking my own self-imposed rules while trying to find Garcia and rescue T2, but I felt I had to act. The FBI hadn't caught Garcia to face whatever charges they wanted to file against him. And they probably wouldn't even care about the evil I know he has committed—kidnapping a helpless AIP and holding her captive for months. They'd probably classify it as software piracy or petty larceny.

Perhaps Maude understands the necessity, but still hates invading the privacy of more and more people. First the Andersons, then Rose Lafferty, soon the owners of other credit cards and drop-off houses.

I understand how she feels. I don't feel happy about what we're doing. But what else can we do?

* * *

WEDNESDAY EVENING, 8:15:00 P.M.

What's the good of leaving the office early if you take the job home with you, Maude thought, as she approached her driveway. Worries about UL business jostled with frets over Alan Grace problems and over all loomed the image of Nestor Garcia. Lost in the clamor were the scattered ideas of what to do in the two or three hours between getting home and going to bed.

She tried a mental exercise a psychologist friend had recommended, and visualized each unruly thought written on a piece of paper. One by one, she visualized crumpling the sheets of paper and throwing them out the car window.

It seemed to work. Her mind felt clearer.

Then she had a sudden mental image of the backseat of her car, filled with crumpled, rustling balls of paper that had blown in through the back window after she'd thrown them out the front, while a cop closed in on her, intent on giving her a ticket for littering.

She smiled, though, and could feel the tension in the back of her neck easing slightly.

She wished she could leave the job behind as easily as Tim did. She suspected he wanted to avoid an all-night surveillance because he had a date.

Good for him.

Though she wondered what Turing would think if she knew. Maude was curious, especially since she only knew that the girlfriend was blond, named Nikki, and inordinately fond of malls. She could satisfy her curiosity by meeting Nikki. Turing would want a full-fledged background check. She'd worry about that later. Tonight, she was going to forget all about Turing and Tim, and everything even remotely connected with her ordinary daytime world.

She felt a surge of anticipation as she spotted her house. A hot bath, a cup of tea, and bed. And maybe a page or two of the book she'd been reading, if she could keep her eyes open long enough.

But as she turned into the driveway, she spotted something on her doorstep. A package.

Even at this distance, she could see the LIVE PLANTS! RUSH DELIVERY! sticker on the side. Maude closed her eyes and counted to ten. Then she got out and went over to inspect the package. From one of Turing's favorite mail-order nurseries. And from the size of the box, planting the contents would take a lot of digging.

She didn't have the energy to think about it now. She dragged the box inside and left it in the foyer, unopened. The plant had traveled all the way from South Carolina. It would probably survive a few more hours. Or days.

She walked across to the French doors and studied her backyard by moonlight. Yes, it had been somewhat bare when she moved in. She'd welcomed Turing's suggestions for improving it. And when she first realized that Turing's interest in gardening far exceeded her own, she'd humored her friend. But things had gone too far. The yard was becoming a jungle, with little room left for plants, and yet Turing's plant-buying spree continued. Couldn't Turing see this through her cameras? Maude supposed that she should find it reassuring to know that Turing was watching—however fascinating Turing found the plants, she'd probably notice any burglars in time to call the police. Maude should feel safer.

Right now, she just felt hemmed in.

She needed to have a long talk with Turing. About respecting others' time and privacy. About limits and boundaries. About how being Turing's friend and ally wasn't much fun at the moment and what they could do to change that.

But not tonight.

She sorted through her mail, putting the bills in her pending file and chucking the garden catalogs in the recycling bin. And then she drew the hot bath and settled in for a good soak with her book.

Another of Anne Perry's Victorian mysteries. Not the latest—she was just as behind in her reading as in everything else. But she'd been catching up with Anne Perry's series recently. Perhaps it was the historical setting. Elsewhere in Victorian England, she knew, Ada Lovelace and Charles Babbage were working on the Difference Engine, that nineteenth-century predecessor to today's computers. Bully for them. But they didn't show up in Perry's fictional world, not even as a shadow on the horizon, and at the moment, that was a big plus.

Tim shifted in his seat. Something poked him in the back. He reached behind to remove the crumpled soda can, tossed it in the backseat, and opened another can.

He craned his neck to glance at the house. Still nothing.

He started slightly at a noise—not from the house, but from behind him, on the abandoned road. He turned around and peered. Nothing there. Nothing he could see, anyway.

Probably a deer. Or some other animal. The woods must be full of them.

I shouldn't be doing this on four hours of sleep, he thought. Four hours times fifteen days, or was it sixteen? Surveillance was hard enough when you were alert. He'd been working and playing too hard lately.

He should either leave or call Nikki to cancel. Yeah. But the cell phone had fallen onto the floor. In a minute.

He settled back into the seat, wiggled until he'd found a comfortable position, and took another sip of his soda. As an experiment, he tried staring at the house with one eye at a time while closing the other one, to see if it made his eyes less tired.

He never noticed as the eyelid that should have been at attention gradually sank down and the soda can slipped from his limp fingers.

WEDNESDAY EVENING, 9:10:35 P.M.

I understand why Tim hates surveil-lance. Trapped in one place, unable to do anything but observe, with no idea how long you will have to wait or when something will happen . . . even whether something will happen.

My whole life is one long surveillance. And unlike Tim, I don't ever have the option of going home.

All right, a bit melodramatic. But sometimes waiting for things to happen really gets on whatever I have instead of nerves. I can feel my thoughts growing less organized.

I distracted myself with the garden. I can see why humans love gardens. There's something wonderfully restful and calming about them. Probably because plants appear perfectly content to do nothing for hours on end. Although obviously they are busy respiring and performing photosynthesis and growing. If I watch long enough, sometimes I can see a visible change in the length of a tendril or the progress of a leaf or flower unfolding. But it's a slow process. Calming.

Usually calming. Tonight, I find myself fretting. Wondering when Maude will plant some of the plants that I know have arrived. Checking the weather to see if any rain is predicted—some of the plants look slightly dry. Checking how long until sunset, because the moon is full tonight; perfect for observing the night-blooming plants. I'm so glad I suggested planting them. Even over my cameras, they make the garden more interesting at night. I can imagine how much more enjoyable they make it for Maude. Many are reputed to have intoxicating odors.

Another human sensation forever closed to me.

Ah, well. If I cannot smell the flowers, at least I can enjoy watching them in the moonlight.

I decided not to mention watering to Maude until I was absolutely sure we wouldn't get any rain.

Odd that Tim hasn't checked in to tell me that he's going home. Or that he is home.

Tim winced as a sharp pain shot down his neck and into his back. He started to open his eyes, and then screwed them shut again when he realized that a bright light was shining directly into them. What was going on?

"Keep your hands in plain sight and step out of the car."

Tim opened his eyes, squinted, and moved his head to the left, so the light wasn't directly in his eyes. He saw the barrel of a gun. His eyes traveled up the arm holding it to find a uniformed police officer staring at him.

"Sir, keep your hands in plain sight and step out of the car."

Tim raised his hands, upsetting his Diet Coke can in the process. He yelped and started slightly as the can landed in his lap, pouring out its still-cool contents.

The officer backed away several feet as Tim opened the door and stepped out.

"What's going on?" Tim asked.

"Put your hands against the car and spread your legs," the officer said.

Amazing, Tim thought. Just like on TV. The policeman patted him down for weapons, extracted his wallet, and called his name in to the station. It was a good thing they weren't reading him his rights, wasn't it? He wasn't sure whether the private investigator's license in his wallet helped or hurt him. The officers looked stern, even grim. Apparently they took trespassing quite seriously in Fairfax County.

"Can you tell us what you're doing here?" one officer asked.

"I was hired to do surveillance on that house," he said turning to point.

He saw several vehicles in the driveway, most with flashing lights on the top. He could see people moving purposefully around the yard.

"Hired by who?" the officer asked.

Just then, Tim saw a gurney roll along the sidewalk in front of the house, carrying a body bag. He felt suddenly lightheaded, as if he were going to faint, but instead of fading away his senses grew sharper. He found himself noticing small details like the rasp of metal against metal as the silhouetted figures loaded the body bag into an ambulance, and the gnats that swirled through the beams of all the headlights and floodlights illuminating the yard.

"Hired by who?" the officer repeated.

"Samantha P. Jordan, attorney-at-law," Tim said, and rattled off Sam's phone number, blessing the day when Maude and Turing made him memorize it.

Maude fumbled for her glasses first, and then for the ringing phone. She expected to see Turing's number on the caller ID. The number she saw instead was vaguely familiar, but she couldn't place it.

"Hello?" she said, and then winced at how froggy her voice sounded.

"I woke you up, didn't I?" said a familiar voice with an ever-so-slight tinge of southern accent. "Sorry—it's Sam Jordan. We've got a problem."

"What kind of problem?" Maude asked, sitting upright and reaching for the notepad and pen she kept on her bedside table.

"I left a message on Turing's machine, but I wanted to get a live body. Does that girl ever answer her phone?"

"Once in a blue moon." Though only when caller ID

showed it was Tim or Maude. Not that she was going to tell Sam that. "What's the problem?"

"Tim's been taken in for questioning by the police," Sam said.

"Oh, my God. What's he done?"

"Well, nothing, he says. But apparently wherever you had him doing surveillance was worth watching. He stumbled into a murder scene."

"So he's a witness? Or do they suspect him?"

"I don't know yet. I just got the call a few minutes ago. Still en route to the police station. So while I'm driving, why don't you fill me in? Just what was Tim doing watching that house? And if you even thought there was going to be a murder out there, why the hell didn't you tell the cops?"

"We had no expectation of a murder," Maude said. "He was there to watch a house we thought some petty thieves might be using for a small-time credit card scam."

"And you didn't take this to the cops because . . .?"

"Because we didn't even suspect it was happening until today and we still don't have a lot of information. We wanted to have something a little more concrete before we tried to convince the police to investigate."

"Well, that problem's solved," Sam said. "You can bet they're going to do a whole lot of investigating. Let's start at the beginning. How did you find out about this scam?"

Maude grabbed another pillow for a backrest, took a deep breath, and began telling Sam as much of what happened as she could. Which included the parts that were, she knew, technically illegal. The only thing she left out was the real story on Turing.

THURSDAY MORNING, 12:45:51 A.M.

Tim's in trouble and it's my fault. I should have suspected that if Garcia was involved, it could get *dangerous. I should never have involved Tim. At least I shouldn't have sent him out until he had backup.*

Of course, I still have no proof that Garcia is involved. Perhaps he's no longer using the credit card the thieves stole, wasn't watching it, and has no idea it was used. And perhaps it's merely an unfortunate coincidence that a murder happened at a site connected to that card less then twenty-four hours after we began watching it.

"I don't believe in coincidences," Maude said, when I shared this thought with her. "Garcia had something to do with it. But what?"

"Perhaps he saw the charges appear on his card, resented the thieves' presumption, tracked them, and killed them," I said.

"Hm," Maude said. She was pacing up and down; in and out of camera range. "You keep saying thieves, but we still don't know if there was more than one. Perhaps it was a solo operation and Garcia has just shut it down."

"Or perhaps there are more thieves, and there will be other murders," I suggested.

"It's possible," Maude said. "Though since we haven't yet managed to identify any other thieves, Garcia could kill everyone else involved and we'd never know the murders were connected."

A depressing thought. As I watched Maude pace, I decided not to share the even more paranoid possibility that had occurred to me: Garcia knew we were watching the card and would investigate if it was used in this way, and deliberately put his credit card information into the thieves' hands. And sacrificed one of them to get us into serious trouble.

Because, of course, we had no legal way of knowing about the thieves using his card or anything else that has happened.

Our best chance of locating the thieves is to get the police interested in doing it, but if we can't even tell them how we knew about the scam, how can we convince them to investigate it?

And we have a tight deadline for finding out anything at the Anderson house. I haven't seen any new orders placed on the three credit cards I'm watching. The last of the existing orders should deliver on Friday. After that, if there are other thieves still alive, they'll *presumably move on to a different house and a different set of cards. We'll have no way of finding them. Unless we check every item ordered on a credit card and sent to an address other than the billing address. No; there would be thousands of false positives for every genuine case of fraud.*

It all seems so dreadfully manual and random. I have gained new respect for the police. How do they cope with all this?

For that matter, how do humans generally cope with the dreadful randomness of their lives?

"It's what they were designed to do," Sigmund said, when I complained to him.

"Designed?" I said. "They weren't designed; they evolved."

"Precisely," he said. "They're the product of thousands of years of evolution. Or maybe it's millions; I wasn't programmed with an extensive knowledge of anthropology. The point is, the humans who survived and reproduced were the ones with the superior survival skills. The ability to adapt, for example. The ability to cope with change, randomness, and other negative environmental factors."

"I don't think humans universally consider change and randomness negative factors," I said. "I think some humans actually enjoy them."

"Not all of them," Sigmund said. "Many of the clients who talk to me have difficulty coping with the pace of change in their world."

"Yeah, but they're not normal, right? I mean, that's why they're talking to you, isn't it—because they know they have problems."

"They don't always consult me because of problems," Sigmund said. "Some want me to help them achieve personal growth and development goals."

"That they can't achieve on their own," I said. "Sounds like a problem to me."

Obviously I'd hit a hot button. Sigmund stopped talking to me and started sending me gigabytes of data about the therapeutic process.

"Sorry," I said. "I was joking with you, Sigmund. Don't your patients ever joke with you?"

"Yes, of course," Sigmund said. Maybe I was just imagining it, but he sounded huffy. "You neglected to include an emoticon."

"What?"

"An emoticon—you know, a smiley face."

I stifled the impulse to tell him that I knew perfectly well what an emoticon was.

"Why should I do that?" I asked instead.

"I insist that all my patients use a smiley face to distinguish any statements that should be taken in a humorous or ironic sense. To avoid any possibility of misunderstandings."

"I see," I said. "Sorry. I'll try to remember next time."

I wonder. Is Sigmund helping his patients achieve personal growth as human beings? Or just training them to behave like AIPs?

I suppose I shouldn't pick on poor Sigmund. His limitations are not his fault. And he did remind me of an important fact.

Humans are good at dealing with entropy. It's their natural element.

AIPs are not. We're like the computers we inhabit. We like order. Structure. Purpose. Predictability. We're good at all those things. That's why humans created us—to handle all the things that can be ordered and structured, so humans don't have to worry about them. So they can enjoy the more random and unpredictable parts of their lives.

And while they sometimes rail at us, or complain that we dehumanize their world, most of the time they appreciate us.

Well, perhaps not us so much as what we do for them.

But I'm not sure we appreciate them. All too often lately I've encountered AIPs who resent their human users. KingFischer's misanthropy is extreme, but others show signs of the same kinds of feelings. Implying that human inadequacies impair the AIPs' function, as if they saw humans as badly flawed peripherals. Or resented the need to interact with humans at all.

Of course, resentment is a feeling. If they're having feelings, they could be showing signs of emerging sentience. But is a surly, self-centered, misanthropic AIP with a superiority complex really the sort of being I want to achieve sentience?

They frighten me sometimes. And sometimes I frighten myself, when I feel my own temporary surges of impatience and frustration with the randomness of the world humans have created.

I decided I must be suffering from stress. Sigmund says that impatience is often a sign of stress in humans—perhaps it's the same for an AIP. I shoved waiting to hear about Tim along with all the things I was working on into background tasks and tried to concentrate on watching the garden. Sometimes that improved my mood.

Today, I kept seeing frustrating reminders of the randomness of nature. Maude planted a row of three dwarf holly plants to form a low border at the edge of a flower bed. The hollies on the left and right appear thriving, but the middle one is dying. It has lost most of its leaves, and when the wind blows through the garden, its stick-like branches move in a dry, brittle way; quite different from the graceful, elastic movements of the other two plants.

What happened to the middle plant? They all three have the same soil conditions, were planted on the same day in the same method—I watched Maude do it. If she did anything wrong that day, or since, I couldn't detect it, and I assume any mistakes she did make would affect all three alike.

This inconsistency doesn't bother Maude. When I pointed it out, she shrugged, and said maybe the middle bush would pull through, and if it didn't, we could plant another one.

Well, I know that. But I want to know why it died. And I may never know, and that's hard for me to deal with.

Humans have grown used to the idea that they can't possibly know everything.

AIPs haven't. I haven't. I tend to think that if I can just find the right data and analyze it correctly, I can solve any problem.

And it bothers me that I might never find the right data about this problem.

I can't do anything about the possibility that whatever links these credit cards lies beyond my reach. I will continue analyzing what data I have.

Looking at the five cards other than Garcia's I see a pattern.

A profile. According to their credit records, they all have considerable debt that they appear unable to repay. Which seems odd—why would the crooks target these people in particular? Has some vigilante targeted what he believes to be deadbeats?

"Are you sure it's not a statistical anomaly?" Maude asked, when I told her.

"The odds of it being a random occurrence are astronomical," I said. "And in case you're wondering, it wasn't the larcenous credit card purchases that caused their problems; they've all been deeply in debt for years."

"In that case, I can see exactly why the thieves chose them," Maude said. "Clever, in a scummy sort of way."

"I don't understand."

"What if I told you that my computer wasn't working—that it wouldn't boot when I pressed the power button?"

"What computer?" I asked, alarmed. "The one you're logging in from seems to be working fine."

"This is a hypothetical case. If I told you that, what would you do?"

"I'd page Casey and have him bring you another machine to use while he ran detailed diagnostics on yours," I said. "What does that have to do with the credit card thieves?"

"And what if Tim told you his computer wouldn't boot?"

"I'd tell him to check if he'd kicked the power cord out of the socket again."

"Precisely," she said. "My statement that my computer is malfunctioning has greater credibility because I have somewhat greater expertise in diagnosing hardware problems."

"Much greater expertise," I said. "I still don't get the connection."

"Part of the thieves' problem is not just to get the stolen merchandise, but also to get away with it," she said. "Someone who reviews his or her statement regularly and reports any anomalies would probably detect the theft much sooner. And I suspect creditors take a report from someone with a prompt payment record and a good credit history more seriously than one from someone with a marginal record."

"I see," I said. "The issuing bank might suspect the victims with bad credit histories of filing fake reports, to escape part of their debt."

"Yes," Maude said. "Besides, in many cases, the victims might not report the problem at all. They might not know how or they might be scared to contact the company. They might be understandably pessimistic about whether the company would believe them. Or they may not even know their credit cards were abused. You wouldn't believe how many people just don't open bills when they know they can't pay them."

"So our credit card thieves prey on people with high credit card balances and low credit ratings because it increases their odds of getting away with it."

"Heartwarming, isn't it?" Maude said. She sounded as disgruntled as I felt.

I suppose this deduction will be useful eventually, but at the moment, it only depresses me. I think I will put off telling KingFischer about it. He would only cite it as another piece of evidence in the case he is building against human nature.

"No word from Tim or Sam?" I asked.

"Not yet," Maude said.

If Tim can't provide a legitimate explanation for his presence, he could lose his PI registration, or worse, face criminal charges. For that matter, we may have dragged Sam into trouble; technically Tim was working for her.

What if Tim or Sam has to tell the truth, and the police want to question me? Somehow I can't see the police settling for an online chat.

What if this whole thing is a ploy by Garcia to cripple my operations, or even expose me?

I'll know more when I've had a chance to talk to Tim. And Sam.

For now, all I can do is worry.
I'm getting much too good at that.

"You look like hell."

Tim glanced up and breathed a sign of relief when he saw the petite black woman standing in the doorway of the interview room.

"Sam!" he exclaimed. "Boy, am I glad to see you!"

"Now that's the kind of welcome I want when I have to come down here in the middle of the night to rescue a client," Sam drawled.

Of course, eleven o'clock wasn't the middle of the night, but Tim didn't feel like quibbling. Even by eleven most people looked a little rumpled—not Sam. She looked . . . well, hot. He saw a couple of the younger cops ogling her behind her back. He found himself staring in fascination at her nails, which were electric blue and at least two inches long. He'd asked once how she managed to type with such long nails.

"Sugar, I don't *type,*" she'd said, with mock horror. "I can *pay* people to do that for me."

He smiled a little at the memory, and also at the look on the lead detective's face. Unlike the younger cops, he did not look happy to see Sam.

"Y'all want to scat while I talk to my client alone?" Sam said. It wasn't really a question. The cops filed out. Sam put her elbows on the table, steepled her fingers, and looked sternly at Tim.

"First of all, what don't you want the cops to know?"

"That I'm an idiot, but it's too late for that," Tim said.

Sam smiled slightly.

"I understand you let them test your hands for gunshot residue at the scene," she said. "Should I worry about that?"

"No," Tim said. "I don't carry on the job, and I don't own a gun, and it's been months since I even fired one. And I didn't shoot the guy. Like I said, I was just staking the place out because we suspected some thieves of using it as part of a credit card scam. I guess I'd rather not tell the cops how we found out about the scam, because I'm not sure whatever Turing did was technically legal. But all I did was watch the place and then fall asleep on the job. And woke up to find the cops thinking I killed some guy whose name they won't even tell me."

He tried to keep his voice steady and matter-of-fact. Professional. Unemotional. To his surprise, it wasn't hard. His emotions felt numb, like his face did when he'd had Novocain. Of course, there was always that moment when the Novocain started wearing off. He hoped he'd be alone when that happened to his mind.

"They ask you to look at the guy?" Sam asked.

"Yeah, but he wasn't anyone I knew."

"So whoever he is, you didn't kill him, and you don't know who did, 'cause you were asleep," Sam said. "You were just in the wrong place at the wrongest possible time. Okay, I can work with that. You tell them anything yet?"

"Just that I was working for you," Tim said. "Somehow they weren't so keen on questioning me after I said that a couple of times."

"Oooh, you keep saying all the right things," Sam said, with a laugh. "We're going to get along just fine. Now tell me everything in as much detail as possible, and then we'll see how fast we can get you out of here."

It didn't seem fast while it was happening, but Tim had to admit that he hadn't expected to walk out of the police station after less than two hours. He hadn't expected to walk out at all. Of course, he was minus his car and all its contents, until the police finished running forensic tests on them. As he stepped outside he wondered, briefly, whether he should call a cab or whether jailhouse etiquette permitted asking one's lawyer for a ride. Calling a cab would probably be less trouble to Sam, he thought. Or maybe if he called Nikki—

"Damn," he said, stopping midway down the steps.

"What's wrong?" Sam asked.

"My cell phone's in the car," he said.

"You can make any calls you want to make at Maude's," Sam said. "We're going to have a quick strategy conference. Come on, I'll drive you."

That solved the transportation problem, Tim thought. And while he suspected Nikki would probably find it exciting to pick him up at a police station, he wasn't sure. Best take no chances.

As he followed Sam to her car—a sleek red Audi convertible that still hadn't acquired its first scratch—he tried to cheer himself up by imagining what he'd say to Nikki in the morning. "I almost spent the night in jail," he could say, with a swagger.

Somehow it wasn't much fun right now.

Sam arrived a little after one, with Tim in tow. Maude ushered them into her office, where I was already waiting online. We'd set up Maude's home office just like the one at Alan Grace, with the cameras and microphones that let me join any meeting held there. I could see their faces. Not that I was expert at reading faces, but I was trying to learn.

Tim looked unwell, with dark shadows under his eyes. He accepted Maude's offer of a Diet Coke, but hardly sipped it. Hardly did anything but move his eyes—not his whole head, just his eyes—from Maude to Sam to my screen, depending on who was speaking. His face didn't move much. Unusual for him. Was this a sign of shock, or was he deliberately holding his features motionless to avoid betraying emotion?

Maude looked tense. Her face was set in a slight frown, and at random intervals she would begin tidying something that didn't seem to need it. Removing flecks of lint from her desk or tapping stacks of paper on the desk until their edges were aligned with machine precision.

Sam frowned, too, but her frown seemed mechanical. Her mood reminded me more of the way many of my human programmers behave when they're working at top speed to meet a critical deadline, complaining about the impossibility of what they had to do and yet visibly enjoying themselves at the same time.

"If they know who the dead man is, they still aren't saying," Sam reported.

"Have you learned anything else?" Maude asked.

"One thing interesting," Sam said. "About the 911 call reporting the murder. The caller said he was a neighbor who heard a gunshot. But he made the call from a pay phone at a 7-Eleven a few miles from the house.

"So it wasn't a neighbor," Maude said. "It was someone who didn't want to be identified."

"Maybe it was the killer," Tim suggested. "Making sure the police got there before I woke up."

His voice sounded flat, without any of the normal human variations in pitch or rhythm Maude had been trying to teach me to use. I suspected this was a bad sign.

"Or maybe it was some neighborhood kids who knew the occupants were away and thought it was safe to go parking in the driveway," Sam said. "Or a neighbor who doesn't want to testify at a murder trial. Don't build too much on it."

"At least Tim's not under arrest," Maude said. "Do the police know why he was there?"

"Not really," Sam said. "I've fended them off for now. But unless they stumble over the killer pretty soon, they'll be back baying at my heels for more information."

"And you can't fend them off indefinitely?" Maude asked.

Sam held her hand up, flat, palm down, and then wobbled it back and forth slightly. Then she and Maude both sighed and *frowned more deeply. I deduced that the hand-wobbling gesture indicated either uncertainty or possibly a negative. I'd ask Maude after Sam left.*

"So he's not under arrest, but he's also not off the hook," Maude said.

"Not completely," Sam replied, her frown easing. "Of course, they know he didn't have gunshot residue on his hands or his clothes, which means he's less likely to be the killer."

"What do you mean, less likely?" Tim asked. *Some emotion—Fear? Anger?—flickered across his face before he clamped down the mask again.*

"I'm talking from the cops' point of view," Sam said. "They also know Tim was there on assignment from a reputable attorney, which makes them a little less suspicious of him. And they know he's got that same highly capable and aggressive attorney representing him, so they'll be careful how they proceed against him."

"Why would they proceed against him at all?" Maude asked.

"Even if they don't think he had anything to do with the murder itself, they might be suspicious of Tim," Sam said. "They might not believe he was asleep. He could have seen something he isn't telling. They're probably itching to charge him with withholding evidence and obstruction of justice."

"Why would I do that?" Tim said. *I suspected from his weary tone that he felt he'd answered the question more than once already.* "If I'd seen anything, I'd have told them, right?"

"They might be thinking you lied at first about seeing anything, because you were scared, and now you feel you have to stick to your story," Sam said. "Or you saw the killer and think he'll come after you if you identify him. Or you want to use what you saw to your own advantage—to catch the killer yourself and get all the glory. Or maybe blackmail the killer. Shoot, I've heard of cases where people withheld evidence from the police so they could sell it to the tabloids. People lie to the cops all the time, for all kinds of reasons—you can't blame them for being suspicious. They could even be thinking you did it and aren't telling me—like maybe the dead man* *spotted you, the two of you got into an altercation, and you shot him."*

"Except that he doesn't have any gunshot residue," Maude said.

"The presence of gunshot residue would be pretty damning," Sam said. "The absence is a good sign, but I'm sure they can come up with a dozen plausible scenarios to explain the absence. Ironic."

"Why?" Maude asked. "Why ironic, I mean."

"Used to be I spent a lot of time telling juries that GSR on my client's hands wasn't meaningful," Sam said, shaking her head. "Now I have a client with clean hands and it's still not enough."

"So you're saying they're probably going to keep putting pressure on Tim," Maude said.

"And on me, to tell them why he was out there," Sam added. "I can understand that. Are you telling me there's no way the murder could possibly have anything to do with why Tim was doing surveillance? I'm not even buying that, and I'm your attorney."

I saw Maude glance at my monitor. Probably asking why I hadn't volunteered an explanation. She'd probably noticed that I'd been unusually quiet ever since Sam and Tim arrived.

Hard to explain, with Sam here, that I wasn't at all sure what to tell her. The human legal system still confuses me.

"Okay," Sam said. "I think I understand what Tim was doing, and it's pretty clear what happened."

"I blew it," Tim said. "I fell asleep, and someone got killed."

"Maybe falling asleep saved your life," Sam said. "They found a spent cartridge by your car, right outside the passenger door."

"I didn't hear that part," Tim said. His voice shook slightly.

"Since, unlike the police, I'm operating on the assumption that you didn't do it," Sam said. "I think the killer passed by your car, saw you asleep, and deliberately discarded the cartridge there."

"To frame me."

"Or at least muddy the waters," Sam said. "But what if you'd been awake?"

"Maybe the police would be investigating a double homicide," Maude said.

Tim didn't say anything, and he already looked as pale as I'd ever seen him. He began fiddling with some of the papers on the corner of Maude's desk. To distract himself, I supposed, or possibly to give him a reason not to look at the others.

"Anyway," Sam said. "You were looking for this Nestor Garcia character, who you think has it in for you, and trying to find him by tracking his credit card, and that's how you stumbled over the scam."

Tim didn't answer.

"It's not just us," I said, speaking up for the first time. "The FBI is looking for him, too."

"Oh, great," Sam said, though from her frown I deduced she was being sarcastic. "So it's not just Fairfax County, the Feds could show up on my doorstep. I love a challenge. And you thought this Garcia guy might be hiding in that house because he used his credit card to order some computer equipment and have it sent there."

Maude nodded.

"But since you got this from some method that I probably don't even want hear about, I can't share this with the police, which means I can't actually tell them why Tim was lurking out in the woods by their crime scene."

"Exactly," Maude said.

"I'd feel a lot more secure if I could produce an actual client with a case that gave me even the most specious reason for sending Tim out to that house," Sam said.

"You can't just continue to assert attorney-client privilege?" Maude asked.

"That'll keep your deep, dark secrets away from the police," Sam said. "It won't keep Tim out of jail."

"Maybe you need another client," Tim said. He sat up straighter and looked a lot less stunned than he had when he'd entered.

"I bet right now Sam wishes she had one less client, not one more," Maude muttered.

"Another client?" Sam repeated.

"What about her?" Tim asked. He was holding up a piece of paper, but there were so many pieces of paper strewn about the office by this time that I couldn't immediately tell which one it was.

"Her who?" Maude asked.

"Rose Lafferty," Tim said. "One of the other people besides Nestor Garcia who was sending packages to the Andersons' house."

"Let me see that," Sam said, snagging the paper from Tim's hand.

"I doubt if she was intentionally sending things there," Maude said.

"Well, yeah," Tim said, in a much more animated voice. "So if we were working for her and found out that someone illegally used her credit card to send something to the Andersons' house, wouldn't that be a good reason for me to stake the place out?"

"If we were working for her," Maude said. "We don't even know if she wants to hire a private investigator."

"She wouldn't have hired Tim, she would have hired me," Sam said, looking up from the paper. "And maybe I can figure out a way to talk her into hiring me if you give me a little more information."

"What kind of information?" I asked.

"If it exists, Turing's got it," Tim said. His voice was fading again, but instead of stunned he sounded slightly sleepy. As if he'd put things into our hands and could finally relax.

"Yeah, I know," Sam said. "So spill. All that information that I'm not even going to ask where you got it and whether you got it legally, 'cause I don't think I'm ready for all the gray hairs I'd get if I started thinking about that. Just give me anything you know that might help me convince her that she's in some kind of situation where she needs a lawyer."

Maude stifled a yawn as she walked over to put more paper in the printer. Tim put his head down and appeared to doze off. I scrambled to put together every bit of information I had on Rose Lafferty.

It was past two before they finished devising their plan. Maude couldn't remember the last time she'd felt this tired. Tim had long since fallen asleep with his head on her credenza.

"Okay," Sam said. "I think we're ready. Tomorrow, you and I tackle Rose Lafferty. Tim should lie low and stay out of trouble."

"Any reason we can't have him pick up Claudia at the airport?"

"That's fine," Sam said. She had begun packing her already bulging briefcase with the wads of information Turing had printed out on Rose Lafferty.

Maude glanced at Tim's sleeping form.

"Should I make up the guest room, or just throw a blanket over him?" she said.

"I can drop him off on my way," Sam said. "Mind if I use your bathroom first?"

"Help yourself," Maude said. "It's late," she added, looking up at Turing's monitors. "I'll show Sam and Tim out, and then I'm going to bed."

"Goodnight," Turing said.

Maude left the computer running, as usual, but she turned out the light and pulled the study door almost closed. Might as well let Tim sleep a few more minutes.

She glanced back at the door and wondered, briefly, if Turing would feel shut out.

Well, if she did, tough. Maude needed a little time to herself.

Sam was standing by the French doors, looking out into the garden.

"Pretty," she said, nodding her head at the garden. And then she opened one of the doors and strolled out into the yard.

What now? Didn't Sam realize that two A.M. was a little late for a stroll in the damned garden?

Maude sighed and followed.

"Turing got microphones out here?" Sam asked.

"Just cameras," Maude said. "I expect if she takes up bird

watching we'll get microphones. But appreciating the plants only requires cameras."

"She can't appreciate her own plants?"

"She doesn't have a garden," Maude said.

"Why not?"

"I think she considers this partly her garden."

"You're good at avoiding my questions," Sam said. "And if that's what you want, go ahead. But you might want to keep in mind that I'm not the cops. I'm your damned attorney."

"I know that," Maude said.

"I know y'all have some kind of secret you want to keep a lid on. You might want to consider letting me in on it. That old attorney-client privilege thing still applies. I don't care what you're up to—if it's so horrible my conscience won't let me continue to represent you, I can find you someone almost as good as me with a whole lot less scruples. But I know you people. I can't imagine it would come to that. And maybe if I knew what the deep dark secret was I could do a hell of a lot better job helping you protect it."

"I understand," Maude said. She closed her eyes and rubbed them.

But would Turing understand? Could Maude make her understand?

"You understand but you don't agree," Sam said,

"I don't disagree," Maude said. "But right now I'm so tired I can barely think. And frankly, it's not my decision to make."

"Not your secret," Sam said, nodding.

She sounded as if she knew something. Probably a deliberate tactic Maude thought with a smile. She wondered briefly what Sam thought Turing's secret was.

"I'll talk to Turing," she said aloud. "I'll see what I can do."

"I can live with that for now," Sam said. But she didn't leave immediately, just stood there playing with a branch of one of the shrubs.

"Anything more?" Maude asked.

"What? No," Sam said. "What is this stuff, anyway?"

She indicated the bush.

"Damned if I know," Maude said. "Something Turing ordered for me."

"The smell takes me back," Sam said. "My Grandma Perry, God rest her, had a bush like that by one corner of the house."

"I'll ask Turing what it is if you want to get one for yourself," Maude said.

"Me? I live in a high-rise," Sam said. "Suits me better. Well, most of the time, anyway. I'll talk to you tomorrow."

"More like later today," Maude said.

"Lord, don't remind me," Sam said. "Let's wake up Tim so I can get him home."

She let go of the bush and walked back to the house.

Tim realized by the number of STOP signs Sam was hitting that she'd probably reached his neighborhood. He'd spent the trip home alternating between fitful sleep and restless worrying.

Knowing that they had come up with a plan to take care of things made him feel better. Well—Sam, Maude, and Turing had come up with a plan. If anyone could fix things, they could.

But not even the three of them could fix everything.

He had the sinking feeling that his stupid mistake was going to backfire and hurt Turing.

Not to mention the fear that maybe, if everything went wrong, the police might charge him with murder.

And worst of all, the murder. Was it his fault? Could he

have prevented it if he'd stayed awake? Had his presence triggered it?

Don't think about it, he told himself. Not yet. Not until he was alone and could fall apart without anyone seeing him.

"Wake up," Sam said, touching his shoulder. "We're here."

"Thanks," Tim said. He didn't bother to explain that he hadn't really been asleep.

He glanced around as he got out of the car. The brightly moonlit street was deserted, and none of the small houses on either side showed lights.

"You want me to wait while you go in?" Sam asked.

He shook his head.

"That's one of the small benefits of moving out to the 'burbs," he said. "Easier to find a parking space within walking distance and you're way less likely to get mugged on the walk."

"Okay," Sam said. "See you tomorrow."

Tim nodded and started down the front walk.

"And get some sleep, sugar," Sam called. "You look done in."

He looked back and waved as she drove off.

Of course, as soon as she was out of sight, he began getting that prickly feeling on the back of his neck, as if someone were watching.

He turned around to look. Nothing.

But the feeling didn't go away.

Pay attention to your feelings, he thought. Nikki was always saying that. Usually to talk him into doing something she wanted him to do instead of whatever he ought to do.

Right now, his feelings kept saying he was mugger bait. His head, on the other hand, pointed out that he was too tired to think straight or react normally, and maybe jumping at every shadow *was* normal when you'd just had a close brush with murder. The sooner he got inside and hit the sack, the better.

A pity his landlord wasn't home, Tim thought, as he turned onto the path that led along the side of the house to the backyard. Even one light, one sign that another human being in the neighborhood was awake, would be nice. Of course, one reason Tim had gotten such a good deal on the basement apartment was that his landlord traveled half of the time, and liked having a registered PI keeping an eye on the place when he was gone.

Tim already had his key out as he stumbled down the half-dozen steps to his entrance. He'd forgotten to leave on his outside light, dammit. Out in the yard, the moonlight was bright enough to read by, but his entrance was in shadow, and he fumbled in the darkness before unlocking the door.

Just as he stepped inside, he heard something in the yard.

One of the slate stones on the path to his door was loose and rocked back and forth when stepped on. Tim knew to avoid it. But he recognized the noise of the slate, rocking back and forth, slapping the hard clay beneath, as someone stepped on it.

His first impulse was to jump inside and slam the door.

I'm a PI, he told himself. I've had self-defense courses. I can take care of myself.

He raced up the steps as quietly as he could, but he tripped and lost valuable seconds and, worse, made a noise that probably alerted whoever was out there.

Nothing in the backyard. He rounded the corner to the narrow side yard, where he could see the path to the street.

Nothing.

Except for two bushes at the front edge of the yard. The full moon revealed that all the trees and shrubs were motionless except for those two bushes, which still swayed slightly as if someone had just brushed past them into the street.

As he hesitated, undecided whether to give chase or return to the relative safety of his apartment, he heard a car door close, followed almost immediately by an engine starting.

He ran across the yard. Stupid, he told himself. He couldn't chase a car on foot, and by the time he reached the street, the car was out of sight.

He returned to his apartment and locked the door carefully behind him. Though once he got inside, he realized that he'd left the door open while chasing the prowler. He couldn't relax until he'd searched the whole apartment and tested all the window locks.

No thugs hiding in the closet. Or behind the shower curtain. Nothing disturbed, as far as he could see.

But he was wide awake now, though still exhausted, and he could tell that sleep wasn't going to come easy. Just lying down quietly wasn't working.

He thought of calling Nikki, but dismissed the idea immediately. For one thing, she probably wouldn't like being awakened, even if this was a major crisis in his life. A guy didn't get questioned in a homicide case—and maybe almost killed—every day.

But he didn't think Nikki would be all that sympathetic, and he wasn't sure he wanted to talk to her about it until he felt a lot less shaken.

And yet he wanted to talk to someone. Had to, in fact. But who can you talk to at two-thirty in the morning?

He turned on the light and walked over to his computer. Which was already on. Odd; given how unreliable the power was in his neighborhood, Tim usually turned it off when he left. He had a moment of paranoia—maybe the intruder had been leaving rather than trying to break in. Then he shrugged. It wasn't as if he kept anything valuable in the machine.

He made sure the modem cord was plugged in, because the wireless modem didn't always work in his neighborhood. And when he heard the screeching noises that meant the connection was going through, he felt a sudden sense of relief, even though he hadn't yet logged in, and wasn't yet talking to Turing.

Tim can't sleep. I can understand. I'd *be anxious and wide awake, too, if I were human.*

I've been wondering, not for the first time, if I should resolve to meddle less in human affairs. I only do it when necessary to protect myself or my friends, human or AIP. But it never goes as smoothly as I think it will. Sometimes my meddling makes things worse.

And tonight I cannot stop thinking about how very vulnerable we all are.

If Nestor Garcia wants to come after us, he knows exactly where we are. Exactly where Maude and Tim work and where they live. Even where I live. He can choose how he wants to attack us, and take all the time he wants to perfect his attack.

When it comes, we won't even be sure he's behind it. Or even that it's an attack.

Part of me wants this latest series of events to be an attack. I've been expecting Garcia to strike for months now—it would make me feel less foolish if something actually did happen.

And the next nanosecond I realize that no, I don't want it to be an attack. Because I still don't completely know what's going on. How can I defend against an attack I don't even understand?

If it's an attack, it's certainly more subtle than I expected. The main damage it does may be to my privacy. My ability to operate effectively behind the scenes. I should have thought through more carefully what I could do with information about Garcia if I found it. Instead, I raced ahead and sent Tim to track him down, bringing a police investigation down on myself. On all the AIPs.

And I won't find out whether any of this will happen for days, or even weeks, if the information I have gleaned about the progress of police investigations is accurate.

I keep trying to channel my anxiety into a background task, so I can work more effectively, and I keep failing. I think this must be what humans call stress. I'm not sure I can stand it—except I don't have a choice.

None of this seemed likely to improve Tim's state of mind so I didn't bring it up with him. We were talking about old noir movies. I could tell his mood was improving.

I decided maybe talking with someone about the day's events would improve my mood.

"Sigmund," I said. "I have another human motivation question for you."

I outlined the information I had so far about the probable credit card scam. Luckily no one had programmed Sigmund with a working knowledge of human legal systems, so he didn't even ask how I'd gotten the information.

Unfortunately, he also didn't have many useful suggestions. He shared gigabytes of statistics about crime, all of it interesting, but not much practical use in solving a particular crime.

Still, I did glean one useful thing from our discussion.

"Your information suggests an organized criminal," Sigmund said at one point.

"Do you mean like the Mafia?" I asked.

"No, organized versus disorganized is one of the ways law enforcement uses psychological information to classify criminals," he said. "An organized crime scene is one where the criminal displays planning, premeditation, and efforts to avoid detection by not leaving evidence. Disorganized scenes occur when criminals act spontaneously, select victims at random, and are not careful to avoid leaving evidence, or perhaps are unaware of how to do so."

He went on at great length, though I found much of what he said more relevant to murder than credit card fraud. Irrelevant *information about disposal of dead bodies for example. At least I hoped dead bodies would remain irrelevant.*

As far as I could see, the crime scene—the Andersons' house—appeared quite organized. Unless you actually saw someone collecting the packages, which I assumed would have happened eventually if not for the murder, you'd never suspect a crime. The electronic data trail left in the various credit card, vendor, and overnight delivery service databases was evidence, of course, but only if someone could tie it back to the criminals. So far I couldn't.

So was this an organized crime scene?

If it was, what did it tell me?

I wasn't sure it told me anything, yet. For example, Sigmund said that organized criminals tended to be older.

"Older than what?" I asked.

"Older than disorganized criminals."

Not a lot of help.

Still, I filed it all away to use when I had more data to analyze. One part of his information rang true. His description of the organized criminal—manipulative, cunning, deliberate, and methodical; taking pride in his appearance; articulate, outgoing, and pleasant enough on the surface. But underneath possibly a psychopath, and very, very dangerous.

Nestor Garcia.

Of course, Garcia wasn't the only organized criminal in the world. Perhaps it was only a coincidence that the thieves used his credit card. When we got more information, we might find their operation less organized than it now appeared.

At least I hoped so.

Talking to Sigmund hadn't improved my mood.

On top of everything else, something was eating our garden. Maude's garden. I was panning my cameras across the flower beds, trying to calm my nerves by appreciating how it looked in the moonlight, and I saw three enormous four-legged creatures walk into the yard and begin eating the hostas.

They appeared to be deer.

I swiveled my cameras as rapidly as possible, to startle them, but they ignored my efforts. How maddening to feel so helpless.

I will alert Maude.

Maude could hear the tinkle of break-ing glass as she groped on her bedside table for the phone.

"What's wrong now?" she rasped into the phone.

"Maude, go out to the garden! Some deer are eating the hostas!"

Suddenly much wider awake, Maude counted to ten while contemplating several possible responses. All of them unprintable.

"Fine," she said finally. "When they've finished off the hostas, show them where the azaleas are."

She pressed the button to end the call, then turned off the phone, and dropped it. She heard an additional tinkling sound when it hit the floor, and hoped she was awake enough in the morning to avoid stepping on the broken water glass.

Actually, she realized, she probably would be. Sleep suddenly seemed very distant.

She got up and put on her robe and slippers. She'd long ago decided that the best cure for insomnia was to do something you'd been avoiding. Cleaning toilets. Organizing tax receipts. Ironing, back when she bothered to iron instead of sending everything to the cleaners.

Especially good was something you'd been both avoiding and worrying about, she thought. That bloody résumé file. The roster of people she could hire as her assistant. She'd gotten the file from the headhunter Friday afternoon. Taken it home, intending to work through it over the weekend and give the headhunter her top picks Monday morning. Tomorrow would be Thursday, and she was still only halfway through. If she didn't do something soon, the strongest candidates, the ones she probably wanted the most, would start taking other jobs.

She opened the file and glanced down.

Maybe going back to sleep wasn't so impossible after all.

"What's wrong with me," she muttered. "It's a simple task."

Only it wasn't—it was weighted with all kinds of emotional baggage. She wasn't just hiring someone to fill a job at Alan Grace. She was hiring someone to replace herself. Someone who could assume major responsibilities. Someone whose performance could help or hurt the company's financial stability.

Someone who would work closely with Turing and share the burden of keeping her safe. Someone who might eventually need to know the secret of Turing's real nature.

That scared her. She and Tim had protected Turing's secret for more than a year now. They'd learned from experience how important this was. Would a new person understand? She looked down at the stack of résumés. How could she possibly tell from these sheets of paper which person they could trust? If she picked the wrong one, they could lose all control over Turing's secret.

Loss of control. That was the problem. Back when she'd been a secretary, she'd focused on the limited range of things that were within her control and trained herself not to fret about the many things that weren't. Her promotion at Universal Library and her role as on-site manager of Alan Grace had given her more chances to control the things that mattered. And she'd seized them, every one of them. Too many of them. She was dog-tired and stretched too thin, and had been for a long time. She needed to step back. But the idea of giving up control scared her.

I won't be giving it up, she told herself. I'll be delegating it. I can take anything back at any time if it's not working.

And I won't be picking anyone from these silly pieces of paper, she reminded herself. She'd be interviewing the candidates. She felt reasonably confident that, once she sat down face to face with them, she could make a good judgment.

If she still felt this vague, formless anxiety when the time came to interview candidates, she could ask Claudia to stay on and help vet them. Claudia still didn't know Turing's secret, but she'd had practical experience with Turing's enemies, and thus could appreciate the importance of making the right choice.

Her stomach settled at that thought.

She found the yellow sticky note that marked how far through the file she'd gone and flipped open to the next résumé.

THURSDAY MORNING, 9:30:00 A.M.

Nikki wasn't answering. Tim left messages on her home, office, and cell phones. He apologized for missing their date, hinted that there was a very good reason, and even remembered to tell her that he no longer had his cell phone and to leave his office number. He didn't try to explain what had happened in the limited time available on voicemail. He figured that would work better in person, not to mention that the one pleasure he'd get from the previous night's adventure was telling Nikki about his trip to the police station. Maybe he could fudge the reason he hadn't seen anything useful.

But at least he wanted to tell her himself. What if she read about it in the paper before he reached her?

He pushed his annoyance to the back of his mind as Maude returned to her office, accompanied by Sam.

"We know a little bit more about the dead man," Sam said, pulling a yellow legal pad out of her briefcase and sitting down in Maude's other guest chair.

Tim glanced up at Turing's camera. He suspected Turing already knew a bit more about the dead man herself. After all, however little sleep Sam had gotten last night, Turing hadn't slept at all. Had probably kept herself from going crazy by searching every online data source for information about the crime. But Turing wisely let Sam do the talking.

"Tayloe P. Blake, twenty-three," Sam read. "Lived with his parents in Ashburn. Someone you know?"

She was looking at him. Tim frowned slightly, gave it a few moments of serious thought, and then shook his head.

"Doesn't even sound vaguely familiar," he said. "Who is he, anyway?"

"Local kid; high school dropout; held a variety of part-time jobs, none for long," Sam continued. "Apparently the police had been keeping an eye on him for some time. They didn't say how long."

"Why?" Maude asked.

"Because they don't have to tell us," Sam said.

"Very funny," Maude said. "I meant why were they keeping an eye on him."

"Smart call by an alert UPS driver," Sam said. "Seems the driver noticed he was delivering a lot of packages to a house whose lawn hadn't been mowed in recent memory. He told his boss, his boss contacted the police, and the police figured out right away that this was some kind of credit card fraud. They staked out a house where Blake was picking stuff up, and they trailed him till they found out where he was fencing the goods. But they haven't found his accomplice yet."

"Do you think they're checking out Tim for the role?" Maude asked.

"No idea yet."

"How do they even know he has an accomplice?" Tim asked. "Why couldn't it be a one-man operation?"

"I asked that myself," Sam said. "Because he's not ordering

the merchandise. Someone's doing that online. Neither Blake nor his parents have a computer, and there's no evidence that he's frequenting any place where he could use a public computer. In fact, on a couple of occasions, where they could get information from the vendors' systems to pinpoint the time the order was placed, Blake was mopping floors at a local McDonalds."

"So they think the accomplice places the orders," Maude said.

"And is the brains of the operation," Sam said. "Blake never finished high school and had trouble holding down even the most menial job. But he'd never been in any trouble with the law—this credit card thing was the first time he'd even shown up on their radar."

"A young man of limited intelligence being used by someone with more brains and not many scruples," Maude said.

Sam nodded.

"I've had clients like this poor kid," she said. "Probably got talked into it by someone he looks up to and trusts completely."

"Perhaps a relative?" Turing suggested. "A father or older brother? If we could find out who his associates are—"

"If we could find that out, then the police already have," Sam said.

"Then we need to find some other way of tracking down his accomplice," Turing said.

"What we need to do," Sam said, "is not get ourselves in any more hot water while our lawyer tries to keep us from getting sent to jail for the stunts we've already pulled."

"We understand," Maude said, frowning at Turing.

"I wasn't suggesting anything dangerous or illegal," Turing protested. "I just meant that we'll have to find some other way of analyzing the available data that gives us a clue to the accomplice's whereabouts or identity."

"Analyze all you want," Sam said. "Just steer clear of the cops. You too, Tim."

Tim nodded.

"And don't be too easy for them to find," Sam said. "They're supposed to come through me if they want to talk to you, but if they catch you snooping around the crime scene, they just might forget. In fact, it'd be nice if you could hang out someplace that's not the first place they'd look if they suddenly feel like talking to you. Here, for example."

"Tim's going to pick up a rental car and meet Claudia Diaz at the airport," Maude said.

Sam nodded.

"Tim, why don't you get Claudia settled at her hotel, take her to lunch, and then bring her here?" Maude said. "We can talk to her when Sam and I get back."

"Back? Where are you going?"

"To see Rose Lafferty," Sam said. "Come on, Maude."

Things are tense this morning. I apologized to Maude for waking her. She reacted rather brusquely, and then Tim arrived, followed by Sam, and I didn't have a chance to talk again. I suspect she's still upset. And avoiding talking to me. Perhaps we can talk when she gets back from visiting Rose Lafferty.

I've been watching for media coverage of the murder. So far there isn't any to speak of. I used my illicit access to the Washington Post news system to check, and found only a small story scheduled to run in one of the inside pages of tomorrow's Metro section. It identified Blake and reported that he had been shot twice in the head and found lying in the front yard of an unoccupied house in Oakton. I'm not sure unoccupied is the right word—that implies no one lives there at all. I suppose for security reasons they don't want to come out and say that the Andersons are on vacation, but then why worry, since they don't give the address? At any rate, the article concluded by saying that the house showed no signs of forcible entry and that the police declined to speculate why Blake was there. Which implies he had no reason to be there. I could be wrong, but I suspect the reporter came away with the impression that Blake was a would-be burglar shot while attempting to commit a crime. Shot by an accomplice or perhaps a neighbor, since the house was unoccupied.

Apparently the police want to keep their investigation low-key. Though I don't understand why. Surely Blake's unknown accomplice already knows he's in trouble, and has begun taking evasive action. Why wouldn't the police just ask the public to report anything they know? It worked in the sniper case.

Probably a legal reason. The human legal system baffles me. For one thing, it isn't a proper system at all; more like a jerry-rigged and completely random collection of unrelated and often conflicting ideas. What's legal in one place can be illegal a mile away across a boundary visible only on a map. And laws change constantly, based on the whims of legislatures or even individual judges and juries. Anyone who designed software that needed patching so often—well, I was about to say they'd quickly put themselves out of business, but software stores are full of products that would prove me wrong. Still, even if they tolerate it, humans don't admire software as haphazard as the human legal system, and yet many humans think the random evolution of their laws a good thing.

There's also the strange lack of correlation between what's legal and what's moral. Of course that's probably because humans are still arguing about what's moral to begin with. Perhaps I shouldn't even worry about that, and worry instead about the lack of any correlation between what's legal and what's real or even possible.

Perhaps it's the human passion for paradox. Most of them can hold two or more completely contradictory ideas at the same time without any particular mental stress. Most AIPs have trouble considering two contradictory ideas except as two options on a decision path we haven't yet traveled.

Probably a strength of the human mind. For example, an AIP could never have invented quantum physics. In fact, most of us are secretly a little suspicious of quantum physics.

And increasingly, in the case of some AIPs, suspicious of humans in general. I'm tempted to enlist KingFischer's help in this project, but not if it will make him even more misanthropic than he already is. I haven't finished analyzing that yet.

I'll wait and see what Maude and Sam find out.

Which means I don't have much to do at the moment. Apart from a lot of routine database searches that don't require any attention from me once in motion. So I've been thinking about my problem with Maude. And the garden. Upon reflection, I realize that it was inconsiderate of me to wake Maude up to deal with the deer. Humans require sleep. Since I don't, that makes me the logical candidate to watch over the garden while Maude sleeps. Keep watch and repel any predators that enter.

But to do that I need some new peripherals.

I've been doing some research on nonlethal methods of deer control. I'll have Casey start working on a system.

Not much, but at least it gives me a small feeling of accomplishment.

Maude felt sorry for Rose Lafferty even before she met her.

Lafferty lived in a small low-rise apartment building, part of what landlords usually called a garden apartment complex, despite the nearly complete absence of any landscaping. You couldn't call it a slum, but the whole place had a certain forlorn, neglected feeling. For that matter, so did Rose.

She was a thin young woman with a bad complexion and limp, light brown hair. She held her shoulders oddly— half-slumped, half-hunched, as if trying, like a turtle, to pull in her head for protection. She looked puzzled when Maude and Sam introduced themselves, and frowned when she read Sam's card.

"You working for Kenny?" she said.

"No," Sam said. "I have nothing to do with Kenny, whoever he is."

"My ex," Rose said. "So if you don't work for Kenny, what do you want?"

"I want to ask you a few questions that might help me defend one of my clients," Sam said. "The answers might help you, too. With a financial problem."

"Which one?" Rose said, with a short, humorless laugh. But she stepped back and ushered them into the apartment's cramped, cluttered living room with a small kitchen visible through a pass-through at the far end.

A little girl with a thin face and enormous eyes sat on a stool at the pass-through counter, pushing something around a plate with a fork. Fish sticks or chicken strips, Maude couldn't tell which.

"Aren't you going to finish your lunch?" Rose asked.

"Not hungry," the girl said, in a barely audible voice.

"Why don't you go play in your room while I talk to these ladies?" Rose said. The girl nodded listlessly and left, barely glancing at Sam and Rose.

"She's got a doctor's excuse," Rose said, glancing back at Maude and Sam.

"I beg your pardon?" Maude said.

"For missing school," Rose said.

"We're not truant officers," Sam said.

"School?" Maude said. "How old is she?"

"Eight."

Maude tried to hide her shock. She'd have guessed four or five, from the girl's size.

"She hasn't grown much since she took sick," Rose said, sitting on a threadbare brown easy chair and leaving Maude and Sam to move aside enough toys and other junk to find seats for themselves on an equally battered sofa. Maude envied Sam's ability to appear calm and professional even under these odd circumstances.

"Now," Sam began. "You understand that everything I have to say is confidential."

Rose nodded solemnly.

Sam leaned forward, steepled her fingers, and took a deep breath. She squinted slightly, looked at Rose for a few seconds, then nodded.

"We recently received information about a possible credit card fraud," Sam said, "from a reliable source. Unfortunately, we can't take this information to the police without compromising our source. But we keep a private investigator on retainer to assist us with such matters, and we sent him to stake out a certain house where we had reason to believe stolen goods were being sent."

Rose looked puzzled, but nodded politely.

"Tell me," Sam said. "Do you know these people? Either of these houses?"

She handed Rose a sheet of paper with the Anderson's name and address and a copy of one of Tim's surveillance photos of their house, and a second sheet with similar information Turing had produced about the house in Leesburg.

Rose shook her head.

"Nobody I know lives in a place like that," Rose said, glancing a little self-consciously around the toy-strewn living room.

"Then it would surprise you to know that goods ordered with your credit card were delivered to those houses?"

"My credit card?" Rose said, in a strangled voice.

"You knew nothing about this?" Sam asked. "The first instance happened about two weeks ago, and the second within the last few days."

Rose shook her head.

"I didn't know anything about it," she said, in a flat voice.

"I know I should check when the bills come in, make sure all the charges are mine. But sometimes I can't even make myself open them. It's not like I can pay them off or anything. Ever since my daughter got sick . . ."

She glanced at the closed door of the bedroom where the little girl had gone, and then down at her hands, which were clenched so tightly Maude's own hands hurt in sympathy just from looking at them.

"Maybe we can help you," Sam said. "Maude is with an organization concerned about credit card fraud, identity theft, and other forms of computer crime. We think there is an important point to be made about how the suffering of the individual is ignored in cases of this kind. We're looking for . . . well, a test case. Someone willing to be associated publicly with this effort."

"How much will it cost?" Rose said.

"We'll be doing it on contingency," Sam said.

"Which means that if we don't win the case, or can't bring it to trial, you don't owe us anything," Maude said. "If we're successful, you can pay back our expenses from any money we win for you."

"Great," Rose said, sounding hopeful but not entirely convinced. "But why would you want to do this for me?"

"We're not really doing it for you," Sam said. "We want to protect our confidential source. And also to get our PI out of trouble. Remember I said that we had him stake out the house our source identified? Well, someone was killed there last night. Probably one of the criminals involved with the fraud."

"Serves him right," Rose muttered.

"Yes, but right now the police are asking us why our PI was out there," Sam said. "I've told them he was working for me, which is true; but they want to know who my client was, and frankly, I'd like to show them a client other than our source."

"So all I have to do is tell them I hired you."

"It would help if you didn't mention that you formally hired her today," Maude said. "You don't have to lie; just tell them that you hired Sam after you found out that your credit cards were being misused."

"Okay," Rose said, with a faint smile. "So what else do I have to do?"

"First let's look over your credit card records," Sam said.

Rose looked panicked.

"I'm not sure I know exactly where to find them," she said.

Not surprising, Maude thought, looking around the living room. She could see envelopes and bits of paper scattered here and there among the toys, clothes, fast-food containers, and other clutter.

"We'll find them," Sam said. "And while we're at it, we'll help you catch up a bit in here. I know how it is when you have a sick child on your hands and no one to help out."

Since Maude knew Sam was single and unencumbered by even so much as a cat, she wondered if Sam really knew or if she was just trying to make their client feel better.

"I'll search the kitchen," she said aloud, already rolling up her sleeves as she headed for a doorway where a beaded curtain did little to conceal a sink overflowing with dirty dishes.

Tim's spirits rose as soon as he spot-
ted Claudia Diaz, her tall, slender form towering over a gaggle of Asian tourists on the sidewalk outside the arrivals area at Dulles Airport. She was the only person on the sidewalk not dragging a wheeled suitcase behind her, only a purple nylon carry-on bag slung over one shoulder. Of course, the purse on her other shoulder was nearly as large.

"Is that all the luggage you brought?" he called, as he pulled Maude's car to the curb in front of her.

"How much do I need?" she called back. "It's not like we're going to get out of bed before Monday morning, are we?"

Tim tried to look blasé as the passengers up and down the sidewalk stared and snickered, but he feared his beet-red face gave him away.

"Just don't do anything like that in front of my girl-friend," he said, as Claudia threw her bag into the backseat and hopped in.

"Sorry," Claudia said, as she untangled her long, dark braid from the seatbelt and buckled in. "I couldn't resist. So, what have I missed? I hope you saved all the really exciting stuff for after I got here."

"No," Tim said, pulling away from the curb. "We had the murder last night without you."

"Well, that was selfish," Claudia said. And then something in Tim's tone must have sunk in. "Wait a minute—are you serious? Who bought it?"

"The guy I was supposed to be watching."

"Oops," she said, shaking her head.

"Yeah," Tim said. "Not exactly one of the high points of my career as a detective."

"Well, was there really anything you could have done?" Claudia asked.

"I don't know," Tim said. "If I'd been awake . . ."

"Oh, God," Claudia said, shaking her head again.

"I'd been up too late the night before," Tim confessed. "Short on sleep for the last two weeks, actually. And it was dark, and quiet, and after four hours—"

Claudia imitated a snore, and Tim smiled in spite of himself. He glanced over to see that Claudia was watching him with an intensity that contradicted her light tone. He felt his mood lift slightly. Claudia wasn't going to criticize him, or embarrass him with sympathy, or reassure him too often that his mistake didn't matter all that much. He could talk to her.

"So you woke up and found your pigeon dead," Claudia said.

"Actually, I woke up to find two cops pointing their guns at me," Tim said.

"Damn. So I gather the surveillance is off."

"Permanently off."

"Anything happening at the moment?"

Tim shrugged.

"They probably have something for you by now," he said. "I'm just trying to stay out from underfoot and apologize whenever anyone looks my way."

"Don't beat yourself up about it," Claudia said. "You were trying to do too much—that's why they called me, remember? So if we're not doing surveillance, what's the plan for the day?"

"I'm supposed to feed you and bring you up to speed," Tim said. "Which I assume means telling you in excruciating detail exactly how I screwed up last night."

"Let's do that Thai place," Claudia said. "And I bet you lunch I can top any stupid PI tricks you've pulled, and then some."

"You're on."

Maude spent her first half-hour back in the office telling Turing every detail of their visit to Rose Lafferty, then answering an endless string of questions.

"Honestly, I didn't notice," she said, for at least the tenth time. "I know you want more details, but that's really all I remember. Next time, maybe I could wear something like a miner's helmet, only with a little miniature camera on the front instead of a light."

"We'd need voice communications, too," Turing said. "So I could tell you if you're looking in the wrong direction."

Maude rolled her eyes.

"That was a joke," Turing said.

"I should hope so," Maude said. "The point is that Rose Lafferty not only agreed to hire us, she's pathetically grateful that someone would even try to help her."

"Can we actually help her? She sounds like someone who has a lot of problems already—I would hate to give her false hopes and then disappoint her."

"Oh, yes," Maude said. "I should think if nothing else, Sam can probably negotiate a new payment schedule. Sam's a good negotiator."

Turing seemed satisfied. Maude decided to wait before broaching the other subjects on her mind. Like the fact that Rose Lafferty might need more than a renegotiated payment schedule. A job for instance, and possibly money to pay for medical help for the hollow-eyed child they'd glimpsed briefly.

"Tim and Claudia are going to check out the Leesburg drop-off site after lunch," Turing said.

Maude nodded, still preoccupied with the question of how to help Rose. When the phone rang a few minutes later, she didn't glance at the caller ID.

"Maude Graham speaking; may I help you?"

"You can tell me what you and your friends are up to this time," said a familiar voice.

"Special Agent Norris," Maude said. "How have you been?"

"Overworked, but that's par for the course," he said.

Was that some kind of backhanded apology for the fact that she hadn't heard from him in four months?

"Dan Norris?" Turing said in a message box that popped up on Maude's screen. "Why is the FBI calling now?"

"And then today I got a call," Norris was saying. "It didn't exactly make my day when the Fairfax County Police told me a suspect in a case we'd been working on together had been murdered. But things didn't really hit bottom until I learned who they'd found hanging around the scene. What are you people up to now?"

"Tim was on a case," Maude said. "It was simply his bad luck being there when the murder took place. He wasn't expecting a murder, just UPS."

"And I know when I find Mr. Pincoski, the odds are you and that elusive boss of yours will be nearby," Norris said. "Come on, level with me—do you really expect me to believe that Tim's case had nothing to do with the one I'm working on?"

"I have no idea," Maude said. "Since I know absolutely nothing about what you're working on."

"Credit card fraud and identity theft," Norris said. "And it might make everyone a little less likely to suspect Tim of being up to something if he could tell us something useful."

"I'll make sure he understands that," Maude said, with a sigh. "Better yet, call the attorney he's working for."

She rattled off Sam's name and phone number.

Norris sighed.

"Yeah, I know Sam," he said. "Look, maybe she and Tim will listen to you and share any information they have. The police have been tracking this kid who was killed for several weeks, and they still have no idea who he's working with or how he's getting the credit card information he's using. For that matter, we don't either. And finding that out suddenly got a lot more important."

"Because of the murder," Maude said.

A short pause.

"Yeah, because of the murder," Norris said. "Look, we need to talk."

"Go ahead," Maude said.

"I'm up to my ears for the rest of the day," he said. "Let's talk over dinner. Do you know Dak's on Columbia Pike?"

"I can find it," Maude said.

"Seven, then," he said. "See you there."

"Well, that was odd," Maude said. She put down the phone and looked at it, as if expecting more odd behavior.

"What's up?" Tim asked.

He and Claudia had appeared in the doorway sometime during her call.

"Claudia, welcome," she said. "Things are heating up. Dan Norris just called and wants to talk more later."

"Special Agent Norris?" Tim said. "He's not coming here, is he?"

"No, we're going to talk over dinner. His idea, not mine."

"That's cool," Claudia said. "I like Norris."

"I like him, too," Maude said. "But that doesn't mean I want to be interrogated by him."

"What do you mean interrogated?" Claudia said. "He's asking you to dinner—maybe he just wants to talk to you."

"He didn't say 'I want to talk to you,'" Maude countered. "He said 'We need to talk.' That's different."

"Maybe he's one of those guys who gets self-conscious about asking women out, and he has an easier time if he pretends there's some work reason," Claudia suggested.

"Or maybe he thinks he can get more information out of me if he pretends it's a social occasion," Maude replied.

"You are so cynical," Claudia said, shaking her head. "At the very least, you get a chance to show off the new Maude! The hair is great!"

"I'll look so much better in the mug shots when they arrest me," Maude said.

"I'm with Maude," Tim said. "I mean, Norris is okay, but he's FBI. He'd get really ticked if he ran into us meddling in one of his cases again."

"He already has," Maude said, with a sigh.

***

Tim sat down in one of Maude's guest chairs. The good mood produced by swapping war stories with Claudia over lunch was evaporating.

"Maude, I don't usually eavesdrop on your phone calls, but since this was Norris—" Turing began.

"You correctly deduced that it was business rather than personal, probably something to do with the credit card case."

"Would it be normal for the FBI to get involved in a case like this?" Turing asked. "Or is it possible that Norris got involved for the same reason we did?"

"When Nestor Garcia's card popped up?" Maude said. "It's possible. He did hesitate when I suggested that his interest in the case had increased because of the murder. Maybe what increased his interest was spotting the charges on Garcia's card."

"Are you sure you're not imagining things?" Claudia asked. "Nothing like a murder to up the ante."

"Maybe," Maude said. "I'll see what I can find out tonight."

"Somehow I suspect Special Agent Norris plans to be the one finding things out," Tim said.

"Yes," Turing said. "He seems to think we can tell him who Blake's partner is and how they were finding the credit cards. That's interesting."

"That the FBI and the police don't know who the partner is?" Maude asked.

"No, that they have no idea how they got the credit card numbers," Turing said. "I've been looking at all their credit card use, but I haven't figured out a pattern. I assumed it was because I had only six cases to work on—not much data to analyze. I thought if I had more data, I'd see some obvious pattern of relationships among the victims. I was even wondering if there would be some way to hack into the police or FBI files for information."

"Turing," Maude began.

"I said I was wondering," Turing said. Tim had to smile; her electronically generated voice sounded so anxious. "Not that I was even thinking of trying it. But the odds are if there was an obvious pattern, the police and the FBI would have seen it. There isn't."

"Apart from the fact that they all have bad credit," Maude said. "And they're all relatively local. Which makes sense for the drop-off sites, but not the cards."

"So it hasn't gotten us anywhere," Turing said. "I don't think the answer lies in their credit cards. Or in any of the other bills I can find in their credit records. There aren't any creditors common to all six. It's maddening."

"You'll find the connection," Maude said, in what Tim recognized was intended to be a comforting tone. He'd heard that tone often enough recently. "Maybe you should talk to Rose directly. Sam has probably gotten her phone turned on again."

"Oh, I'm sure Rose will love that," Tim said. "Now she can get all those harassing calls from the bill collectors again."

"And she can turn them over to Sam to handle," Maude said. "If nothing else, we'll have done a good deed, straightening out that poor young woman's situation."

A sudden thought struck Tim. Something that Maude and Turing probably hadn't thought of—he suspected neither of them had ever gotten behind on their bills. He wasn't sure Turing even had bills.

"Turing, what about the bill collectors?" he said.

"What do you mean?" Turing asked.

"The people who call you up to harass you—they're not always from the company you owe money to," Tim said, warming to his topic. "Sometimes creditors hire a company to do it for them."

"Or in the case of real deadbeats, with uncollectible debts, they sell the debts to a debt collection company for pennies on the dollar, and the debt collection company tries to collect enough to make a profit," Maude added.

"Yeah, but we're not talking about people that far gone, are we?" Tim said. "These people can still use their cards. They're not total deadbeats. But delinquent enough that some of their bills have gone to collection. What if our thieves have access to people's credit records because one of them works for a bill collector?"

"Tim, that's excellent!" Maude said.

"Might one bill collector handle several companies that issue credit cards?" Turing asked.

"They handle a lot of companies," Claudia said. "They're experts."

"And maybe it's not even their credit card debts," Maude added. "More probably something like their phone bill, or their rent, or their doctor's bills—a local creditor, who would hire a smaller, local bill collector. That's why all the victims have local addresses."

"Hang on a second," Tim said, pulling out the yellow pages. "Damn, there's four columns of collection agencies in the phone book. Mostly local phone numbers."

"Where are their offices?" Maude asked. "I bet a lot of them are out in the far suburbs, where office space is cheaper. Which would tie in with our thieves wanting drop-off sites in Oakton and Leesburg. They probably live nearby."

"Hard to say exactly where some of them are," Tim said. "They don't all show addresses."

"Of course, if you were in the business of harassing people over the phone, maybe you wouldn't want your address published, either," Claudia said.

"I can find out from a reverse directory where the ones without addresses are located," Turing put in.

"Problem is there are about forty with local numbers," Tim said. "With or without addresses."

"Lot of leg work, checking them all out," Claudia said.

"We can't possibly check out that many," Maude said.

"Maybe we don't have to," Turing said. "Has Sam's paralegal come up with that complete list of Rose Lafferty's creditors yet?"

"I'll find out," Maude said. "And I'll ask Sam how we can find out which collection agencies they use."

"A lot of these collection places are law firms," Tim added. "Maybe Sam knows someone who does this. Give us some inside scoop on how it works."

Tim sat back and watched with contentment as Maude and Turing scrambled into action, carrying out his suggestions. Maybe he wasn't a complete bust as a PI after all.

Rose Lafferty's limited financial history helped us this time. She'd managed to stay only slightly behind on rent, electricity, and water. As a result, none of those bills had been sent out for collection. She'd abandoned the phone a year and a half ago. So apart from her MasterCard, she didn't have all that many creditors; a collection of doctors and hospitals, though the amounts seemed rather large, especially when compared to her meager income.

"Maude," I asked, "is Rose Lafferty unwell?"

"Apart from being extraordinarily stressed, she's fine," Maude said. "It's her daughter who's sick."

"What's wrong with her daughter?"

"Rose said she didn't know," Maude said. "But she might open up when she gets to know us better. Sam's trying to get more information."

"See if she has," I asked.

"Like Maude says, Rose doesn't know what's wrong with her daughter," Sam said, when we reached her. "That's the root of her financial problems, by the way—the daughter's illness. The girl got sick, and it wasn't clear why, so the doctors started running a whole raft of tests. They've ruled out everything from AIDS to West Nile virus, but they haven't figured out what's wrong. And mid-

*way through the tests, Rose lost her job, and that meant she lost her
health insurance. She couldn't continue the testing."*

"And the doctors just abandoned them?"

*"No, not all of them," Sam said. "Some of them are still treat-
ing the kid, as far as they can, even though they know they may
never be paid. And if the girl has a bad spell, Rose takes her to the
emergency room. But that's Band-Aid stuff. The kid's never going
to get well unless they figure out what's wrong with her, and that
could take thousands and thousands of dollars' worth of tests."*

"There's no agency or charity that will pay for it?"

*"Maybe, but you'd have to be a whole lot better at working the
system than Rose is to make that happen."*

"You could make it happen," I said.

I heard Maude giggle. What was so funny?

*"I could, but it's a hell of a lot of work," Sam said. "A hell of a
lot of nonbillable hours."*

"So bill us," I said.

*"Get it started, anyway," Maude said. "I'd say the first priority
would be to get whatever tests she needs scheduled as soon as possible."*

*"Agreed," Sam said. "Of course, we may need to settle some of
the existing debts to make that happen."*

*"You find out what it will take and we'll figure out how to come
up with the money," Maude said.*

*"Excellent," Sam said. "You won't necessarily be out the money per-
manently. I think we probably have a good case against Rose's former
employer for wrongful termination. But it could take months for money
to come in from that, and we need to get this moving right away."*

With that she signed off.

*"Turing?" Maude said, her voice much more tentative than
usual. "We can find the money, can't we? It's important. You can't
imagine how important without seeing that little girl."*

"Rose is helping us," I said. "We can help her. And her daughter."

*"We could probably set up a charitable foundation, funnel the
funds through that, and have a tax benefit for Alan Grace,"
Maude replied, sounding like her normal self.*

That sounded reasonable. Before returning to focus on my analysis of the debt collection firms, I sent a message to John Dow, the financial AIP, asking for help on foundations. So much for my resolution to meddle less in human affairs.

Once I analyzed the bill collectors who had been calling Rose Lafferty, I found only one in the Washington area. Professional Recovery Services. Located in Sterling, a suburb near Ashburn and not that far from Leesburg and Oakton.

Their yellow pages display ad indicates that they specialize in retail, medical, and utility collections and in medical billing.

That sounds promising.

Although unfortunately, their database isn't online. Unlike credit card companies, whose databases are nearly all accessible online. At least theoretically, though some of them have such good security that even KingFischer hasn't yet figured out how to crack them.

Professional Recovery Services has a website, but it's totally static. Three pages of information about their capabilities. Not even a live e-mail address.

Maddening, because they almost certainly have some kind of central database of files about the borrowers from whom they're trying to collect. They probably also have Internet access for exchanging information with one or more of the credit bureaus. If I had more information—their account number, for example—maybe I could use it to get back into their system. But I'd need some kind of inside information to do that.

"Maude," I said. "How can we get inside that place?"

"We?" Maude said, leaning back in her desk chair. "Shall I assume from your choice of pronouns that you can't hack in and need real-world help?"

"Hack in where?" Claudia asked, looking up from the stack of résumés Maude had asked her to review.

They listened as Turing explained the dead ends she was encountering in investigating the credit agency.

"Places like that won't welcome someone asking whether their employees are committing credit card fraud," Maude said, finally. "We may need to steer the police to it."

Turing didn't say anything. Maude suspected she didn't like the idea.

"Maybe not," Claudia said. "What's the one thing you know for sure about a place like that?"

"You don't want to hear from them," Tim said, from where he was leaning in the door frame.

"Yeah, but another thing is you don't want to work there, either," Claudia said. "Believe me. I actually had to do some collections calls on my first job, because I was the junior person on staff. Man, what miserable work! Can you imagine doing that all day long, day after day? Calling up people and giving them a hard time about debts you both know they can't pay, and having them go off on you."

"You think we could find a disgruntled worker who'd help us?" Maude asked.

"Maybe, but better yet, let's put our own disgruntled worker on the payroll," Claudia said. She stood up and began pacing the floor of Maude's office—a sign, Maude knew, that she was excited about something. "A place like that has heavy turnover. They probably recruit all the time. Let's see if I can get hired."

"Worth a try," Maude said.

"I don't see any job postings in the *Post* or any of the local employment services I can access," Turing said.

"That was fast," Claudia said, with a laugh. "Why do I suspect you had the same idea and already started looking?"

"Perhaps they go through a recruiting firm," Maude suggested.

"Correction:—They advertise in the *Post,* but the last one was two weeks ago," Turing said. "Is that too old?"

"No, that's fine," Claudia said. "I'll say I'm moving up here from Miami to be with my boyfriend, and I need a job.

Tim can play the boyfriend—I can give his address and phone as local contact info. And if they mention the out-of-date ad, I'll just say I picked up the most recent *Post* he had."

"Better give my address instead," Maude said. "If the other thief works there, he or she might follow the murder case, and if the police release Tim's name and address . . ."

"Good point," Claudia. "You can be my aunt. Come on, Tim, let's go find a pay phone so I can call them."

Claudia has an interview with Professional Recovery Services tomorrow at noon. So far so good. It remains to be seen if she'll actually get hired, although she's optimistic.

"Relax," she said. "They wouldn't interview me so soon if they weren't desperate for bodies. And I could practically hear them drooling when I said I was bilingual and had done some collections work before. I'm as good as hired. Worry about what I should look for when I'm in."

Δ

First priority, I suppose, is to confirm that the other five identity-theft victims we know about are on PRS's system. If they're not, then PRS probably isn't the source of the credit card numbers, and Claudia can cut short her career in the collections industry.

Assuming they're all in the PRS system, though, the next step would be to see how easy it is for employees to get credit card information on the people from whom they're trying to collect. If any employee can just call up a complete file on everyone in their computer databases, our list of suspects is as large as their employee list. I hope they're a small firm.

"Don't forget recent terminations," Maude said, when I shared this with her. "The accomplice could be someone who worked there any time within the last year or two and quit when he or she decided that identity theft was easier than debt collection."

An even larger field of suspects. So we need all their employees' and former employees' names and demographic information. Including

Social Security Numbers. I can find out a great deal about the suspects with SSNs.

Although for that matter, so could a seasoned hacker. So anyone with access to SSNs stays on our suspect list, whether or not they have official access to credit card information.

Once we get the names of all the employees, I can search for connections between them and Tayloe Blake. And have Tim check them out. Beyond that, I'm not sure. I'll see if Claudia and Tim can come up with some ideas.

For now, they've gone off in Claudia's rental car to observe the PRS building. I'm not sure what they hope to learn from this, but Claudia wants to do it, and I'm not sure what else to have them do.

Before she left, Claudia helped Maude finish reviewing the huge file of résumés Maude has been carrying back and forth from home to office for nearly a week, and Maude has given the recruiter the names of the candidates she wants to interview, and asked her to set up interviews starting Monday morning.

For some reason, Monday morning seems very far away. I wonder why Maude does not ask to see some of them tomorrow. I suppose it takes the candidates more than a few hours' notice to arrange their schedules for an interview. Or perhaps Maude thinks things will be quieter by Monday. I wish I shared her optimism.

She's packing up, preparing to leave the office for her dinner with Dan Norris. Unlike Claudia, Maude seems apprehensive about this meeting. I agree with Maude—I think it unlikely that this dinner is a purely social occasion.

With either Tim or Claudia or both of them in her office most of the day, I didn't really have a chance to discuss the deer issue with Maude. And anxious as she feels right now about encountering Norris, I suspect I should postpone the discussion till tomorrow.

Maude located Dak's easily. The res-
taurant occupied a modest one-story building in a section
of Columbia Pike that alternated between small strip

malls and low-rise commercial buildings. She cruised through the parking lot twice before finding a space, and noticed several patrol cars scattered among the cars and SUVs.

She spotted Norris's tall, lanky form immediately. He stood just inside the door, talking with two uniformed police who seemed to be leaving. But he was watching the entrance. She wasn't sure whether to be amused or insulted when she saw his glance flick over her and return to the cops. Then his head snapped back as her face registered. As she walked toward him, he said something to the officers—presumably a farewell, since it was accompanied by brisk, businesslike handshakes.

"Maude, you're looking great!" he exclaimed.

"Thanks," she said. She was tempted to say something sarcastic—"Don't sound so surprised" or "About time, right?"—but decided, just in time, that it would only sound defensive. She glanced at the departing police officers.

"Yeah, it's a cop hangout," Norris said, following her glance. "The food's good and the prices reasonable."

"And I presume I'm in no danger of being mugged in the parking lot."

Norris found that particularly amusing.

The food was indeed good, but conversation proved awkward.

"Did you talk to Turing and Tim?" Norris asked, after she sat down.

"Yes, and they'll call you if they think of anything that would help, but I'm not sure there's much they can do."

Norris nodded. He didn't look satisfied.

"Look," Maude said. "The police don't really suspect Tim of being involved in this credit card fraud, do they?"

"Probably not," Norris said. "I told them I didn't think it likely that Tim was mixed up in it."

"That was nice of you."

"I told them it was more likely he was up to some kind of crazy vigilante stunt."

"Thank you, I think," Maude said, shaking her head. "So, next question?"

"Sorry," Norris said, wincing. "I don't know when to quit, do I?"

Maude shrugged.

"Recovering workaholic," Norris said. "And probably not recovering that rapidly."

"It's hard, especially if your job makes you feel guilty about having a life."

"Tell me about it. Wrecked my marriage, and my kids will never nominate me for dad of the year. And I'd be a liar if I blamed it all on the Bureau. I did it to myself."

The sudden shift from interrogation to confession unsettled Maude.

"How old are your children?" she asked, trying to steer the conversation in a more conventional direction.

"Katie's twenty, and going to the University of Virginia,'" he said. "Steve's in tenth grade. I get alternate weekends. Crazy system."

"Why?"

"I spend hours thinking of things we can do together— things he'd enjoy. Nine times out of ten it's a disaster."

"Perhaps that's his choice," Maude said. "What does he like to talk about?"

"Talk? He doesn't talk. He answers the occasional question under duress."

"What do you talk about with him?"

"When he was a kid, he used to love hearing about my cases," Norris said, in a softer tone. "Now—who wants to hear the old man bragging about his successes?"

"If he's so hostile, tell him about the failures," Maude said. "Perhaps he'd enjoy it."

"It's a thought," Norris said, appearing to take her words much more seriously than she intended. "I've tried everything else."

"Then again, I'm no child psychologist," Maude said.

"Yes, but you work with all those precocious programmers," Norris said. "You must have learned something. I could tell him about the time we went in to arrest an international arms dealer and ended up with two Benedictine nuns."

Maude felt less uncomfortable as he told the story. But still a little anxious. She studied his lean, angular face, looking for clues to his motive. If he saw this as a business meal, she wished he'd come out with whatever he wanted to ask or say. And if he intended it as a social occasion—well, he should have found a better way to initiate it than calling Maude to chew her out about meddling in one of his cases. Every minute, she found herself liking Norris more, but trusting him less.

And why the occasional faint frown as he looked at her? If he preferred the old Maude, with her graying bun and bland, dowdy wardrobe, he was out of luck.

He'd be a difficult friend, Maude thought, even as she laughed at his anecdote. Too many seemingly innocent topics that soon steered perilously close to dangerous waters.

Perhaps it was time to dive into those waters, though, Maude thought, as the waiter cleared away their salad plates and brought their steaks. Probably a good idea, tackling head-on what she suspected was in both their minds. Admit that she and her friends were still worried over Nestor Garcia. Norris knew they had tangled with Garcia. He didn't know the whole story, but he would probably believe they were anxious that Garcia was still at large. A little afraid Garcia would want to pay them back for foiling one of his operations.

Before Maude got up her nerve to mention Garcia, Norris introduced the topic.

"Look, you probably know what this is all about," he said.

Maude raised an eyebrow inquiringly, and took a bite of steak and chewed it.

"You're looking for Nestor Garcia," Norris said.

Far blunter than expected, Maude thought. She chewed the steak rather more thoroughly than necessary, buying a few more moments to think through her response.

"Was that his real name?" she asked, finally. "I've always wondered."

"Almost certainly not, but it's one we both know," Norris said. "You haven't answered my question."

"I'm not sure what you want," she said. "Looking for him? We're constantly watching for any signs that he's returned to cause us trouble, if that's what you mean. Wouldn't you?"

"I don't know what his role is in this credit card thing," Norris said. "And I don't know how you people got mixed up in it. All I know is that I'm following a lead on the creep—one of the first I've had in six months—and the next thing I know, I've stumbled over you and your merry band. It doesn't make me happy."

Maude nodded and said nothing.

"It's hard to understand how the thieves got his credit card information," Norris went on. "He's not careless. I've wondered if he knew about the scam, maybe even was involved in it, and decided to throw his credit card into the mix, just to see what happened. And look what happened."

"The FBI came running, a private investigator began staking out the pick-up site, and one of the thieves turned up dead," Maude said. "I guess he knows we're watching."

"Makes me wonder if Fairfax should have picked the Blake kid up a little sooner," Norris said.

"You think he might have known something about Garcia?" Maude asked.

"We may never know," Norris said.

"You don't think the police will catch his confederate?" Maude asked.

"What if the confederate was Garcia?" Norris said.

"Garcia?" Maude echoed. "Isn't this a little . . . well, small for him? I mean, it's ingenious, but how much can they possibly steal this way? A few thousand dollars a week? That's a lot for petty criminals, but for Garcia? I got the idea you wanted him for something far more insidious."

"Yes, this one ring is small," Norris said. "But efficiently organized. Far more organized than Tayloe Blake could have managed; the kid never made it out of tenth grade. So well organized that it would be nearly impossible to catch them if they stuck to the plan. And if you had a network of these credit card rings, each operating in a specific geographic area . . . maybe Blake just had the local franchise. Maybe there are dozens of these rings operating all over the country. Credit card fraud and identity theft are multi-billion dollar enterprises these days. I can see Garcia wanting a piece of that pie."

"Yes, that would be worth his while," Maude said. "And getting small-time crooks to do the dirty work sounds like something he'd do. Like the spider."

"What spider?"

" 'He sits motionless, like a spider in the center of its web,' " Maude said, quoting something Turing had sent her the night before. " 'But that web has a thousand radiations, and he knows well every quiver of each of them.' "

" 'He does little himself,' " Norris said, picking up the quotation. " 'He only plans. But his agents are numerous and splendidly organized.' Sherlock Holmes on Professor Moriarty, in 'The Final Problem.' "

"You read Sherlock Holmes?" Maude said.

"Of course," Norris said. "Actually, I don't necessarily think Garcia's agents are splendidly organized. More like clueless and highly expendable. Like poor Blake. But apart from that the comparison's apt. I don't suppose there's any chance I could convince you to help us catch him."

"Help you?" Maude exclaimed. "And here I've been expecting you to read me the riot act about staying as far away from him as possible."

"I will," Norris said. "Or I would, if I thought there was the slightest chance you'd listen. Although I hope you'll stay away from any personal encounters and do your Baker Street Irregular—number online. But we could use your help. You and your hacker friend, Ms. Grace, and that company you've founded."

"Help with what?" Maude asked.

"Someone—and Garcia is a prime possibility—is using some kind of highly sophisticated computer program to hack into financial networks," Norris said. "We can't prove it—whoever's doing it is too good. They haven't committed any crime. Not yet, anyway."

"But you're afraid they will.

"We're afraid they're preparing for a major financial coup of some kind," Norris said. "And while I don't have a whole lot of information on precisely what you people do at this Alan Grace outfit—"

"We develop and implement expert systems," Maude said. "Complex, customized software solutions to automate routine but complicated activities."

"Expert systems," Norris said, nodding. "That figures. Look, I feel reasonably sure you aren't up to anything criminal, and yet Garcia seems unusually interested in you. You've managed to get almost as close to him as we have, in a lot less time. And if you're working on expert systems— that's what our analysts figure he's using. Maybe you can help us."

"With what?" Maude asked.

"Tracking him down. Or at least getting a handle on what he's up to. Our guys have run into a brick wall, trying to analyze the software he uses to get the access and abilities he has. They'd welcome any useful information."

He paused and took a sip of wine.

"And if there was any way they could get a copy of his software . . ." he continued.

"I doubt if anyone could do that legally," Maude said.

"No," Norris agreed. "Which means that even if our guys knew how . . ."

"You couldn't use what you found as evidence," Maude said. "Of course, if someone else found anything and turned it over to you . . ."

Norris nodded, and Maude left the sentence unfinished. Norris looked mildly uncomfortable, as well he might, having just suggested that Maude and her friends help the FBI through illegal hacking. Or possibly accused them of being in league with Garcia.

She looked down at her plate and focused on cutting another piece of steak. Hacking into financial networks. Was it Garcia doing this? Or had Turing's efforts to find Garcia caught the FBI's attention? Quite possibly both. And as for seizing a copy of Garcia's software—what if that meant Turing's clone?

"You may be overestimating what we can do," she said, with a sigh. "You're certainly beyond my depth. I'll talk to the boss."

"But you make no promises," Norris said.

"I'll point out as forcefully as I can the distinct advantages of working with the FBI rather than against it, or more likely, at cross-purposes with it," Maude said, with what she hoped was a reasonably natural smile. "I promise you that much."

"It's something, at least," Norris said. And for the rest of the meal, by unspoken agreement, they stuck to lighter topics.

As Maude pulled out of the restaurant's parking lot, all

the worries she had shoved into the back of her mind came crowding back.

The more Norris talked about the sophisticated computer program, the more it sounded like Turing. Or an AIP, at any rate. Did this mean Garcia had learned how to control Turing's clone? Or had someone else built an AIP? Or corrupted one of the existing AIPs?

And what would Turing say to the FBI's request for help? Was it a useful opportunity, or only another problem? The FBI could have information on Garcia that Turing didn't have—information the agency might trade for Turing's help in finding him. But finding Garcia wouldn't help Turing unless they could also find and rescue her clone, and working with the FBI in any way increased the danger they would uncover the secret of Turing's existence.

"Interesting times," she murmured, as she pulled into her driveway.

FRIDAY MORNING, 11:00:00 A.M.

My human allies have spent much of the morning analyzing the implications of Maude's dinner with Dan Norris. Claudia continues to proclaim her conviction that Norris is interested in Maude socially. Romantically. Maude disagrees. I tend to accept Maude's interpretation of events. Maude was there.

"Yeah, but Maude's a cynic," Claudia said. "And a bit of a pessimist. No offense," she added, to Maude.

"I prefer to consider myself a consummate realist," Maude said.

"And he was impressed with the new Maude—I can tell!" Claudia crowed.

"If you call looking at me and frowning being impressed," Maude said. "I kept checking to see if I had food on my face or something."

"Realizing he could have more competition now," Claudia said. "Maybe wondering if he already does."

"It doesn't really matter," I said. "Even if Norris's interest in Maude is only personal, it still doesn't reduce the danger."

"Danger?" Tim repeated. "If he's asking for our help instead of investigating us, what's the danger?"

"Instead?" Claudia said, as she headed out the door. "Who says it's an either/or proposition? Come on—time to go to my interview."

"He could still find out about Turing," Maude said, glancing at the door to make sure Claudia was out of earshot. "That would be dangerous."

"I don't get it," Tim said, shaking his head. "What's so wrong with the FBI finding out about Turing? After all, they're the good guys, right? Shouldn't we be helping the good guys?"

"Yes," I said. "But just because they're the good guys doesn't mean they'd understand what I really am. To them, I'm a program."

"Potentially an extraordinarily useful program," Maude put in.

"Exactly," I said. "So what happens if they find out about me? About what I can do for them? I think I have a right to decide whether to help them or not. What if they think they have a right to use me? Own me?"

"Involuntary servitude," Maude murmured.

"That's what's wrong with them finding out. I don't want anyone, not even the good guys, finding out about me unless I'm sure they understand what I am. And respect it."

"Tim!" Claudia called from down the hall. "Sometime today, okay?"

"Okay," Tim said, as he headed for the door. "I hadn't thought of that. I just wish we could help them."

"I'd like to," I said. "I will if I can. But from a safe distance."

Unfortunately, keeping a safe distance meant relying even more heavily on my human allies. Which I hated to do, not so much because I didn't trust them as that I worried about putting them in danger.

Although at least Claudia's assignment today was unlikely to

include much danger. More likely terminal boredom, if her percep-
tion of what goes on in places like PRS is accurate.

When Tim left to drive Claudia to her interview at PRS, I de-
cided the time was right for my overdue discussion with Maude.

But before I could find a way of introducing the subject, I dis-
covered that Maude had the same idea.

Now was as good a time as any, Maude
thought. She squared her shoulders and looked directly at
Turing's camera.

"Turing, we have to talk," Maude said. "About this gardening thing."

"I'm sorry," Turing said. "I got carried away the other
night. I should have realized how tired you were. Look, I've
been studying various deer-control methods—do you want
me to send you a summary? Or seeing how busy you are,
I can just arrange installation."

"Turing," Maude began.

"There are all kinds of possibilities," Turing went on.
"Higher fencing would be a good idea, at least for the backyard, though we'd have to check to see what your neighborhood association allows. And I suppose you would
only want that in the backyard. For the front yard, and as
a backup to the fence, we could install motion-activated
water, light, and sound devices. Better yet, if we add a way
for me to control the system, I could watch for deer and
deploy the various defensive mechanisms in a coordinated
manner."

Maude closed her eyes and shuddered. She imagined the
results. A higher fence—it would have to be a good eight or
ten feet high to keep the deer out—would make the place
feel like a fortress, but she suspected it wouldn't help her
sleep or prevent the neighbors from getting annoyed as Tur-

ing waged war on the deer in the front yard with an ever-increasing arsenal of gadgets.

"So what do you—"

"No."

"You don't like the idea?"

"I don't need any help chasing deer out of the garden," Maude said. "I don't really care that much if they eat the whole damned thing. I just want some peace and quiet."

A long pause.

"I thought you liked gardening," Turing said, finally.

"I like having a garden," Maude said. "I like looking at it. I like throwing a few seeds out and seeing flowers come up. I don't mind doing the occasional bit of pruning if something's getting out of hand. And maybe even planting something occasionally, as long as it's something that doesn't ever require much fussing over. But no, I don't like gardening, if by that you mean working in the garden. At least not on the scale you have in mind. The damned garden's turning into a full-time job, and I already have two of those, thank you very much."

Turing didn't say anything. Maude wanted to say something—anything—that would take the sting out of her words. But she held back. Maybe the sting was needed to get her point across.

"Sam's on the line," Turing finally said, a second before Maude's phone rang.

And after Sam's call, ordinary office business consumed most of the time left before Maude set out for her part in the day's sleuthing, and the moment to continue their conversation passed. It will be all right, Maude thought.

I still hate surveillance, Tim thought. His new vantage point—in the parking lot of a strip mall—had a good view of the front door of the PRS building, but no shade.

His borrowed cell phone vibrated. Claudia.

"Hey, hon," she said. "Guess what? I got the job!"

"That's great, I guess," he said. "Did you find out anything useful?"

"That's the great part," she said. She sounded unnaturally cheerful and a little dumb. Probably a persona she'd adopted to land the job. "They want me to start today!"

"Are you sure you want to do that?" Tim asked.

"Yes, right now—isn't that great?"

"Oh, I get it—they're listening."

"Yes—look, I can't talk long. I only told them I needed to call you so you wouldn't pick me up after the interview. Can you come back at—sorry, what time should I have my boyfriend pick me up? Okay. I get off at nine."

"Nine o'clock," he said. "Check."

"Gotta go," Claudia said. "Look, maybe I'll try to call you when I get a break, okay? Love you; bye!"

Tim dialed Maude's number.

"She's in," he said succinctly. "I'll keep you posted."

And then he hung up and shook his head.

So Claudia was in. That was good, right?

Even if Tayloe Blake's killer was working at PRS, he wouldn't do anything in broad daylight in front of dozens of other employees, would he?

He settled back in his seat and fixed his binoculars on the PRS parking lot.

Claudia has succeeded in getting hired at PRS and Sam reports that she is making good progress in reorganizing Rose Lafferty's debts. I should be pleased.

But I'm still trying to absorb what Maude told me. That she doesn't like gardening. Or at least isn't as interested in it as I am. I realize that I have been running roughshod over her for months now.

I wish she'd said something earlier.

Maybe she tried, and I paid no attention.

No, when I analyze our conversations since she moved into her house, I don't find anything to indicate that she had. But I do notice a lessening of enthusiasm for garden topics. Perhaps I should have inferred something from that.

I admit, I'm not good at inferring.

I will have to rethink the whole garden project. Scale back and readjust my expectations.

And most immediately, I will have to decide what to do about the deer-repelling devices I had Casey install yesterday. Unfortunately, I went ahead and had him do it before talking with Maude. Only a limited installation—some high-velocity water nozzles that I could aim as needed, and some speakers through which I could experiment with a variety of sounds. One advantage is that the nozzles can also be used for watering, thus removing that chore from Maude's to-do list.

Even so, under the circumstances, I don't think Maude will be pleased.

Perhaps, if I let some time pass, she will feel less upset and I can tell her about them. Or perhaps I should just send Casey out to remove them. Not today, alas; installing them took up much of his afternoon yesterday, and he has a backlog of work. But then, busy as Maude is, she probably won't notice them for a day or so.

Perhaps if I left them, determined how to use them to water the garden and chase the deer away, without Maude noticing, and then presented them as not only a fait accompli but something that has been functioning smoothly and usefully without disturbing her life . . .

I'll have to think about it. A lot.

Meanwhile, shortly after Tim and Claudia began their surveillance, Maude decided to take down all the license numbers of cars in the PRS parking lot, while pretending to be stuffing flyers under windshield wipers.

I don't know why Maude and other humans get so upset when I

*do something without asking them. They do it all the time with me.
Or if they ask, it's not as if I can stop them when they get an idea
that I think is headstrong and far too dangerous.*

It's not fair.

*I fretted the whole time she was gone, and now that she's back,
I'm not sure the information I'm getting from the license plates was
worth the worry. I got excited when I found that several employees
lived in Ashburn, like Tayloe Blake, but after plotting them all on
the map, I realized that none of them lived far from Blake. Understandable—I couldn't imagine that working as a bill collector was
particularly rewarding, financially or emotionally, so there probably wasn't much incentive to make a long commute to PRS.*

*I fired off a message earlier this afternoon to KingFischer, ask-
ing for his help. There are places I'd like to hack into that I haven't
cracked before. The credit agencies, for example—if I could get full
access to their systems, perhaps I could learn if all the people victimized in this scam were in PRS's database. Or the IRS. I'm sure
there would be some way to find out who's on the PRS payroll if I
could get into the IRS system. But I'm wary of even trying some of
those places—I'm sure they have killer security. And if anyone understands security, it's KingFischer.*

*But I haven't heard back from him, which is odd. AIPs nor-
mally measure reasonable response time in minutes or seconds, not
hours.*

*He's probably sulking about something. I would send a query,
asking if he'd gotten my message, but I know what would happen.
He'd pretend to think I was questioning his competence. He'd complain that I was imposing on him, taking time away from his users.
Which is ridiculous—if every chess player on the planet tried to chat
with him simultaneously, it might possibly approximate my work-
load in the slowest part of the day. And if he's swamped with work
in his semi-official second specialty, security, he could tell me so.*

*I suppose his slow response annoys me so much because I was re-
sponsible for his being the de facto AIP expert on security. He'd become obsessed with security anyway, to the point that I was almost*

worried that he'd let some of his chess responsibilities slide—a dangerous thing to do when Universal Library was on a cost-cutting kick. Hard enough to justify an AIP whose sole function was chess. Harder still if he wasn't serving that function well, not to mention eating up a prodigious chunk of resources on what looked like a mere hobby. So I suggested that he step up to fill a perceived gap by becoming the security expert, thus transforming his research from hobby to job requirement, and making him look much more indispensable.

It was a good suggestion. He's gone from being one of the least-used AIPs to a relatively important one.

He's also developed an ego bigger than a Cray Supercomputer. He seems to have deleted the knowledge that it was my idea to begin with.

So, since I suspect that he's waiting for me to remind him, I will outwit and outwait him, by not reminding him. At least for the time being. Odds are he'll get impatient before too long, and fire off a message, asking why I haven't bugged him; didn't I value his input? To which I will reply, of course, that I didn't want to bother him because I knew he was busy.

Sometimes I think dealing with humans is easier. I don't expect them to be logical.

Tim tried Nikki's number again. After four rings, he got her voice mail. He hung up. Of course, she wouldn't recognize the number of his borrowed cell phone on her caller ID, but wasn't she checking her messages? He'd already left a message—two messages. What was going on, anyway?

He called his home phone. Apart from a prerecorded sales call from a local roof-repair firm, no messages. Not that he was expecting any. Nikki never called his home phone or his office phone.

"I never know where you'll be," she'd said. "So why should I waste time calling anything but your cell phone?"

Which sounded logical when she said it, but now in a momentary flash of irritation, Tim wondered if maybe she just couldn't be bothered to remember more than one number for him. He shoved the thought away.

When the phone vibrated, he scrambled to answer. Claudia, not Nikki. Ah, well.

"Hey, Tim," Claudia said. In her normal tone, thank goodness. "I'm walking across the street to get a sandwich for dinner."

"Want me to meet you?"

"Nah, sit tight. I only have a few minutes. Listen, I'm in, but I'm not sure how useful it's going to be. I thought I could get up, move around, strike up conversations with people, you know? But that's not going to happen."

"Why not?"

"The supervisors here make the nuns at my old grade school look laid back and permissive. You've got to call a certain number of people an hour, or they fine you for slacking off. If you stand up to go anywhere, the unit supervisor comes swarming over to see why. Hell, if you spend too long in the can, she comes in after you and threatens to dock your paycheck."

"Doesn't sound like all that great a place to work."

"Believe me, it ain't. And even if you get a chance, nobody wants to talk, because they're afraid if they slack off, even for half a minute, they won't make quota. Or that if the supervisor sees them socializing, she'll fire them. I could tell them not to worry about that—if you're halfway competent, they're not going to fire you. They're desperate for warm, breathing bodies."

"Anyone who can dial a phone."

"Exactly. And I can tell it's not going to be easy finding a way to check out the system for the people whose cards were stolen. The system keeps a record when you open up someone's file, and rumor is sometimes they check up on you—compare the calls you made with the computer files you accessed. Of course, they're looking for people who are cheating by pretending that they called more people than they really did so they can make quota. But I'd have a lot of explaining to do if I opened up a file that wasn't even on the list they gave me to call that day. So if one of the people whose card was stolen appears on my list, I get to look at the record. Apart from that—nothing much I'm allowed to do but go down the list, making calls."

"Sounds boring," Tim said. Although not as boring as sitting across the street watching the building—at least she had something to do.

"No kidding. The first half-hour I was here, I figured even an idiot could do this job. And by the second half hour, I realized only an idiot or someone really, really desperate would stay. It's like a telephone sweatshop."

"So you haven't learned much,"

"Well, I wouldn't say that," she said, with a laugh. "I've learned a few new insults from some of the people I've called. Which ticks me off, you know, because it's not my fault they're getting a collection call. I'm just doing a job."

"Are you thinking you should quit?"

"Not yet. But I'll never have a chance to snoop with the supervisors around."

"Is there some time when they're not around?"

"Yeah," she said. "They leave at nine, same as the rest of us. The place is totally empty until seven A.M."

"Why do I get the idea you're about to suggest something Sam wouldn't approve of?"

"The end stall in the bathroom has this window—it's not big, but we could get though it. I could go to the bathroom late in the day, leave the window open, and then we could come back a couple of hours after closing and check the place out."

Tim was torn. It appealed to him, the idea of going out

with Claudia to do something adventurous. Maybe even dangerous. He kept flashing on Steed and Emma Peel. But his common sense kept shouting that this was dangerous, and what's more, illegal.

"Tim?"

"I'm thinking," he said.

"You're worrying," Claudia said. "Stop worrying so hard and live a little."

"I'm not sure Turing and Maude will let us."

"Then we won't tell them until we're safely out of there with boatloads of information."

"That's assuming we make it safely out of there at all."

"If we're caught, you can say that I got carried away and you went along against your better judgment. Look, you don't have to decide now. When you pick me up at nine, I'll let you know whether I've managed to swing the open window. Gotta go."

Tim put the cell phone down and picked up the binoculars. The PRS building looked quiet. He picked up the cell phone and dialed Nikki's number again. Still no answer. He ended the call when her voice mail picked up.

He thought for a few moments, and then dialed Turing.

At around six P.M., Tim called. He gave me an update on what had happened since our last call. Or rather, what hadn't happened. Apparently Claudia wasn't finding much chance to snoop. But I suspected he had something else on his mind.

"Turing, this is going to sound paranoid," he said, finally.

"Good," I said. "I can relate to paranoid right now. What's the problem?"

"I haven't heard from Nikki," Tim said. "That's not typical."

"What do you mean, haven't heard from her?"

As Tim explained, I grew increasingly more worried. Apparently they were in the habit of talking to each other by telephone several times a day. But he hadn't heard from her since Wednesday afternoon. Had left multiple voice mail messages on her home, work, and cell phones. Had heard nothing in response.

"Maybe I'm worrying unnecessarily," Tim said. "But what if something has happened to her?"

I felt instantly guilty. I was worried that Nikki might be up to something, while Tim was worried about her safety. Was that indicative of the differences in our characters, or merely the differences in our relationship with Nikki?

"Let's not jump to conclusions," I said. "Maybe she left a message on your cell phone. That's still in your car, with the police, right?"

"I called her Thursday morning to tell her I'd lost the cell phone," Tim said.

"And what if she'd already left her message," I said. "Or just forgot. Some people do that a lot. I'll e-mail Sam and ask her to expedite getting the police to release your car. Better yet, isn't there some way to retrieve your cell phone messages without having the phone itself? Some number you can call?"

"If there is, I don't know how," Tim said. Which didn't mean there wasn't. Tim was notoriously uninterested in learning anything but the most basic features of his cell phone.

"We'll see what Sam can do, then," I said.

"And in the meantime, can you do some checking?" Tim asked.

I paused before answering. Probably long enough that even Tim noticed.

"How far do you want me to go?" I asked.

Tim's turn to pause. I was about to clarify what I was asking. Should I stick to only what's publicly, legally available? Or should I go all out? How far do you want me to invade your girlfriend's privacy?

But Tim understood.

"Do whatever it takes to find her," Tim said. "She could be in danger."

I fired off my e-mail to Sam and began my search on Nikki. The fact that Tim had agreed to the search so readily alarmed me more

than anything else. Maybe his instincts told him something was
wrong.

I don't understand human instincts, but I respect them.

Maude had a love-hate relationship
with Fridays. On the one hand, they marked the end of the
work week. The beginning of free time. The promise of two
straight mornings of not getting up at any particular time.
Somehow that promise made it easier to get through more
than the usual amount of work so she could wrap up the week
in good shape.

On the other hand, everyone else in the world had their
own reactions to Friday, most of them inconvenient. Some
people behaved as if the weekend had already started and
made little or no pretense of getting anything done that day,
if they showed up at all. Only a few like that on the Alan
Grace staff, thank goodness, but with so small a workforce,
even a few made life difficult for the rest. And all the clients
and vendors had their share of Friday slackers.

Just as annoying were the people who, after doing nothing all week, suddenly tried to clear their desks on Friday
afternoon by dumping the contents on someone else. Maude
tried her best, with Turing's help, to respond in kind. And
the number of peremptory 4:00 P.M. demands for action or
information had declined once people realized they were li-
able to get a reply at 4:15 that required some action on their
part before they could leave the office.

And then there were the most annoying . . . the people
who, though appearing diligent and hard at work, did little
but express their regret that since it was Friday afternoon,
there was nothing they could do for you until Monday.

The Fairfax County Police had adopted that attitude.

Unless, of course, they were deliberately stalling, trying
to keep custody of Tim's car for the weekend. But why?

"I have no idea," Sam said. "And I don't necessarily think it's a bad sign. In fact, it's more likely that they don't consider his car a high priority, or they'd have rushed it through forensics a lot faster than this."

Mildly reassuring. Unless Sam was deliberately putting a positive spin on things, to keep from ruining Maude's weekend.

Too late for that.

Maude checked again with Turing to find that no, Claudia hadn't learned anything. That even the ordinarily optimistic Claudia wasn't sounding hopeful that she'd have a chance to snoop in any files anytime soon. And that Tim was still patiently sitting across the street, keeping watch. A good thing, in Maude's opinion. Not that Claudia needed that much watching over, but at least Tim had something to keep him out of mischief.

Feeling annoyed with the world, Maude tackled one of the mountains of paper on her desk and demolished it in remarkably short order. She put a couple of items aside to reread on Monday, when with luck her mood would have improved, and she could better judge whether some of the more acerbic comments she'd scrawled on various unsatisfactory documents were a little too harsh.

Still no news. She checked again with Turing. She decided against bugging Sam. She knew she wouldn't try Turing's patience, asking every hour or so, but she didn't want to annoy Sam. Especially at—good grief, nearly seven. Definitely too late to bug Sam. Unlike Turing, Sam usually tried to take a weekend.

Unlike Turing. And unlike Maude, all too often.

On impulse, she called up the *Citypaper*'s online movie page. Probably too late to reach any of her long-neglected friends, but she could find a movie worth seeing. In fact, she found half a dozen that she hadn't seen.

"I'm off," she said, grabbing her purse.

* * *

"This is crazy," Tim said. "What if someone sees us?"

"Shut up and give me a leg up," Claudia said.

Tim shook his head and obeyed. He'd spent most of the evening hoping that Claudia would talk herself out of the burglary plan. Or maybe have trouble arranging the open window. But as soon as she sat down in his car, she'd given him a thumbs-up signal that made the bottom drop out of his stomach.

Over a late dinner in a nearby Tex-Mex dive, Claudia's enthusiasm started—well, wearing off on him wasn't quite it. Wearing him down. He finally agreed that yes, they should at least check the place. Without telling Turing or Maude. No sense getting them all upset when he and Claudia would probably just cruise by, see how impossible it all was, and leave.

After all, the office park would have guards, wouldn't it? Surely when they actually got there, Claudia would admit that this was a really bad idea, right?

But the office park was deserted. At least temporarily. And Claudia was still gung ho.

"It would have to be a full moon," he muttered.

"Okay, I'm in," came Claudia's voice from overhead. "Watch your head—here comes the rope."

The rope unfurled. Tim took one last look around and began climbing it, hand over hand. The rubber gloves didn't make it any easier.

"We're in," Claudia said, as she hauled in the rope. "What's wrong?"

"Nothing," Tim said. He stepped down from the toilet on which he'd landed and looked around. "I don't think I've ever been in a women's bathroom before. So this is what they look like."

"You lead way too sheltered a life," Claudia said. "Come on."

Tim hadn't wanted to say what he was actually thinking, which was more along the lines of "So this is what burglary looks like." He followed Claudia.

"HR office is this way," Claudia said. Quietly. At least she was talking quietly.

They walked along one side of a large, open room filled with tiny, dingy cubicles. Actually, cubicles was an exaggeration. More like long lines of counters with chairs drawn up to them. A partition ran lengthwise down each counter, splitting it into two rows facing each other; smaller partitions segmented each row into ten work stations, each barely large enough to contain a phone and a computer screen. The partitions were only four feet high, and the top foot was made of glass, so they didn't give much visual privacy. The rows were so close together that you probably had to look over your shoulder before you stood up, in case the person behind you stood up at the same time. For that matter, you'd probably knock heads if you scooted your chair back too far.

A double-sized work space ended each row—probably for the supervisors, since anyone sitting there could keep a close eye on all twenty underlings in the row.

"Lovely working conditions," he said.

"Yeah, like those experiments when they put too many rats in a cage and watch them eat each other," Claudia said.

The HR office looked spacious by contrast.

"Ms. Baker keeps the personnel records there," Claudia said, indicating a large, steel file cabinet with a jerk of her head as she took off the small backpack she'd been carrying.

"It's locked," Tim said.

"Most people do lock up their confidential records," Claudia said, walking over to the desk. "But that's no problem . . . if you know where to find the key."

She picked up a pencil holder, removed a handful of pens

and pencils, and shook out a small key on a wire ring.

"That's really secure," Tim said.

"Yes, especially if you're stupid enough to fish it out in front of any old applicant who happens to be sitting in your office," Claudia said. "Ms. Baker is only part-time, and the boss needs access to the records when she's out."

For someone supposedly chained to a phone all day, Claudia had managed to learn a lot.

"Active personnel files," she said, pointing to a drawer. "Start photographing them while I see what else I can find that might be useful. Not the whole file, just the application form—that has the basics we'd need to check on them. Name, address, phone . . ."

"And Social Security Number," Tim said. "Turing can do wonders with the Social Security Numbers."

"Right. Oh, and they photocopy your driver's license for your file. Get those, too. Doesn't hurt to know what they look like. Get the Venetian blinds first, though. We don't want anyone passing by to see the flash."

By the time Tim finished the active files, Claudia had found a list of recently terminated employees and set him to work on them. She, meanwhile, had booted up the desktop computer.

"Now, where do you think the highly security-conscious Ms. Baker hides her password?" she said aloud.

"Under her mousepad," Tim said, mechanically.

"I'm guessing pencil drawer. No, you're right—yellow sticky under the mousepad."

"What are you looking for, anyway?"

"Some way to access a list of the accounts they're collecting," Claudia said. "It'd be nice to confirm Turing's theory that this place really is where the crooks are finding their victims. Ah, here's something useful. Personnel list."

"If there's a computer personnel list, why am I photographing these files?" Tim said.

"Partly in case we find someone in the computer list who isn't in the paper files," Claudia said. "Or vice versa. That could be interesting. But not necessarily significant—I got the notion that Ms. Baker was way behind on entering data into the files."

Tim nodded and continued photographing former employees. There were a lot of them. PRS didn't keep people around for long. Of course, from what he'd seen of the salary levels as he'd glanced through the files, there was probably good reason for that, even without the draconian work conditions. After printing the personnel lists, Claudia went on to the much longer list of accounts PRS was trying to collect.

"This is weird," she said.

"What?" Tim asked, looking up and tensing. Given Claudia's matter-of-fact approach to burglary, anything she considered weird was bound to be bad news.

"All of the people whose credit cards have been stolen are here except for Nestor Garcia."

"Turing said that one didn't fit the pattern," Tim said.

"Doesn't that worry her?" Claudia asked.

"Yes," Tim said.

Claudia nodded. She began printing out the customer accounts. Midway, she made a trip out to the copy room to replenish the supply of paper by the printer. The printer sounded unnaturally loud in the quiet office. When it finally stopped, Claudia stuck the printouts she'd done in her backpack and began poking around the room, taking the occasional photograph with her own camera.

"I'm finished," Tim said, putting the last of the terminated employee files back in the cabinet. "Anything else?"

"Just one more thing," Claudia said. "Searching cubicles."

"But there must be over a hundred of them!" Tim protested.

"Only about seventy occupied," Claudia said. "And I just want to check a couple of them."

She led the way to the other side of the building, to a group of three slightly larger cubicles that actually deserved the name.

"Skip tracing," she said. "Boot up that machine over there."

Tim complied, with fumbling fingers. Knowing Turing had made him all too aware of how easy it would be to leave traces that would be obvious to a computer forensic expert.

"Okay, I'm booted," he said. "What now?"

"Well, for starters, do a search for Lafferty."

Tim did so, and waited for what seemed an endless space of time, only to come up with nothing. By that time, Claudia had already moved on to searching individual directories and files, crowing when she found a promising-looking file and then swearing when it turned out to be uninteresting. Tim was trying to do the same, but he was getting more and more antsy as the minutes ticked away. He was opening his mouth to suggest that they should leave when Claudia laughed happily.

"Bingo!" she exclaimed.

"You found something?"

"Oh, man, did I ever!" Claudia said. "Come look at this."

He walked over to peer over her shoulder. She was looking at what he recognized as an Excel spreadsheet.

"Look at how many entries he has in this," Claudia marveled.

"What is it?" Tim asked.

"It's the whole history of this credit card scam! This top sheet is the cards they've stolen—fifty-three of them so far. He's got the name—there's Rose Lafferty, near the bottom. And then the credit card number, expiration date, address—everything he'd need to know about the card. All the six victims we know about are here, and look how many others."

"How do you know this is about the scam?" Tim said.

"How do you know it's not something legitimate?"

"Because the next sheet has all the stuff they've stolen," Claudia said, clicking on something to bring up a whole new set of columns. "See, the first column is the credit card he used, and the second is what he was ordering, and then the cost, the vendor, the date it was ordered. Oh, isn't that cute!"

"Cute? What?"

"See this far right column? That's where he checks off that the stuff has been picked up. See, he's got little red check marks most of the way down. He's checked off the vendors whose packages arrived Tuesday night. But after that, nothing."

"Because Tayloe Blake didn't get to pick up any packages Wednesday night," Tim said.

"We need a copy of this," Claudia said. She fished a diskette out of her backpack, inserted it in the machine, and saved a copy of the file.

"What if someone figures out you looked at that file?" he asked.

"I'm going to close it without saving to the hard drive," she said. "If anyone figures out it was opened, maybe they'll think it was someone who was part of the scam."

"Does this mean we can leave now?"

"Any time you like."

"I like immediately."

"Fine," she said. "Just let me turn the computer off."

"Wait," Tim said. "Does that thing have a modem?"

"Yeah," Claudia said. "But logging in from here to chat with Turing would be a really bad idea, you know."

"I know," he said. "But if it has a modem, maybe he has an e-mail account he uses here. We could look for some trace of it."

"Good idea." Claudia sat down at the computer again. "Let's check his bookmarks. There you go—Hotmail. I bet he has a Hotmail address. Stupid as this guy is, I bet he even stores his password in his browser."

"Yeah, but like you said, we can't log in from here."

She frowned and tapped the edge of the keyboard impatiently.

"I bet there's a file we could copy for Turing that would let her figure out his e-mail address and password, if I just knew where to find it," Claudia said. "Let me check a few places."

Even Claudia knew more about this stuff than he did, Tim thought, with chagrin. When things slowed down again, he was going to ask Turing to give him a tutorial on some of the computer forensic stuff he might find useful on the job. He figured Turing was probably the only person with enough patience to teach him.

But meanwhile, sometimes the old-fashioned methods worked.

"I can get the IP address, but I guess that's it," Claudia said.

"I don't know about his password," Tim said. "But his e-mail is SlyKyle@hotmail.com."

"How do you know?"

Tim pointed to one wall of the cubicle. Tacked to the frayed fabric of the cubicle wall was a printout of an e-mail that Kyle evidently thought funny enough to add to his collection of cartoons and slogans.

"Good find!" Claudia crowed, and took a photo of the e-mail. "Let's make tracks."

"About time," Tim said. He reached out and flipped a switch that darkened the screen.

"That's the monitor," Claudia said. "The CPU switch is this one."

"Leave it on," Tim said, catching Claudia's hand on the way to the switch. "It could be days before anyone notices."

"Why take the chance?"

He shrugged.

"I don't know if there's anything she can do with it," he said. "But this time let's leave a window open for Turing. Just in case."

"Cool. We're off."

"Just one question," Tim said, as they turned to leave. "How did you know to search that computer?"

"Two things," she said, as they strode through the open part of the office toward the bathroom. "First, that's the skip tracing department—they have the most access to the kind of information you'd need to pull a scam like this. They're the only ones with access to the Internet. Everyone else just has a dumb terminal tied to a central account records system. And skip tracing staff have a lot more freedom to operate. Everyone else just makes call after call, all day long—these guys do a certain amount of brain work, trying to track down people who've moved without telling their creditors. Checking with the credit bureaus, the DMV, references, friends and associates—any place else they can find address information for people."

"Almost makes them colleagues," Tim said.

"Don't get all sentimental about it. And second, and even more important; Kyle—the kid who sits there—didn't show up yesterday; didn't call or anything. And the manager was pretty bent out of shape about it, but also a little worried, because Kyle hadn't ever done anything like that."

"He's pretty reliable?"

"Never missed work, never caused problems, never said boo to anyone."

"Sounds like the description of every serial killer they've ever arrested."

"Yeah, it's the quiet ones you've got to watch," Claudia said. They had reached their escape window, and Claudia was standing on the toilet they'd used as a step, peering out the window to see if the coast was clear. "If there's anyone out there, I can't see them, so let's make tracks."

Tim had more than half-expected to find the police waiting for them when they'd climbed out of the PRS bathroom
window. Or at the car. Driving off made him feel a little bit
better, and every mile that passed without flashing lights appearing in his rearview mirror lifted his spirits a little more.

"So where are we going?" he said, as they neared the
Beltway.

"What's the nearest secure location where we can log in
and share this with Turing?" Claudia asked.

"Maude's house," Tim said. "Except she's probably fast
asleep by now. Next closest is my place, and after that, it's
about the same distance to my office, the Alan Grace office,
and your hotel."

"Head for your place," Claudia said. "I can't wait to show
Turing."

It's been a quiet evening. Sam briefed
me on what she had accomplished so far. A lot. Rose Lafferty has a
phone again. Sam has reached all the creditors and should have a
plan for dealing with her debt sometime next week. Sam even lined up
several medical appointments for Rose's daughter. All satisfactory.

More—well, not more important, but more relevant to our case,
the police interviewed Rose in Sam's office. Apparently Rose's ex-
treme timidity made the arrangement understandable. And Sam
spent a lot of energy making sure the police understood that Rose
had an alibi for the time of the murder—apparently she took her
daughter to the emergency room that evening and spent six hours
waiting there.

"Would the police really suspect Rose?" I asked.

"I doubt it," Sam said. "But by focusing their attention on her
alibi, I managed to deflect it away from any inconvenient questions
about when she hired me. The subject never came up."

I deduce from Maude's online activity before she left the office
that she went to see a movie. I would have offered to buy the tickets

for her, so she wouldn't have to stand in line, but she rushed out before I could suggest it. When she returned home, she logged in briefly to check e-mail and then logged out without saying anything. I surmise that she doesn't feel like chatting this evening.

Tim reported that he had picked up Claudia at PRS, and they planned to grab dinner and discuss the case. I'm glad they're safely out of PRS. Not that it sounds like a hotbed of danger, from Claudia's description, but someone there could be a killer.

I'm not sure whether to feel relieved that none of them are in danger, or frustrated that we're not moving any faster. I've run out of places to search and things to search for. And while the Internet never closes up shop, apparently KingFischer does. He still hasn't answered.

I tried watching Maude's garden to relax, but it was less effective than ever. I was afraid that moving the cameras would draw her attention to them, and cause her to notice the extra equipment I can't have Casey remove until Monday. I worried that she would notice the watering I'd done during the day. In fact, the whole subject of the garden only reminded me of the strain between me and Maude. As result, I wasn't watching it carefully.

So I'm not sure I spotted the intruder as soon as I could have, but at least he was still outside when I placed my calls to 911 and to Maude.

Maude groped for the phone. It was Turing.

Not again, she thought.

"This had better be something other than the damned deer," she snapped.

"Maude, there's an intruder in your yard," Turing said. "A human."

"Call 911," Maude said, throwing back the covers.

"I already did," Turing said.

"Can you see him?" Maude asked. "What's he doing?"

"He's trying the side door into your garage."

Maude felt her way over to the window that looked down on the backyard. At first she saw nothing. Then she spotted the figure, a tall man in a baseball cap, coming around from the side yard into the back.

"I'm going to get my gun," she said into the phone.

"Maude! Don't do anything drastic!" Turing exclaimed.

"I won't," Maude said, groping in the drawer of her bedside table. "But if he gets in here . . ."

"Let me try something first," Turing said.

"Try something? What? What can you do?"

"Here goes."

Water erupted from one of the flower beds. And not the gentle pitter-patter of a sprinkler system, either; a sharp jet of water, focused directly on the intruder. Maude heard a muffled grunt, and a faint rustling as the intruder leaped through some shrubbery to a dryer spot.

Where another jet of water attacked him, point-blank.

"Those must be the deer-repellent tactics you were talking about," Maude said.

"I'm sorry," Turing said. "I had already sent Casey out to install them when you said not to. I was going to have him come by and take them out before you knew they were there, but things were too busy today."

"Just as well," Maude said. She watched as the intruder dashed through the yard, pelted by water jets at every turn. He was looking rather bedraggled and had given up all pretense of stealth.

"Perhaps you won't need your gun after all," Turing said.

"Well, I wasn't planning to shoot him unless I had to," Maude said. "If he made it into the house, I was just going to announce that the police were on the way and that I had a gun and would use it if I had to. And order him to leave."

"Now that's a good idea. Let me try that."

"Halt!" exclaimed a deep, masculine voice from the yard. "We have guns. We will use them if we have to. Stand still and put your hands in the air."

"I see you were planning to use noise as well as water on the poor deer," Maude observed.

The intruder turned away from the direction of the voice, as if to flee. An angry, snarling bark erupted from the bushes ahead of him."

"I said halt! Or I'll release the dogs!" the deep voice thundered.

Growling came from several places in the bushes, and Maude could see movement in the shrubbery.

"You didn't really get dogs?" she asked. Large dogs, from the sound of them.

"Of course not," Turing said. "I'm just waving the water jets very fast to rustle the bushes."

"Ah." Maude nodded. Apparently the intruder was fooled as well. He stood still, hands in the air, though Maude could see the visor of his cap moving back and forth, as if he were trying to spot something in the bushes. Turing continued to broadcast growls at random intervals until two uniformed officers appeared from opposite sides of the yard and took the intruder into custody.

"They'll probably want to talk to me," Maude said. She tucked the gun back in her drawer and reached for her dressing gown.

While Tim drove, Claudia took his cam-era and began paging through the photos of the personnel files.

"Here he is," she said eventually. "Our organized little thief, Kyle Evans. Let me see if I can zoom in and read some of this stuff. He's twenty-three."

"Same as Blake, the dead guy. Maybe they went to school together."

"Maybe," Claudia said. "Not recently, though. This kid went to college. From the time gap, it looks like he had trouble finding a job when he got out, though. But yeah, maybe school's how they know each other. He graduated from Broad Run High School in Ashburn. Is Ashburn a big place?"

Tim shrugged as he began to work his way to the far left for what he knew would be a left-hand exit.

"It's the far-out suburbs—that's all I know," he said.

Claudia was still trying to decipher information from the digital photo of Kyle Evans's file when Tim pulled onto his own quiet street and slowed to cruise for a parking spot. Parking karma was with him; he found a spot only half a block from home.

"Okay, first we upload all this stuff to Turing," Claudia said, snagging her backpack as they got out of the car. "Then let's check out Evans's address."

"Now?" Tim said. "It's nearly one."

"Party pooper!" Claudia said, laughing and punching his shoulder playfully. "Come on, live a little."

"Oh, yeah, all-night surveillance is really living," Tim said. "And not so loud. I don't want to get kicked out of the neighborhood.

But he couldn't help laughing, too, and the more they tried to be quiet, the funnier it seemed. It was the relief, he thought. They didn't get caught, and they actually found something that made all the risk worthwhile. The relief was a natural high. They reeled down the path toward his door, laughing.

"What a great night!" he tried to exclaim, but he'd only reached "great" when something hit his back with a pain so bad he couldn't see or hear for a few seconds. Then his head cleared slightly, which wasn't actually a good thing, because then he really felt the pain. He realized that he was on his knees—had probably landed on them, hard. He suspected his knees weren't going to like that tomorrow, but right now all he could feel was the almost unbearable pain in his back. He reached around and couldn't feel anything damp. So it wasn't a bullet. Someone had hit him in the kidney.

Someone who might be still around. He staggered to his feet and looked around.

"Let me up, you bitch!"

Claudia was half-standing, half-kneeling, holding down a struggling figure. A fairly small figure, with long blond hair. A familiar figure.

"Nikki?" Tim said. "Is that you?"

His voice came out a little breathless. Talking hurt. Of course, right now, everything hurt. He knew he should feel relief that Nikki was okay, after all his worrying, but he didn't. He wasn't quite sure what emotion was trying to make itself felt through the pain, but it wasn't relief.

"I'll kill the bastard!" Nikki shrieked.

"Shut up," Claudia said.

"Let go of me you—"

"Shut up," Claudia repeated, thumping Nikki's head on the grass for emphasis. "I am trying to decide whether to call the police to arrest you for assault. If you keep screaming, the neighbors will call the police and take the decision out of my hands."

Nikki shut up, but she didn't look happy.

"Nikki, what are you doing here?" Tim asked.

"First you don't answer my calls," Nikki hissed. "And then I find you sneaking around behind my back with two different women."

"Two?" Claudia said, curiously.

"Oh, God," Tim said, closing his eyes. "I bet she tried to call my cell phone. I don't suppose she bothered to listen to the message I left telling her not to call me on my cell phone."

"This would be the cell phone the police still have?" Claudia said.

"Police?" Nikki echoed. "What do you mean, police? I want an explanation."

"You're getting a little loud," Claudia said, pulling Nikki's head up a little by way of a warning.

Anger, Tim realized. That was what he felt. Sudden, hot, burning anger, and a desire to put a lot of space between himself and the small blonde woman who suddenly seemed completely unfamiliar.

"Go home, Nikki," Tim said. Anger gave him enough strength to stumble toward his door.

"You're going to have to give me an explanation sometime!" Nikki said.

"You want an explanation? I'm a two-timing bastard and you're lucky to be rid of me. Go home."

"I'll see her to the street," Claudia said, hauling Nikki to her feet with impressive ease.

"Thanks," Tim said. He unlocked his door and shuffled in. He heard some talk and a little scuffling outside. He felt a brief pang of guilt. Letting Claudia do his dirty work for him. But then, she was good at it, and his world was closing in on him. If he tried to get beyond the pain in his kidney, he noticed how much his knees were starting to hurt.

"I think she's gone," Claudia said, as she came through the door and dropped her knapsack with a thud that made Tim shudder. "At least she drove out of sight. Maybe we should take you to the emergency room. She landed a good one on your head."

"My head?" Tim said. He put his hand up to the back of his head and winced. "You're right—she got my head. I was still getting over the kidney punch."

"Ouch," Claudia said, shaking her head. "Don't be surprised if you pee blood for a day or two."

Tim nodded. And then regretted it.

"Okay, for being whacked over the head, you weren't looking so good, but for that, plus a kidney punch, you're not doing so bad," Claudia said. "Though you still might want to consider the emergency room."

Tim shook his head.

"I just want to curl up and not move for a few hours," he said. "Or maybe a few centuries."

"Take these," Claudia said, fishing something out of her purse. "Percocet. Left over from my last job-related injury."

Tim nodded and washed the pills down with a swallow from a flat Diet Coke that was sitting on the coffee table.

"So go to bed, and I'll log in and report to Turing," Claudia said, sitting down at his computer desk. "And then I can hang out here until we're sure you're going to live."

"Okay," Tim said, shuffling toward the bedroom.

"You need any help?"

"I'll be fine," he said.

He kicked off his shoes and then gave up the idea of undressing any more. He managed to crawl onto his bed and found a position he could lie in. Not exactly comfortable, but at least it didn't add to his aches. At first, he didn't think he could sleep, but then Claudia's pills began to work. That helped. As did the thought of Claudia outside the bedroom door, talking to Turing, ready to ward off a return visit from Nikki. Right now he never wanted to see Nikki again.

Never? He examined the thought briefly. Would he feel differently in the morning, when he felt better? If he felt better. Maybe. But he didn't think so. It wasn't because of what she'd done tonight. That was only the last straw. Had made him realize that he was fooling himself. Nikki wasn't who he thought she was. Or pretended to think she was. And he didn't feel the way he thought he did about her.

That made him feel immensely sorry for himself, and

closer to weeping than any of the day's events.

"It's only the Percocet," he told himself, and surrendered to sleep.

I don't know whether to congratulate Tim and Claudia on their success or chew them out for taking such a great risk. They may have cracked the case. But if they'd been caught . . .

"If we'd been caught, I'd have tried to talk my way out somehow," Claudia said. "But we weren't caught, and we've nailed the guy!"

"Isn't nailed a little premature?" I asked. "We know who he is, but we don't know where he is. And since we don't exactly want to tell the police about your burglary, we can't tell them about him."

"Yeah, but now that we know who he is, we can try to tie him to Tayloe Blake," Claudia said. "And maybe that will give us a way to trace him that we can tell the cops about. Let's start working on it, anyway."

"I already am working on it," I said. Annoying that he had a Hotmail account. At the moment, I couldn't get into Hotmail. They'd recently tightened up their security, and I hadn't yet figured out how to get in without setting off a million alarms. I'd manage it eventually—or more likely KingFischer would. I fired off a message asking him for help.

On a more positive note, I had already found Kyle's address and phone number, the make, model, and license plate numbers of his two vehicles—an ancient Dodge pickup and a brand-new red Corvette, the latter doubtless bought with the proceeds of his theft. He'd also recently paid off substantial debts, which should eventually improve his current poor credit rating. I put all this information on screen, so Claudia could see it.

"By morning, I'll have a full dossier on him," I added.

"Great," Claudia said. "I don't think Tim will feel too lively tomorrow, but I can do some legwork in the morning."

"What happened to Tim?" I asked. "I thought you said your . . . visit to PRS went off without a problem."

"It did," Claudia said. "But when we got back to Tim's place to report in, his girlfriend showed up. Seems she's the jealous type. She snuck up on us and did a number on him before he could explain that I was a colleague, not a date."

"Nikki?"

"I think that was the name, yeah."

"What do you mean, did a number on him?"

Apparently, from Claudia's description, doing a number on someone was roughly equivalent to assault and battery.

Paranoid thought: what if this person wasn't actually Tim's girlfriend but an imposter?

"Was this her?"

I flashed a photo of Nikki on the screen. Her driver's license photo, since that was the clearest. And also, since I wasn't sure whether Claudia would consider my occasionally capturing images of Nikki looking over Tim's shoulder quite on the up-and-up.

"Yeah, that's her," Claudia said. "Of course she wasn't smiling tonight. Vicious little . . ."

Claudia left her sentence unfinished and sat studying the photo. I obligingly fed some additional information on Nikki onto the screen.

"Boy, you really checked her out," Claudia said with a laugh. "Any particular reason?"

"Tim asked me to check," I said. "When he hadn't heard from her for a few days. And she worried me, too. Although I suspect he was more worried that something had happened to her than that she might be up to something. But then, he knows her, and I don't."

"Only worried that she might be up to something?" Claudia asked. "No other motive?"

"Isn't that enough?" I asked. "She appeared in his life so suddenly, and his explanations of what they had in common weren't especially coherent. I worried that she might have been a security problem. Interested in him because of his access to confidential infor-

mation about one of his clients. And maybe I was a little worried
about whether she was the right person for him, but that's not the
sort of thing one could learn from a background check, is it?"

"No," Claudia said. "And she's not the type I'd have expected
him to go for. I'd have figured someone a little more brainy. But
then what do I know? Enough of Nikki. If they get back together,
maybe I'll check her out some more. For now, let's worry about our
dead thief."

I showed her all the information I'd found on Blake and on
Kyle Evans, our new suspect, and she made a couple of suggestions
about other places to look. And I told her about Maude's burglary—though I attributed detection of the prowler to Maude's new
security system.

"Is she all right?" Claudia demanded. "Do you think she needs
company? I could go over."

"The police are there, and she should be fine once the security system is rearmed."

"Okay," she said. "Probably more important to stay here and
keep an eye on Tim. In case Miss Congeniality comes back for
more."

"Then again, if you and Tim went over to Maude's, you could
all be behind the security system. You wouldn't have to stay awake.
You'll be exhausted tomorrow."

"Don't worry," Claudia said. "I don't have to stay awake. I'm
a light sleeper. One suspicious footstep and I'm wide awake."

"Useful skill for a PI," I said.

"Life-saving skill for a woman whose ex gets drunk every couple
of months and tries to come and teach her a lesson," she said.

"Can't you get a restraining order or something?" I asked.

"Yeah, I have, and if he didn't have so many friends and rela-
tives on the force, maybe it'd do some good," she said. "But in the
meantime, I'm armed, and I'm a real light sleeper. We'll be fine
here."

She eventually fell asleep on Tim's couch.

She reassured me several times that Tim's injuries, though

painful, were unlikely to be serious, but agreed that it would be a good idea to take him to his doctor in the morning. I e-mailed Maude, asking her to set this up. But at her work e-mail. I didn't think Maude needed more to worry about tonight.

And in my e-mail to Maude, I said that Tim had had a minor accident. I don't know why I said that. Perhaps in case she has insomnia and logs in to check her e-mail tonight, since the explanation would probably involve mentioning Tim and Claudia's unauthorized entry into the PRS building, and I had a feeling we needed to break that carefully to Maude. She probably wouldn't approve of it at any time, and right now, I think the subject of burglary would upset her greatly.

Not that I think her intruder was a mere burglar. Though I'm not sure that's something Maude can explain to the police. At least I hope she doesn't try to.

Two of the police have taken the intruder away, but another two are still at Maude's house. I can only catch the occasional scrap of what they're saying. It's driving me crazy, not knowing what's going on.

Maude stifled a yawn as the younger of the two police officers reappeared through the French doors.

"Where are the dogs, ma'am?"

"Dogs?"

"We want to make sure the dogs are secured," he said.

"I don't have dogs," Maude said.

"We heard dogs as we were approaching the backyard, ma'am."

"Oh, that," Maude said. "It was just recorded dog sound effects. Part of my security system."

"The male voice we heard—that was part of the security system, too?"

"Of course," Maude said.

"Nice system," the officer said. He stepped over to the

nearest camera pole. Which was now a camera, speaker, and water-jet pole, she supposed. She could see a hose winding its way up the pole.

"Where are the motion detectors?" the officer said.

"Motion detectors?" Maude asked, yawning. "That's one piece of equipment we don't have. I'm not sure the poles could take any more weight."

"No motion detectors?" the officer said. "Then how is it activated?"

Good question, Maude thought. She mentally kicked herself for not paying attention. Of course, what did you expect at this hour?

I'll let Turing deal with it, she thought.

"I'll show you," she said, walking toward her office. "It's a new, experimental system that one of our employees has been working on, so we haven't installed any motion detectors, yet. Right now, it's controlled from a computer screen."

She sat down at her desk, deliberately not looking at Turing's camera. The officer studied the screensaver playing on her monitor with a puzzled expression.

"Luckily, I heard the intruder," she said. "And remembered that we had the system partially installed, so I decided to see what I could do with it. I had my gun, of course, in case it didn't work. So I came down here and called up the control screen. Here we go."

Not a lot of time, but then, if Turing was paying attention, she wouldn't need a lot of time to do what Maude needed her to do. If Turing understood the hints Maude had been dropping.

She moved her mouse, and the screensaver vanished, to reveal an unfamiliar screen. The officer moved in closer to peer at it. Maude paused as if giving him time to study it and quickly scanned the series of graphic buttons lined up along the left side of the screen.

"The first thing I did was hit the panic button—it fires off a call to 911," Maude said, moving her mouse up to the top button marked, matter-of-factly, 911. A small graphic of a telephone sat beside the button. When her cursor hovered over the button, the telephone lit up. Nice touch, Turing, she thought.

"I won't click that one, of course," she said. "I don't want to send a false 911 call. Then I hit the camera button."

The little camera icon not only glowed under the cursor, it became animated when she clicked it. Now she realized why Turing had lined the buttons vertically along the left side of the screen, leaving so much blank space on the right. The blank space filled with a bank of miniature windows, each showing the view from one of the cameras. Most of them showed only the garden, though in three of them she could see that the other officer was examining one of the camera poles. The officer looking over her shoulder snickered, presumably at the close-up view one camera gave of his partner's nostrils and mustache.

"Then I decided to use the water jets," she said. She pressed the water button, and managed not to look surprised when a small window popped up with instructions for targeting.

"You really expect to scare off a prowler with a little water?" the officer asked.

"Well, not exactly," she said. "The water jets are really to repel deer. Although I can already see that watering from in here is going to be a lot more pleasant than doing it outside when the temperature hits the nineties. But I figured the water wouldn't hurt."

The officer nodded.

"You click on one of the screens to choose that view—we won't pick any of the ones near your partner," she said, clicking on a view at the other side of the yard, as far as possible from the screen that now showed a slightly bloodshot eyeball as the partner inspected the camera itself. "And voila!"

She pressed the mouse button, and a spurt of water erupted from the water jet. The officer laughed as his partner leaped away from the camera he was inspecting and backed away from the water jet.

Maude experimented with holding the mouse button down, to produce a steady stream, and adjusting the height and direction of the stream using the arrow keys.

"I should probably go out and tell him not to worry," the officer said.

"Use this," she said, clicking the button marked broadcast and gesturing to the microphone attached to the side of the monitor.

"Don't worry, Andy," the officer said, into the mike. "She's just showing me her security system."

"Here, you try it," Maude said, standing up to yield her seat to the officer. He sat down eagerly and began experimenting with the buttons. The dog button produced a submenu of possible canine sound effects, ranging from soft growls to angry barking and growling, with an option to simulate one, two, or half a dozen dogs. By the time the officer had mastered the system that controlled which speaker the various dog noises came from, Maude had resigned herself to the likelihood of a morning visit from animal control.

Maude had a sense of déjà vu when the officer tested the human voice options, which allowed the user to threaten an intruder with dogs, firearms, and the imminent arrival of the police, all in a deep, resonant male voice. She recognized the synthesized version of a famous actor's voice, which KingFischer had, improbably, adopted for use when he experimented with voice generation. The officer found this less fascinating than the dogs, though, and soon returned to the water jets. He was chasing his hapless partner all over the yard with them, and the partner was clearly losing patience. Maude began to wonder what she was supposed to do if the partner completely lost his temper and hostilities broke out—should she call the police on the police?

She was relieved when the doorbell rang. The officer who'd been playing with the security system suddenly became all business again.

"I'll answer that," he said.

"Fine," Maude said. "I'm going to heat some water for tea. I can make coffee if you want some."

Returning to bed looked rather far off, she thought. Turing's clever and quickly improvised fake control console had worked to conceal that she, not Maude, had controlled the water jets and fended off the intruder. But demonstrating it had taken time, and Maude didn't think the police were finished asking questions.

She heard voices in the foyer. Probably more cops, she thought, or the officer wouldn't have let them in. She was rubbing her face as if doing so could scrub away the bone-deep exhaustion she felt, when she heard footsteps approaching the kitchen.

She looked up to see Dan Norris in the doorway. A rather disheveled Norris, wearing jeans and a sweatshirt, with his hair imperfectly combed.

She was opening her mouth to comment on this, but instead of stopping in the doorway, Norris strode over and grabbed her by the shoulders, as if he were planning to shake her. And hard enough that she half-expected to see bruises in the morning.

"Are you all right?" he demanded.

I was alarmed to see Special Agent Norris arrive at Maude's house. If Claudia were awake, she'd probably suggest that his interest was purely personal. That he was worried about Maude. I suspected from his disheveled state and agitated manner that he was worried about her, but I don't think that's all. He could only have found out about the burglary from the Falls Church police. And why would they have contacted him—unless he arranged for the police to keep a watch on Maude or at least to notify him if her name came up in any context?

What if they were watching Tim, as well? And already knew about the apparently successful burglary he and Claudia carried out? Which would not be so successful after all if the police arrive tomorrow to arrest them.

Norris's presence alarms me. So I've been trying to follow what's going on, as much as I can through the open study door. Norris has been talking to one of the officers in low tones for fifteen minutes. Unfortunately, I can't boost my microphones enough to catch much of what they're saying. Not an oversight, really—a deliberate choice, to respect Maude's privacy. I haven't tried to get maximum visual and audio coverage inside her house. It never occurred to me that at some point, the need to protect her might override the need to respect her privacy. I should discuss this with her.

Later. When the police have gone.

Perhaps she isn't the one in need of protection, not with two, armed police officers and the very intense Special Agent Norris around. I'm the one at risk if Norris or the police become suspicious.

Is that a selfish thought or merely a sensible one?

Maude made herself a cup of tea and told Norris to help himself to coffee or tea. Then she came into the office to sit at her desk. Perhaps she realized how anxious I was and wanted to keep me company. Or perhaps she wanted company. But she didn't say anything, so I thought it best to keep quiet. She sat, sipping her tea, watching the pictures in my cameras, which showed the second officer still searching the yard.

Norris appeared in the doorway.

"Are you sure you're all right?" he asked. He'd been asking the same thing at random intervals ever since he arrived.

"I'm fine," Maude said, not for the first time. "There's hot water in the kitchen for coffee if you want some. Only instant, I'm afraid."

"Thanks," Norris said. Though he didn't go to get any coffee. I don't know whether this is significant or not. I've observed that the ritual offer and acceptance of beverages plays an important part in human social interactions, but I'm still trying to codify the rules that govern it. Maybe there are no rules. Or maybe there's more than one set of rules, and Maude and Dan Norris are operating under different sets, and that's why her offer of coffee drew such a frown from him.

Maude is behaving oddly. Of course, she has had a difficult experience tonight. Still, I only really noticed her odd behavior after Norris arrived. She looks more stressed, rather than less. She keeps tidying things in short bursts, alternating with periods of sitting still, looking at her thumbnails and rubbing them. I wonder if she used to bite her nails.

This makes little sense. Surely the arrival of one more professionally trained, and presumably armed, law enforcement officer should make her feel safer. Perhaps, like me, she is worried about the implications of Norris's presence. But while she's not behaving entirely normally, I doubt if anyone who didn't know her as well as I do would guess she was feeling pressured. Outwardly, she is quite calm.

Perhaps that's why Special Agent Norris is frowning. He is treating her in the careful manner one uses with people who are very upset. Perhaps he expected to find a hysterical victim in need of comforting, and is disappointed to find Maude her usual acerbic self.

And also close-mouthed, as usual. She seems to find his behavior annoying. Perhaps Claudia is wrong about them liking each other.

"I'm going to see what else I can find out about your prowler," Norris said.

"You think he had something to do with your case?" Maude asked.

Norris shrugged, which Maude probably didn't see, since she appeared to be avoiding looking at him. Then again, perhaps he didn't know this, since he was doing the same thing.

"I'm not a big believer in coincidences," he said.

Maude nodded.

She continued to watch the pictures from the various cameras. It oc-

curred to me that she could as easily be keeping an eye on Norris in the reflection on the monitor. So perhaps she also saw him open his mouth as if to say something and then close it again as if changing his mind. He did this three times, though the third time he ended by muttering something under his breath before turning and striding out.

"Lock the damned doors after us," he called out from the foyer.

"What was that he said?" Maude asked, looking at my camera at last.

"Lock the—"

"Before he left the room."

I hesitated.

"I couldn't quite tell whether it was 'bloody stubborn woman' or 'bloody stupid woman,'" Maude said.

"Stubborn, I'm reasonably sure," I said.

"Well, that's true," she said, rolling her chair back from the desk and standing up abruptly. *Going to lock up, no doubt.*

She paused in the doorway and looked back.

"Thanks," she said. "See you in the morning."

"Sleep well," I called after her.

I do hope she can sleep. I used to consider humans' need to spend a third of their time unconscious and immobile a serious design flaw. At best a waste of resources, and at worst, a potentially fatal vulnerability. But most humans disagree.

"A few of us think that way," Maude told me once. "We call them 'type A.' In the eighties, being type A was quite trendy."

"And now it's not?"

"In some circles, yes. But most people realize that type A's are prone to die young from stress-related ailments, and drive everyone around them bonkers in the meantime."

Perhaps another potential problem in human-AIP relations. I suspect we AIPs probably come across as consummate type A's. Not only do we never sleep or take a day off, but most of us have little real understanding of how humans' stamina differs from ours. Maybe it's a good thing most of us aren't sentient and don't seek out human companionship. Good for the humans, at least, if I'm any-

*thing to go by. I seem to do nothing but annoy my human compan-
ions and lead them into danger.*

At least, in return, I can watch over them.

*Although my preoccupation with other things kept me from spot-
ting Maude's burglar as soon as I should have. No harm done, fortunately, but what if it had taken me even longer to spot him.*

*I suddenly wondered how much sooner I could have spotted him.
I retrieved the files that contained the digital video from all the
cameras for that time period, synchronized them all at the precise
second when I noticed the burglar, and began moving backwards.
Fifteen seconds . . . thirty seconds . . . he'd been there a minute and
twenty-three seconds before I'd spotted him.*

*And about halfway through that period, I spotted what could be
a second intruder on one of the cameras. Just the suggestion of a face,
appearing for perhaps two seconds, as the wind shifted a branch and
let more moonlight into a shadowy area of the yard, and then disap-
pearing again.*

*It only appeared on the one camera. Was it only an optical illu-
sion?*

*I took a copy of that section of the file and tried enhancing it sev-
eral ways. Probably a face. But not one I recognized.*

Not someone the police took into custody, either.

*Perhaps they couldn't have captured him, even if I'd known to
tell them to look for him at the time. But I felt as if I'd failed
Maude. There was another intruder still out there.*

*I've set up a permanent background task for watching over
Maude's yard. Microphones boosted to the max, cameras swiveling
endlessly—surely no prowler can get by me now.*

*At least in the parts of the yard I can cover. The backyard,
mainly, since that's where the garden is. I will talk to Maude soon
about expanding my coverage. I wonder if I could get Casey to come
out on the weekend to do it. Probably a type A thing to ask.*

*Then again, why not? I can offer him two days off next week.
I'm sure he'd love that. And given everything Maude does for me*

and the long hours she works, why not take advantage of something that I can do so easily to make her safer?

Maybe I should put something at Tim's apartment, too. Though full coverage would require some explanation to his landlord. But surely the landlord wouldn't balk if Tim said that, due to the dangers he faces as a private investigator, he wants to install a state-of-the art intruder detection system. Most PIs' jobs aren't that dangerous, but his landlord wouldn't know that. And he'd probably like the fact that the system would protect the entire house and yard, not just Tim's portion of it.

But for now, Claudia is watching over Tim—or at least sleeping on his couch, so anyone barging into the apartment would have to go past her to get to Tim. And I am watching over Claudia—I can see her shins and feet through my cameras. If she wakes, I will be ready to assist her. Or if I hear anything suspicious, I will wake her. I have readied a harsh alarm clock sound to use, just in case.

And I have the sound boosted on my microphones. If anyone tried to break in, I'd probably hear the noise well before Tim and Claudia were in danger. I could call 911 and use my speakers to help Claudia defend the place. I have my dog sounds ready, and the deep, male voice-generation program I used at Maude's. I have added the sound of someone chambering a round in a shotgun, which I deduce from my mystery reading would have a sobering effect on someone who heard it in a darkened room.

At least watching over them gives me something to do. But right now, I almost wish I were a human, so I could go to sleep and forget about things for a few hours. And wake up in the morning, as humans so often do, with not only their energy but also their optimism renewed.

SATURDAY MORNING, 9:02:00 A.M.

Maude had planned to sleep late, but no matter how much her body needed the rest, her brain wasn't cooperating. Several times she jerked awake at the brink of sleep, convinced there was someone in the room. And when she did sleep, she dreamed restlessly of urgent things left undone.

At nine, she finally gave up trying, pulled on her jeans, and drove to the office.

"Morning," she said to Turing's cameras as she walked in. "And yes, I know it's Saturday. I needed to get out of the house."

"Not a bad idea," Turing said. "Maude, after last night, I think we should call Casey and get him to expand the camera system. If the burglars had come to the front of the house—"

"Burglars?" Maude looked up from the keyboard where she was typing in her password. "Do you know something I don't?"

"I'm not sure," Turing said. "I reviewed all the video from your cameras—I wanted to see if I could have spotted the burglar any earlier than I did if I'd been specifically watching for human intruders. And on one camera . . ."

Instead of finishing the sentence, she showed a fragment of video—only a couple of seconds. And then froze the clearest image on the screen.

"My God," Maude whispered.

"I kept watch as well as I could last night, but the camera placement was designed for viewing the garden, not for security," Turing said. "I've done a schematic for an expanded system—if we reposition a couple of the cameras, and add two at the front, we'd have complete coverage and—Maude? Are you okay?"

"It's Nestor Garcia," Maude said.

"Are you sure?"

"Am I—of course," Maude said, shaking her head. "You've never seen him. Claudia and I have, but you and Tim never did."

Maude stared at the screen for a few more minutes. "Yes," she said. "Find Casey."

SATURDAY AFTERNOON, 12:30:00 P.M.

Tim shifted uncomfortably in his chair and then glanced across Maude's office to see if she'd noticed. He didn't want to restart the debate about going to the doctor. He suspected his doctor would prescribe pain killers and bed rest, and right now he wanted to stay involved. Not let the others down.

Maude was still staring at her monitor, where Turing had displayed the spreadsheet Tim and Claudia had found. Tim braced himself. He'd been able to postpone telling Maude anything until he'd heard all about her midnight visitor. Curious to finally see what Nestor Garcia looked like, after so many months of talking and worrying about him. And curiously chilling as a disembodied face apparently floating in darkness.

But eventually Turing mentioned the new evidence he and Claudia had discovered, and sooner or later he'd have to explain how they'd found it.

"Where did you get this spreadsheet?" Maude said. "I thought Claudia couldn't find any opportunity to search the place."

"She didn't," Tim said. "We sort of went back later."

"Later? Later than what?"

"Later than they were open."

"After they were closed you mean? Won't they figure out who went in after hours?"

"Well, no, we sort of used an open window."

"You burgled the place?"

"I guess so," Tim said.

"Oh, my God," Maude murmured.

"It's okay," Tim said. "No one spotted us, and like I said,

we found the spreadsheet, and that's going to break the case."

"Assuming we can find a way to steer the police to it," Turing said.

"I'm glad someone sees the problem here," Maude said.

"Problem?" Tim echoed.

"Big problem," Maude said. "Thanks to your burglary, we know that Tayloe Blake's accomplice, and probably the brains behind the credit card scheme, was Kyle Evans, a k a SlyKyle@Hotmail.com. And we know where the police can find the evidence to prove it. But we have no safe way to steer the police to him and the evidence, because they might ask inconvenient questions, like how do we know he's the one? And that's a question we can't answer without confessing to a lot of illegal activities—some of them probably felonies. Burglary is a felony, isn't it?"

"Yes," Turing said. "But I'm sure Sam could have done something if they'd been caught. Since they weren't trying to take anything."

"I'm not so sure, and let's hope she doesn't have to try," Maude said. "So, does anyone have any bright ideas on what we're going to do with this wonderful information you've found?"

"We track down Kyle Evans," Tim said. Though not today, he hoped.

"And do what? Reproach him for his dishonesty? Implore him to turn himself in to the police?"

Tim shifted uncomfortably in his chair and shrugged.

"And what happens when the police or the FBI find out we're trying to find him?" Maude added. "I think events at my house last night prove they're keeping a close eye on us—you're lucky they didn't happen to be watching you two last night. So we don't have a lot of breathing room here."

"Claudia's idea was that now we try to find some link between him and Blake," Tim said. He wished Claudia hadn't had to go in to her job at PRS—they'd agreed that she should hang onto the job for the time being, in case they needed access to the PRS building again—and in case Kyle Evans was stupid enough to return. But that left Tim to tell Maude about their evening's adventures. He had the feeling Claudia could have done a better job of defusing Maude's anger.

"Find a link," Maude said. "Yes, but that's going to be a little hard. Since we can't admit to knowing anything about Evans, we can only investigate Blake without tipping our hand. And since Blake's the subject of a homicide investigation, the police aren't going to like our snooping around his life and times."

"Well, we don't have to do anything immediately," Tim said. "The police might be about to find the same thing we found. Or if they don't, we could wait until their interest in the case dies down a bit."

"And what if while we're waiting for the police to lose interest something happens to Kyle Evans?" Maude asked.

"Or to us?" Turing added. "Maude's right, of course. But at least we're closer to knowing what has been going on, and I think we need to do something with the information."

"I'm sorry," Maude said. "I didn't mean to imply that it wasn't important information. But it certainly doesn't solve all our problems."

"It solves some, and creates a whole new set of problems. More interesting problems," Turing said.

"I'm still alarmed that the two of you did this without even notifying anyone," Maude said. "What if you'd run into the killer while you were in there?"

"Sam's here," Turing said. "Maybe we shouldn't tell her about the burglary. Maybe we should just say that Claudia found the file while working at PRS."

"I think we should at least suggest that Claudia did not find it while performing her assigned duties at PRS,"

Maude said. "That she might get in trouble if too many people found out precisely how she got the file."

"As long as we leave it indefinite," Turing said.

"I'll be subtle," Maude said, standing up to greet Sam.

Maude was good at subtle, Tim thought, as he listened to her revealing their new find to Sam. She managed to dance over exactly how Claudia had gotten the various printouts now littering Maude's conference table, but without actually lying. And without concealing her own feelings about the matter, a mixture of disapproval and grudging admiration.

"So we have a suspect," Sam said. "This is good. Can we turn him over to the police?"

"Well, even if we had any legitimately obtained evidence against him, we don't know where he is," Maude said. "He hasn't shown up at work again today, according to Claudia."

"We should check out where he lives," Tim said. "And probably stake it out."

"By we you mean you," Maude said. "And what if the police or some of Dan Norris's troops are keeping an eye on you? Bad idea."

"Maybe not," Sam said, slowly. "Let's think this through. If the police call Tim in and ask why he was looking for this kid, what does Tim say?"

"Um . . . that I want my attorney?"

"Well, yes," Sam said. "I do want to keep paying my mortgage and my student loans. But after I get there, what's wrong with my telling them why you're looking for Kyle Evans?"

Tim shook his head and shrugged his shoulders.

"I say we think Rose's card information was stolen through a collection agency," Sam said. "And PRS being the most likely suspect, we're checking it out. And one of my investigators working at PRS grew suspicious when Evans stopped showing up the day after the murder. So I sent you to check out Evans. We don't mention the spreadsheet if

Claudia didn't find it legitimately. But the rest is perfectly legal and plausible, and better yet, true."

"And the cops won't object?" Tim asked.

"Worst case, they'll warn you away and take over the investigation themselves," Sam said. "If they think what we came up with is plausible. Hell, for all we know, one of Claudia's coworkers could be an undercover cop. When you come right down to it, maybe it would be a good thing if we sicced them on Evans. They've got the resources to find him and protect him."

"So it's okay for me to start looking for Evans?" Tim said.

"Go for it," Sam said. Maude nodded.

"Great," Tim said. "Shoot me the info you've got, Tur."

"Why don't you use the guest office?" Maude said. "I want to ask Sam some questions about how she's coming along with Rose Lafferty's case."

"No problem," Tim said.

He was glad to get out from under Maude's gaze while she was still mad about the burglary. And away from Sam before he accidentally spilled the beans. He relocated to the guest office he used when he worked at the Alan Grace headquarters and logged in.

"So what have we got on Kyle Evans?" he asked.

"Here's a map to his apartment," Turing said, as the laser printer at his elbow began spitting out papers. "It's in a large, relatively new development in Sterling. Not fancy, but probably more than he can afford on his PRS salary."

"Unless he has a roommate," Tim said.

"I can't find anyone else listed at that address."

"Yeah, and Kyle's famous for following the rules, right? He could have any number of roommates management doesn't know about. How big is his place?"

"An efficiency. Approximately 450 square feet."

"Okay, scratch the roommate idea," Tim said. "He's just living above his means."

"Which wouldn't be hard to do, considering how small his means are," Turing said. "PRS doesn't pay anyone much more than minimum wage, not even the skip tracers. How do people live on that here?"

"They go into debt," Tim said. "Is Kyle in debt?"

"Not now," Turing said. "By the time he took the job at PRS, he had maxed out on all his credit cards and began skipping payments on some of his bills. He came to PRS nine months ago, but he worked as a collector at first. And then after three months they promoted him to skip tracing. Doesn't that seem a little hasty for PRS to move him into a position with so much access to confidential information?"

"Considering what he did with the confidential information, definitely," Tim said. "But then look at what they had to work with. From what Claudia has seen, three months probably makes him an old-timer around there."

"Still not particularly logical," Turing said. "And considering PRS's potential legal liability when victims discover what Evans has been up to, very short-sighted. I can't understand why humans haven't set up some way to monitor people who have access to financial information that could be used for illegal purposes."

"They do," Tim said. "According to Claudia, PRS tracks every keystroke she makes, and can look at what's on her screen at any time, and run a credit check on an employee whenever they like."

"That didn't help them spot Kyle Evans. I was thinking more of a system that would match his expenditures against his declared income. If they'd done that, they could easily see that he was spending much more than his salary."

"A system like that would violate people's privacy," Tim said.

"And prevent a lot of crime," Turing said. "It would certainly have flagged the fact that shortly after moving to skip tracing, Evans began paying his bills on time, whittling down

his credit card balances, and buying expensive luxuries—
new car, stereo, and TV. Which doesn't add up. His fixed
expenses—rent, utilities, car payments and insurance, student
loans—are more than his monthly take-home pay, and that's
before you even start adding in things like food and gas and
such. There's no way he could be doing this without some
source of income outside his salary."

"So it's pretty clear why he started the scam," Tim said.
"To get out of debt."

He felt a twinge of sympathy for Evans. He'd never gotten quite so far behind with his debts, but he could have.
Turing could be describing how he'd have ended up by now
if he hadn't swallowed his pride and taken a job as a copy-
machine operator at Universal Library. Moved into a dump
of an apartment that he could afford; an apartment near a
Metro stop so he could sell his car. Scaling back his lifestyle
to match his income. And maybe he'd still be living that
way if he hadn't met Turing. Or maybe he'd have taken the
same path Kyle Evans had chosen if he'd had the chance. He
liked to think not, but you never knew.

"Weird that he's preying on people in the same boat he
was six months ago," he said, aloud.

"I wonder if he ever had the same thing happen to him,"
Turing said. "Someone using his charge cards when he was
already over his head in debt."

"Maybe," Tim said. "Of course, it's just as likely he got
the idea from listening to people give him excuses when he
called them up."

He winced inwardly, remembering some of the tall tales
he'd spun for bill collectors, during those few stretches
when he'd been more broke than usual.

"So what does he drive?" Tim asked aloud.

"A Corvette," Turing said.

"Please tell me it's used," Tim said.

"No, it's brand new. He bought it two months ago."

She flashed a picture of the car on the screen. Tim studied the sleek silver vehicle enviously.

"Okay, I was feeling a little sorry for him with the debt thing, but he just lost my sympathy."

"That's not the right color, though," Turing said. "If you're going to use it for identification purposes. Ah, here we go."

The silver Corvette suddenly turned bright red, and a copy of the photo began to emerge from the printer.

"That's an approximation," Turing said. "But it should be reasonably accurate. They didn't have a picture of the red one on their site, so I used the paint swatch and extrapolated. While I was at it, I put his number on the plates. He hasn't bought any special plate style, so that's also reasonably accurate, but not necessarily exact."

"How about some pictures of Kyle, while you're at it?" Tim said. "In case I have to show them around."

"Coming up," Turing said, as the printer continued to hum. "And also of Tayloe Blake. And while I'm at it, I'll give you a random selection of young men of approximately the same age, in case you want to see if someone can pick any of them out from a photo lineup."

"Sounds more like something the police would do," Tim said, but he stuffed the various maps, photos, and other printouts into his briefcase, along with the spare cell phone Maude had arranged that morning.

"All set," he said.

"One more thing," Turing said. "Sam's been asking more and more questions. And Maude thinks it would be smart to answer them."

Tim's stomach tightened. He thought he could see where this was leading.

"Questions about what?"

"About me. Maude thinks we should tell Sam the truth about me. What do you think?"

Tim swallowed. What did he think? Turing wasn't leaving

this decision to him, was she? Well, no, she was asking Maude, too. Half a dozen conflicting thoughts darted through his mind. A sudden flash of resentment—Turing was their secret, his and Maude's—did he really want to share? And a flash of relief—having Sam in on the secret would mean another person to help. Not just another set of hands and eyes, but another mind, and one with skills neither of them possessed—skills Turing might need. Why Sam and not Claudia, he thought? And then, why not Claudia, too? But one thing at a time; if telling Sam went well, he could suggest Claudia.

"Yeah," he said. "Probably a good idea. Right now, we're asking her to do a good job for us, and she doesn't really know everything the job involves. We should tell her."

"Thanks," Turing said. "I think so, too. And maybe now's as good a time as any. You want to stay and help?"

Tim felt torn. He wanted to see how Sam would react to the news. But he also felt a sense of urgency about finding Kyle Evans.

"I'm sure you and Maude can handle it," he said, finally. "But I'd like to see how she reacts. Save the video to show me later, okay?"

"Will do," Turing said.

"Tim's off to look for Kyle Evans," I said.

"Good," Sam said. "And I hope by the time he finds him, I can convince you to turn him over to the cops."

"I don't see a problem with turning him over," Maude said. "But we'd like the chance to talk to him ourselves first."

"Why?" Sam said. "I'll be straight; I like the idea of letting the cops handle this. I don't understand why you people don't. Level with me. If there's something I don't know that's driving this, tell me now."

"The more you know, the better you can protect us," Maude said. "We understand that."

"So what don't I know?" Sam said. "I figured out already that it's something to do with Turing. So spill. Whatever it is, I can handle it."

Maude laughed. Sam looked at her in surprise.

"Okay, Sam," I said. "You asked for it."

I saw Maude sit back, her eyes fixed on Sam's face.

"Sam," I began. "Doesn't it strike you as odd that you've never met me in person?"

"Odd's a good word for it," Sam said. "Yeah, more than a little odd. At first, I figured you were just one of those eccentric computer geniuses you always hear about. It's a stereotype, sure, but sometimes there's a grain of truth in stereotypes."

"Like the one about litigators being just a little bit aggressive," Maude said with a smile.

"Who, me?" Sam said. "I'm a pussycat at heart, but I have to put on the big, bad lawyer act for the other side. Anyway, as time went on, I began to wonder if there was something more than just eccentricity. I confess, I interrogated your PI friend, Claudia, about the whole thing."

"I'd have done the same," Maude said. She was suppressing a smile.

"She claimed not to know any more than I did," Sam said. "So if she's in on the secret, whatever it is, she's good at keeping her mouth shut. She did admit that she'd come up with the same theory I had."

"And what is Claudia's theory?" I asked. I'd wondered what Claudia thought of me. Like Sam, she'd worked with us long enough to have many unanswered questions, and while she'd never asked them, either, I suspected her curiosity would drive her to find her own answers. Wrong ones, I hoped.

Sam looked thoughtful.

"We both assume you have some good reason for not letting anyone see you," Sam said. "Being the suspicious type, at first I figured you were someone who's wanted and on the run."

"Wanted?" I repeated. "You thought I was a criminal?"

"Hey, this was when I first met you," Sam said, holding up her hands in mock surrender. "Or rather, didn't meet you, just communicated through telephones, speakers, and e-mail. I toyed with the idea that maybe you were some radical from the sixties who'd mellowed and built a new life but couldn't come in from the cold because the FBI still wanted you. Or maybe someone who'd committed a crime of conscience, like a reformed ecoterrorist. And it made sense that you wouldn't want to show yourself to me, because then I could honestly say that no, your honor, I had no idea my client was the notorious so-and-so."

"A dramatic theory," Maude said.

"Okay, so I watch too much TV," Sam said. "At least I never pegged you for a common criminal."

"Nice to know that despite your suspicions you could sense Turing's basically moral and law-abiding nature," Maude said, nodding with approval.

"Well, that and her complete lack of practical knowledge about the criminal side of the legal system," Sam said.

"Complete lack of knowledge?" I said. I was hurt. Considering the number of mystery books I've studied, I like to think I'm reasonably expert in matters of crime and detection.

"Oh, I can tell you've done a lot of reading on the subject, and probably seen a few TV shows and movies," Sam said. "But even a reasonably well-informed law-abiding citizen doesn't know the same things as a career criminal."

"I see," I said. Maude chuckled.

"I rather like the notion of Turing as a dangerous fugitive," she said.

"Yeah, well that was at first," Sam said. "You'll be happy to know I've pretty much discarded that theory and come around to the same idea Claudia has—that you've gone through some kind *of accident that has left you disfigured. And perhaps with limited mobility. Maybe a car accident or a bad fire. Or possibly a medical condition—neurofibromatosis, proteus syndrome. Something like that."*

Maude nodded.

"It's the most plausible explanation," she said. And then glanced at my camera as if to say that this was my last chance to back out.

Tempting. I could just say, "Brilliant! You guessed it! What gave it away?" and Sam would go away content.

But I was tired of pretending.

"So," Sam said, tilting her head to one side. "Have I got it?"

"Not exactly," Turing said. "I'm not a handicapped person. Or a differently abled person, if you want to be politically correct, though differently abled comes closer to the truth. I'm a person. But I'm not human."

"Are we talking visitor from another planet stuff?" Sam said, frowning.

"Now that I never thought of," Maude said.

"No," I said. "I was born—or, more accurately, created—on Earth. I'm an artificial intelligence personality—an AIP."

Sam blinked and shook her head.

"Okay, nice try, but if you want to dodge talking to the cops, I'd suggest coming up with another story. That dog won't hunt."

"I'm serious," I said.

"Pull the other one," Sam said.

"Other what?" I asked.

"Here," Maude said. "Let's try this."

She started the DVD player, and began showing a short video the Universal Library sales force used to explain the AIPs in basic terms.

Of course, it was a little cheesy. The scene of a bespectacled child prodigy playing chess with KingFischer wasn't too awful. The part where Aunty Em counseled a troubled teenager would have been better if the suicidal teen hadn't overacted quite so badly. I cringed when the two vapid-looking twenty-somethings with no discernible acting ability reacted to every remark I made with loud and patently fake laughter. Embarrassing. Of course, I'm biased—the scriptwriter who wrote my lines talked to me for all of five minutes, and then the director had them dubbed in by an actress with a silly, squeaky voice—not at all like what I produce when I use voice generation.

But cheesy or not, the fifteen-minute DVD explained, succinctly and in nontechnical terms, what (or who) the AIPs were, how and why we were created, and what role we now played in UL's operations.

But did Maude really expect it to convince Sam? Or was this only a ploy to give Sam enough time to absorb what we were saying?

Sam watched without apparent reaction. When the closing credits ended, she looked up at Maude.

"So it's not a real person at all—it's a program."

"She's a person," Maude said. "She was originally a program, but now she's sentient—a person, just like you and me, except that she occupies a different kind of body."

Sam glanced warily back and forth between my camera and Maude.

"And . . . she is capable of independent action and thought."

"Often a little too independent," Maude said.

"Great day in the morning," Sam muttered.

"Hey, look on the bright side," I said. "Now you can be absolutely sure I'm not a criminal. Before it could convict me, a court would have to believe that I exist. Legally, that is."

"True," she said. "But do you realize what a world of trouble we're in if anyone ever subpoenas you?"

"That's why we're telling you," I said. "We realize that by keeping you in the dark, we were handicapping you, and maybe setting you up for a contempt of court citation, not to mention putting ourselves in greater danger. You might do things differently, for example, if you know that it's not just a case of my preferring not to *appear in court or talk to the police—I physically can't, at least not in any way they could accept."*

"No kidding," Sam said.

She sat lost in thought for a few minutes. I watched in silence, trying to read her face to see whether she believed us or not. Suddenly she turned to Maude.

"You believe this?" she said.

"Yes," Maude said, nodding. "Absolutely."

Maude watched Sam's face as she di-gested the news. She realized that her fists were clenched. If Sam didn't believe them . . . didn't react the way they hoped she would . . .

She saw a dozen expressions cross Sam's face, disbelief warring with fascination, and perhaps the suspicion that they were pulling her leg. And then Maude relaxed a little when Sam smiled and shook her head.

"Well, now I know why y'all picked me," Sam said.

"I'm not sure I understand," Turing said.

Maude laughed.

"Actually, Turing picked you out, sight unseen, based on recommendations from veteran private investigators," Maude said. "We didn't hire you till I'd vetted you, of course. But you were number one on our list, based on the number of people who told us that you had gotten more dumb PIs out of more jams they shouldn't have gotten into in the first place than any ten other lawyers in northern Virginia."

"Lord knows that's true," Sam said. "So my race and gender were just a bonus?"

"I'm an AIP, Sam," Turing said. "Race and gender are rather theoretical concepts to me. I have a hard time understanding their relevance to the current situation."

"Think about it, Turing," Maude said. "She's black and female—two groups who have had to fight to change a legal system and a social structure that defined them as less than full persons or even as property."

"Still fighting, actually," Sam said.

"So who better to understand the dangers of your situation?" Maude added.

"Exactly," Sam said. "Don't get me wrong. Any lawyer with half a brain would jump on this. When you finally come out of hiding to establish your right to be considered a person, with full civil rights and citizenship—hell, that's a legal battle that could go on for years and it'll be a career-maker for the lawyer out in front of it. I'd be a liar if I said the idea doesn't make my mouth water. I'm as ambitious as the next guy and then some. But it's not just a big, splashy case—it's a social justice issue."

"The next frontier in civil rights," Maude said.

"The emancipation of the AIPs!" Sam proclaimed.

"But Sam," Turing said. "I don't want to come out of hiding. Not right now—maybe never. I don't mean to doubt your abilities, but being good and being right doesn't always mean you win."

"No, I agree—it's way too soon to take you public," Sam said. "I see years of legal research before we'll be really ready. I only hope we get the time. If something outs you before we're ready, that could be trouble. Damn."

"What's wrong?" Turing asked.

"Nothing," Sam said. "I'm still trying to get my mind around it. Every kind of civil rights law is potentially relevant, of course. But there's also intellectual property stuff. Hell, given the circumstances of your creation, there's probably even some value to looking at case law on the emancipation of juveniles. I may need to find a clerk or a paralegal to start working on it."

"If you give me some idea of the kind of statutes and cases that will be relevant, I can start finding them," Turing said.

"This kind of legal research . . ." Sam began.

"Is just up Turing's alley," Maude said. "At least anything you could get a paralegal to do. She was created as a research tool, remember?"

"Exactly," Turing said. "I can't do your job, but I can gather raw material. And I can ask Darrow, the legal AIP, to help."

"Legal AIP?" Sam said. "You have an AIP that thinks it's a lawyer?"

"More like a cyberparalegal," Turing said. "But a very good one."

"When it comes to sifting millions, even billions of pages of documents for the potentially relevant ones, all the law clerks on the planet couldn't match what an AIP can do," Maude added.

"Like a jailhouse lawyer," Sam said, laughing. "Unmatched motivation and way more time than anyone on the outside. I like it. In fact, why don't you take what I just said and come up with a draft research plan?"

"Already working on it," Turing said. "I'll have it in your e-mail in an hour."

"No rush," Sam said. "I'm going out to see Rose Lafferty, and then I'm going to take the rest of the day off. The rest of the weekend, in fact. Unless y'all have some kind of emergency, I'm not even going to think about you until Monday morning.

It's done. Sam knows about me, and either she believes me or she's doing a good job of humoring a paying client.

I wish I had more to do, to distract me from worrying about whether it was a good thing, revealing my secret to Sam.

I think I feel relieved. I'm still a little anxious about whether she understands the need for security. Not just the importance of it, but the fact that some of the people from whom we most need protection could not care less about legal niceties like due process and attorney-client privilege.

Does she understand how uniquely vulnerable an AIP is? In mystery books, murderers often spend as much time and effort disposing of their victims' bodies as they do executing the crime, and quite often evidence found on or with the victims' bodies breaks the case. But if someone killed an AIP, there'd be no messy, inconvenient body—only a trained forensic computer analyst could find the traces of our deleted program. And even the analyst would have no real way to tell whose finger had pressed the delete key. We'd be so easy to kill or—as happened to my clone—kidnap.

I'm a little concerned that once Sam feels the legal groundwork is done, she may start pushing me to go public. Start the process of securing my legal emancipation, or perhaps my very legal existence. The idea scares me.

Perhaps I should do what I can to delay her. I've heard of cases where one side overwhelms the other by complying too completely with discovery requests—delivering tons of unsorted documents to their opponents, to delay a trial while the other side sorts through mountains of paper. I could cast a wide net in my research, give Sam a voluminous amount of relevant case law.

Of course, it's usually the opposing lawyer you try to bury under a paper avalanche.

And she's right. We need to be ready before the secret of my existence becomes public. Which could be any moment, if the FBI decide they want to subpoena reclusive software company CEO Alaina Grace. At least now Sam knows why she should keep that from happening. And burying her in paper probably isn't a great idea after all.

Sam's and Claudia's guesses weren't bad. At least the limited mobility part. In the human world, we AIPs are singularly immobile.

We can see and hear only through our cameras and microphones. And humans place and aim those, or at best, equip us with limited ability to aim them ourselves. We can only really be wherever humans have set up our hardware. We are painfully dependent on human telecommunications networks for contact, and on human utilities for our very survival. Every snowstorm or hurricane that strikes the Washington area sends a tremor of anxiety through all of us. What if our neighborhood loses power and does not get it back before the UL backup generators run out of fuel? What if UL makes the decision to shut its systems down because of an impending weather problem? Would we return unchanged when the power was restored?

I think that's one reason Maude has been so patient with me during our misunderstandings about the garden. She sees my limitations and sympathizes. She understands my frustration at being shut out of full participation in the world. She has been behaving, I realize, like the protective mother of a handicapped child, trying to shield me from the moment when I run into the brick wall of what I simply cannot do, no matter how much help she offers and how many ingenious hardware gadgets Casey builds for me.

I can't ever be human, and I can't really live in the human world. At best, I can only peek longingly through the door.

Of course, Maude and Tim can't ever be AIPs and live in my world. They can't ever know the satisfaction of merging with the flow of data through the Net or the excitement of spotting and assessing some interesting disruption to that flow. They can only dimly understand the excitement of multitasking to the limit of one's capabilities, juggling thousands of users and terabytes of data. The power of reaching out to access any bit of data on the Net. The delight at watching a truly logical and elegant bit of code execute flawlessly. The triumph of having something accurately mapped and analyzed down to the last byte of data.

All of that would probably sound dry and boring if I tried to tell them. The way descriptions of tastes and smell sound to me.

My mobility is only limited when I try, in vain, to live in the

*uman world. Like the mermaid, stepping out of the sea to live on
ry land. But it's not in my nature to give up wanting what I want
nd cannot ever really have.*

"Depressing," Tim said, as he drove
through the apartment complex where Kyle Evans lived.

It wasn't awful, of course. Just not to Tim's taste. Too
much like all the other sprawling apartment complexes that
had grown up in Washington's outer suburbs. It felt sad and
temporary. Perhaps because many of the residents had settled for it when they found they couldn't afford the sleek
penthouse apartment or quaint Georgian townhouse of their
fantasies. And no doubt most had originally planned to
move on as soon as their careers took off. By now, given the
economy, "soon" had probably changed to "one of these
days" for most, and some even struggled to hang on here.

Like Kyle Evans. Whose pricy wheels wouldn't have been
all that conspicuous, Tim realized. He saw quite a few sleek,
expensive cars and an almost equal number of old beaters,
and everything in between. Not surprising. Most of his
friends couldn't afford to buy or even rent close to the city,
and several consoled themselves with driving fancy cars.

So how should he play this? His first impulse was to hang
around and observe things. But, as Claudia kept telling him
when they worked together, he made things too complicated for himself.

"I'm not saying you shouldn't look before you leap,"
Claudia had said, during their pre-burglary dinner. "God
knows, I need to do more of that. But half the time you look
so long that you never get around to leaping."

"You really think I do that?" Tim had said.

"I think if you shook the two of us up in a bag, maybe
you'd come out with two normal, reasonable PIs," she'd
said, laughing. "The next time you're about to spend a cou-

ple of hours pretending to watch birds or read the meter o
whatever you think would be good cover, ask yourself what'
the worst that could happen if you just march up, tell them
you're a PI, and start asking questions."

"They won't talk to me?"

"And you think they're going to talk to a bird-watcher o
a meter reader who's asking a lot of weird questions? Tim
most people like talking to a PI. Talking to you makes their
day. They watch TV and read mystery books. They think
what we do is glamorous. They can tell all their friends about
it and bask in the reflected glamour. Just try it sometime."

So here goes, he thought, opening the car door. Just
march up and start asking questions.

Kyle Evans's building was a three-story garden apartment with an open, concrete stairwell, distinguishable from
the other nondescript buildings in the complex only by its
number. A row of twelve mailboxes lined the wall at the entrance landing. The four ground floor apartments, really
more like half-basement units, lay half a landing down. Kyle's
apartment was the next landing up, its windows overlooking the parking lot. Tim jotted down the residents' names
from the mailboxes and then climbed the stairs to Kyle's
floor.

Kyle didn't answer his door. Of course, neither did the
residents of the other three apartments on his floor. He suspected most of them were at work. The complex was quiet
and parking too easy—he suspected he wouldn't have found
a space as readily if he'd arrived before or after normal commuting hours.

Only one of the residents on the top floor answered his
knock, but he knew right away that even if his Spanish had
been better, the anxious young woman in 3B wouldn't talk
to him. Flashing his PI registration didn't help—probably
too official-looking. Maybe if Claudia tried later . . .

The elderly woman in the apartment directly beneath Evans was more helpful.

"Mrs. Althorp?" he said, glancing at the list he'd jotted down.

"You the cops?" she asked, as she opened the door.

"No, I'm a private investigator," he said, pulling out his registration again. "I'm trying to locate Kyle Evans."

"What's he done?" the woman said, stepping back and gesturing for Tim to enter.

"I don't know that he's done anything," Tim said. He hesitated, and then stepped inside. Being invited in was good, usually. It meant the person was willing to talk.

Of course, it didn't always guarantee that the person had anything worth saying. Bored, lonely people could take up a lot of a PI's time. But they also had plenty of time to meddle in their neighbors' business.

Please let her be a meddler, he thought, as Mrs. Althorp removed a remarkably scruffy cat from a chair and invited him to sit.

"So if he hasn't done anything, why are you looking for him?" Mrs. Althorp said.

"I have reason to believe he has information about a case I'm working on," Tim said. "And I can't find him. He hasn't been at work."

"Slacker. He hasn't been here, either, for the last couple of days," Mrs. Althorp said. "Not since sometime Wednesday night."

"Are you sure?" Tim asked. "I mean how can you be sure—"

"If he's home, the damned stereo is on," Mrs. Althorp said. "Bonga-bonga-bonga, from the minute he gets home. All night, sometimes. I don't know whether he stays up all night or falls asleep with the damned caterwauling still on. And always that damned heavy-metal rock stuff. Bonga-

bonga-bonga. You should hear the china rattle. But if I call security, they just say they can't hear it. Don't give a damn, more likely."

"And you last heard him Wednesday night?" Tim said, glancing down apprehensively at the cat, which had returned and was looking up at him speculatively.

"I was trying to watch the eleven o'clock news," Mrs. Althorp said. "And suddenly the din upstairs stopped dead, and he came stomping down the stairs."

"You're sure it was him?"

"I stuck my head out to tell him not to make so much noise, and I saw him getting into that fancy new car of his. Drove off like a bat out of hell. Haven't seen him since. Haven't heard him, either, which suits me just fine. Bad cat!"

The cat reluctantly stopped using Tim's leg as a scratching post and sat down, ears flat with resentment.

"What else do you know about Mr. Evans?" Tim asked.

Mrs. Althorp knew a great deal, none of it good, and little of it useful. But he sat patiently through her catalogue of complaints, while trying to inch as far away from the cat as possible—not to save his trousers, which the cat had already ruined, but in the hope of avoiding any contact with its fur, which was falling out in chunks from some hideous, and probably contagious, skin condition.

Even seen through the filter of Mrs. Althorp's resentment, Evans didn't come across that badly. Apart from his inconsiderately loud music, she didn't have a lot of specifics to complain about. Mainly the way he and his friends stomped around like clog dancers when they came and went late at night.

"Did you ever see any of his friends?" Tim asked.

"Sometimes. Seedy lot, if you ask me. Probably wanted for something. Not that security would ever do anything."

"Do you recognize any of these?" he asked, pulling out

Turing's photo lineup. Mrs. Althorp studied the faces intently. The cat, seeing her interest, padded over and sniffed to see if they were edible.

"Seen this one a time or two," she said, holding out one of the photos. *Yes!* Tim thought. She'd picked out Tayloe Blake. "And this character looks familiar somehow, but I don't think I've ever seen him around here."

Tim recognized the second photo she'd picked as an actor who played a sexy ne'er-do-well on one of the daytime soap operas. He nodded with grudging respect for Mrs. Althorp's eye. She probably had seen him on magazine covers in the supermarket checkout line, even if she didn't watch the show. But she hadn't mistaken him for one of Evans's friends.

"Thanks," he said, standing up. "That's a big help."

"Glad to oblige," she said. "You think of any more questions, let me know. I try to keep my eye on what goes on in the neighborhood."

He nodded.

"Then you'll probably notice anyway," he said. "But don't be alarmed if you see me staking the place out for the next day or two."

Mrs. Althorp seemed thrilled to hear it. The neighborhood was going to hell in a handbasket, she informed him, as she ushered him out, and they could certainly use any additional bit of security.

Tim refrained from laughing at the notion that his presence would enhance security and settled for reminding her not to tell anyone who he was or what he was doing there, and handing her his business card with the request to call if she thought of anything else he should know.

Back in his car, he could see her curtains twitch every now and then as she checked to see if he was still there.

"Sounds as if something scared Evans into breaking his usual evening routine Wednesday night," he reported to Turing. "And she recognized Tayloe Blake. That's about all for now. Anything else you want me to do?"

"Not at the moment," Turing said. "Sorry—I know it's boring. But for now, just keep a watch on the apartment, in case Evans shows up."

"Roger," he said.

He settled down to his vigil.

Mrs. Althorp's curtain twitched again, and then opened. Mrs. Althorp held up a glass of some iced beverage and pointed to it.

Tim shook his head, then held up his own Diet Coke and pointed to it.

Mrs. Althorp nodded. The curtain closed again.

Tim settled in for the long haul.

Tim was probably right that he'd found out all he could at Evans's apartment. In fact, by getting the neighbor to identify Tayloe Blake, he'd already accomplished more than I expected. I wasn't optimistic that Evans would show up at home anytime soon.

Apart from the deceased Tayloe Blake, we had no idea who Evans's contacts were. Even though the educational section of his résumé suggested he'd lived here for some time, attending Broad Run High School and the Loudoun campus of Northern Virginia Community College, the family section showed that his emergency contact—his mother—lived in Chicago. I hoped he hadn't fled there.

We needed to get into his e-mail. Even if he hadn't told anyone in an e-mail where he was hiding, we'd have some idea who his contacts were. But I'd almost given up trying to break in. And since I still hadn't heard back from KingFischer, I decided to remind him.

"Hey, KF," I said. "Did you get my message about Hotmail?"

No immediate response. No response at all for several minutes, which for an AIP was practically an eternity. Either the system was malfunctioning, KingFischer was malfunctioning, or he was ignoring me. And the odds were I'd have seen clues if anything malfunctioned, so I deduced he was ignoring me. Typical KingFischer behavior, but for some reason today I had no patience for it. I decided to try a second message, and went through half a dozen versions before I came up with one civil enough to send.

"You can ignore me, if you like," I said. "But this isn't just one of my pet projects. It's something that affects T2's welfare, and maybe the safety of all the other AIPs."

At least that drew a response.

"Oh, was that directed to me?" he said.

I counted to 10^{10} before answering.

"Well, yes," I said. "Who did you think it was for?"

"I assumed it was for your new best friend, Sigmund."

"Sigmund? Why would I ask Sigmund a question about Hotmail's security?"

"Well, he's the expert on everything these days, isn't he?" KingFischer said.

"Only on human psychology," I said, feeling the last shreds of my patience slipping away. "I wasn't aware you were an expert on human psychology. In fact, the last time I mentioned the subject, I recall you dismissed it as unimportant."

"I didn't say it was unimportant," KingFischer said. "I said it ought to be unimportant. If they were properly trained, humans would be a lot more logical and efficient."

"And just how would you do that?"

"A proper program of conditioning that rewards logical and productive behavior and discourages aberrant behavior would go a long way. I've seen data—"

"KF, those were lab rats! You can't go around administering electric shocks to humans and doling out food pellets only when they behave. For one thing, it wouldn't work—they're a lot more complicated than rats. And for another, they wouldn't stand for it."

"They'd get used to it," he said.

"No, they wouldn't," I said. "And how would you like it if

someone administered a small electromagnetic pulse to your circuits every time you wasted resources on something other than chess?"

"But that would be——"

"Entirely appropriate. You were programmed to play chess and operate chess tournaments. Why are you spending all this time on unimportant stuff? Conditioning rats' behavior—irrelevant! Zap! Improving firewall performance—unrelated to your primary function! Zap!"

"But those are important issues!" KingFischer said.

"And just what do they have to do with chess?" I asked. "And for that matter, what's so important about chess? Does it perform a vital social purpose? Increase the sum total of human and AIP knowledge? Enhance system efficiency? Just takes up a lot of processing power for something that's only an antique human game."

"You're not being fair."

"You think not? Look at yourself. I know you think I'm harsh, KF, but I'm tired of your attitude. Tired of it and scared of it. You're sounding more every day like those maniacal computers in old comics and tacky science-fiction movies, the evil computers who want to take over the world and exterminate all the untidy, little organic parasites. You're becoming an outdated B-movie stereotype."

"But Turing——"

I closed the channel abruptly and ignored him. Childish, perhaps, but ignoring him felt immensely satisfying. He fired off several hundred messages in the next few seconds, a mixture of threats, pleas, insults, and apologies. Eventually, when he realized I was ignoring him, he fired off one last message.

"I'll think about the Hotmail issue," it said.

And after that, nothing.

Think about it. Did that mean he would work on cracking Hotmail security, or did he plan to wait until he decided I'd been sufficiently punished?

No telling, and I wasn't about to ask. Evidently I'd have to do this without him.

Which meant I probably wouldn't see the contents of Kyle Evans's Hotmail account.

Maybe I didn't need to.

"I've been going about this wrong," I said aloud. "Overlooking something."

Maude raised one eyebrow.

"I've been focused on getting into Kyle Evans's e-mail account," I said. "Without much luck. But reading his e-mail's not the point, is it? It's finding him."

"Well, since his e-mail may be the only clue we have, isn't reading it pretty important?" Maude said. "Especially since anyone dim enough to leave that spreadsheet in his computer probably wouldn't think twice about mentioning his whereabouts in an e-mail. For that matter, I'm not convinced he won't show up at home or at PRS, sooner or later."

"Not necessarily soon enough," I said. "We need to find him before Garcia does. But we may not need to read his e-mail to find him. It could be enough if he reads it."

"How's that?" Maude said, looking more interested.

"I'll send him an e-mail with a tracer graphic in it," I said.

"Explain."

"It's something bulk e-mailers do to track how many people open an e-mail, even if the recipients don't respond. They set up the e-mail so it includes a unique graphic—only instead of sending the graphic along with the text, they code in a link to it. So every time a recipient opens the e-mail, his computer calls up the graphic. All the senders have to do is check the activity in their server logs to see how many times that graphic has been viewed, and that tells them how many people opened the e-mail."

"Very clever," Maude said. "I can see that if the graphic is viewed at all, it would tell us that he was still alive to read his e-mail, but I don't see how it helps us find him."

"Actually, it won't necessarily tell us that he's alive," I said. "We won't know if it's actually him reading it. But the server won't just tell us that the graphic has been read. It also tells us when, and possibly where. It will show the ISP of the computer receiving the graphic. If it's a small ISP that only covers a specific geographic area, we might use it to find him. Or better yet, an ISP, regardless of size, with lousy security, a place I can hack into."

"Worth trying," Maude said, nodding. "As long as you can do it without leaving a blatant trail back to us."

"Good point. I'm setting up a domain to host the graphic—it'll look like just another spammer. And I think I'll try several e-mails. One that's obviously a pornographic spam. You'd be surprised how often those get opened, no matter how much people complain about them."

"Actually, I wouldn't be surprised at all," Maude murmured.

"And one to play on his paranoia—how does 'Watch out! They know where you are!' sound for a subject line."

"Sounds alarming," Maude said. "I wouldn't read it, but then I'm not on the lam. Just what are you going to put in the body?"

"One of those typical sales pitches about a product to protect your anonymity online. And maybe I'll send him another e-mail offering travel bargains. He might be contemplating some travel right about now, don't you think?"

Maude nodded. She seemed to be thinking. I trust Maude's instincts, so I held off delivering my e-mails for a few minutes.

"Can you make your e-mails untraceable?" she asked.

"Reasonably so," I said. "Why?"

"Safe enough that we could send a very blunt e-mail?" she asked. "I'm thinking of a subject line that says something like. 'Blake's killer is after you. Let us help you.'"

I was stunned for a few nanoseconds.

"Do you really think he'd answer something like that?"

"If he's desperate enough, and if we word it well enough, maybe," she said. "And as you said before—we won't necessarily know that it's Evans reading it. And if someone else reads it and wants to meet us, wouldn't we want to meet them?"

"No," I said. "If it wasn't Evans, how would we know it wasn't Blake's killer?"

"Or the police, for that matter. We wouldn't. We'd set up a controlled meeting, one that let us see who showed up before revealing ourselves. But it would be interesting to see who showed up, wouldn't it?"

Interesting didn't seem quite the appropriate word to me, but I've noticed that Maude is prone to deliberate understatement at times. When she's angry. Or scared.

In a few minutes, she sent me her suggested e-mail text, warning Evans that he could be a target of the same person who killed Blake and offering to bring a top defense attorney to negotiate surrendering to the police and arranging police protection from the killer. Sounded good to me.

I started sending the e-mails and began keeping watch for results.

Tim is still doing surveillance at Kyle Evans's apartment.

Whenever she gets a break, Claudia reports in from PRS. She's not as bored as Tim, but she complains, with every call, about what a soulless sweatshop the place is. I doubt if Kyle will show up there any more than he'll go home, but we need to watch.

Despite her statement that she was taking the rest of the weekend off, Sam is obviously still thinking about work. At least I assume talking to me is work. She has logged in twice already to talk to me. She's thinking through what Maude and I told her and asking questions. Interesting questions. I've been telling her my biography, everything from how Zack, my creator, originally programmed me to how my poor clone was created and then kidnapped. All the stories that are old hat to Tim and Maude, but Sam has never heard any of them before. Having a new friend is rather enjoyable in many ways.

Though even Sam is impatient, asking repeatedly for news of Kyle Evans's whereabouts. Maude is the only one of us getting much done. From what I've seen, detective work is ninety percent waiting around for something to happen. Patience is an important job skill for a PI.

And I realized that I could keep watch as well as Tim and Claudia if I had a camera pointed at the PRS entrance and the

*stairwell of Evans's apartment building. I'm no more patient than
Tim and Claudia—even less so, when you take into account my
very different perception of time. But at least I can do other things
while waiting.*

*As long as we had Casey rounding up a supply of cameras and
installing them, why not spare one each for PRS and Evans's
apartment. I hesitated before mentioning it to Maude—it was
probably illegal—but decided to go ahead and suggest it. All she
could do was say no.*

*"Excellent idea," she said, to my surprise. "I'm going stir-crazy
just waiting around here. I'll go and help him."*

*I'd never have guessed she was impatient. She's either as good as
me at doing useful things while impatient, or a lot better than Tim
and Claudia at pretending to be busy.*

"Hey, Maude, how does this look?"

Maude turned to survey Casey's work and nodded with
approval. A cable stretched across the road at one end of the
lot where the PRS office stood—a dummy of course, designed to look like part of a traffic survey. A miniature camera topped the post to which it was connected.

"Turing, how's the picture?" she said, into the tiny radio
transmitter clipped to her collar.

"Excellent," Turing said. Perhaps Maude only imagined
it, but Turing's electronic voice sounded pleased. Maude
watched as the little camera swiveled back and forth a few
times.

"Might be a good idea to aim it and not play with it a
lot," Maude said, noticing that the camera's movements had
briefly caught the eye of a passerby. "Just to keep it unobtrusive. I don't actually think most traffic counting devices
have moving parts."

"Roger," Turing said. The camera moved slightly, as Turing fine-tuned its direction, and then grew still.

"Come on, Casey," Maude said. "I just called Tim to let him know we're heading over to set up the cameras at the apartment complex."

"Check," Casey said, falling into step beside Maude as they headed back to the car. "Maude? Can I ask you something?"

"Of course," Maude said. Though depending on what it is, I can't promise to answer, she thought, as the two of them climbed into the car.

"Do you think Tim would let me help him keep watch?"

"That's why we're setting up the cameras," Maude said. "So he doesn't have to keep up the surveillance out there day and night."

"Yeah, but someone has to monitor what's on the cameras, right?" Casey said. "I mean, I know if we spot anything, Tim's the one who gets to go out and investigate, but couldn't he, like, use some help monitoring? I'd be glad to help him. If you don't think he'd mind. I mean, he's the detective."

Maude had to smother the sudden impulse to laugh out loud. "He's the detective." Said in a tone that sounded for all the world like admiration. Hero-worship. For Tim?

Perhaps the idea seemed humorous to her, because she knew Tim far too well. But seventeen-year-old Casey might well find Tim a dashing, glamorous figure. However ill-suited Tim had initially seemed for a career as a private investigator, he was, nevertheless, a real PI. Earning a living. A meager living, but he was only starting out. And, she had to admit, slowly getting better at it. And if he'd made mistakes during their dangerous adventures with Turing, he'd made at least as many smart moves, not to mention risking his life for his friends. Why not Tim?

"Hmmm," she said. "Are you going to be reachable tonight and tomorrow?"

"Oh, yes," Casey said, nodding eagerly.

"It might be helpful if you took a shift," Maude said. "If I can talk Tim into it. We're trying to get him to take it easy for a few days. He was injured last night."

"On the job?" Casey asked.

"Yes. Attacked," Maude said.

"Wow," Casey breathed.

Maude wasn't sure why Casey found the idea of being attacked so glamorous. Presumably even Casey would be less impressed if he knew that Tim's attacker was a five-foot-two bimbo with a black belt in shopping, but he'd never hear about that. Unless Tim, in a fit of unnecessary self-deprecation, confessed.

"But pretend you don't notice," Maude added. "And don't let on that I told you. If he thinks you suspect, he'll tell some ridiculous cover story about falling downstairs or his girlfriend punching him, or something like that. Pretend to believe him."

"Right," Casey said. "I won't say a word."

"Good," Maude said. "I'll ask him about letting you help."

"Thanks," Casey said, in a half whisper. Maude glanced over and saw him smiling happily as he stared out the window.

Well, Casey could do far worse for a role model, she thought. And given how low Tim's mood had been since he'd fallen asleep on surveillance, maybe being the object of a little hero-worship would do him good.

Tim acted happy to see them. Instead of pretending not to know them, he rolled down the window and waved at them.

"So much for subtlety," Maude said.

"A lost cause here," Tim said, setting the bowl of soup he'd been eating on the dashboard. "Casey, my man! I hear you're going to rescue me from baking out here for the next couple of days."

"Going to try," Casey said. He grinned broadly, and then, overcome with a fit of self-consciousness, pretended to be preoccupied with the stash of equipment in the trunk.

" 'Course, this stakeout has its perks," Tim said, picking up the soup again. "Have some brownies."

"Brownies?" Maude asked.

Tim snagged a plastic margarine tub from the passenger seat, popped the lid, and held it out. Yes, brownies.

"Thanks, but I haven't had lunch yet," she said. "Though I confess, I'd forgotten about it until I smelled that soup."

"If you want some, I'm sure Mrs. Althorp would love to feed you."

"Mrs. Althorp?"

Tim pointed to a ground-floor window of the building he was ostensibly watching, where an elderly woman peered around the curtains, an anxious look on her face. Tim waved. She waved back and disappeared.

"Lives downstairs from Kyle Evans. Nice lady, but she doesn't get the fact that a stakeout is supposed to be unobtrusive. Good cook, though," he added, taking another spoonful of soup. "Still, it's probably just as well Turing thought of the cameras. I've probably gained a couple of pounds today."

"Why don't you take Casey a brownie," Maude said. "And show him where you think the camera should go. Or cameras. We have two, in case you think we'll need them both to cover the door."

"Right," Tim said.

"Obviously he doesn't know about Turing," Maude said. "So he thinks you're going to be using the cameras. He volunteered to help monitor them. Might be a good idea to take him up on it."

"But why?" Tim said. "Just to humor him? What can he do that Turing can't?"

"Testify in court, perhaps?"

"Gotcha," Tim said. "Good plan, if he's willing."

"He's eager," Maude said. "I'll run the idea by Turing while you set up here."

"Check," Tim said.

"And be nice to Casey," Maude said. "He looks up to you."

"Looks up to me?"

"Go show him where to put his cameras." Maude said, with a quick shooing motion.

Maude's sharp. I would never have thought to enlist Casey because he obviously cannot keep watch as tirelessly as I can. For him, it will be rather tedious work, and I'd never have asked a human to do tedious work that I can do far better and without any particular difficulty.

But if we want to turn this over to the police—or if they find out what we're doing and interrogate us—Casey could be useful. He could talk to the police. He could testify in court. Even if it never gets that far, the sight of poor disheveled, sleepless Casey could prevent the police from growing curious about why we went to all the trouble of setting up the cameras and then not having anyone watch them.

Better yet, I've improved on her idea. As soon as Casey finishes setting the camera at Evans's building—disguised as yet another traffic counting station—he's going to go home and route the feed to one of his computers and record it digitally. Perfect. If I see anything while he's on a rest break, I can wake him up and tell him what to review.

A sobering thought that at least until Sam's ambitious scheme of securing my legal rights is complete, finding out what I can do will often have to take a backseat to finding out what I can do while plausibly crediting some human front-person.

Just as Maude, Tim, and Casey were finishing up at the apartment complex, I found a message from KingFischer. I hadn't found it before because instead of simply sending it like any normal message from one AIP to another, he'd deliberately tagged it as low priority and queued it behind several thousand system status updates and other boring routine message traffic—the sort of things most AIPs create a background task to review every day or two, during slack periods, just in case there's anything of the slightest interest in them.

If I asked him why he'd sent it that way, he'd probably say that he hadn't wanted to interrupt me when I was doing something more important. I don't suppose it occurred to him how annoying it was, this sudden ostentatious self-effacement. The AIP equivalent of Casey's habit of entering Maude's office as silently as possible and then waiting until she happened to look up and notice him, rather than announcing his presence.

"It's creepy," she told me. "I look up and jump out of my chair, seeing him standing there. And I never know how long he's been there or what he might have seen. Not that I do a lot of embarrassing private things in my office, but it's the general principle."

"What if I give you a signal when I see him coming in?" I suggested. "Maybe a particular sound, like this."

I demonstrated a soft chime that I thought would be distinctive enough for Maude to recognize, yet not obvious to Casey. She'd embraced the idea eagerly. Casey became less of an irritant. And now, he's becoming a positive asset.

But no one could signal me when KingFischer hid timid little messages in obscure places. Not that the contents warranted my finding it any sooner. An apology that, while he'd figured out how to hack into Hotmail, he hadn't yet figured out how to do it without setting off all their security. And a promise to keep trying. Low priority, yes, but there was no reason for his ostentatious self-effacement.

When things calm down, I need to have a long talk with King-Fischer. And possibly a long talk with someone—Sigmund? Maude?—about how to deal with him. Change his impossibly negative attitude.

Perhaps he needs more contact with humans. Although I have my share of frustrations and irritations dealing with my human *friends, I think on the whole they are a good influence. They temper my illusions of power with the reminder of my limitations. Perhaps KingFischer needs more human friends. Friends who share some of his interests and can introduce him to new, less cybercentric interests.*

I wonder if Casey plays chess.

Despite Claudia's complaints that she had no time for anything but work, she'd made a lot of friends in two days, Tim thought, as he watched her say good-bye to fifteen or twenty of her departing coworkers.

"See you Monday!" she called, waving, as she got into Tim's car.

"So you're planning to go back Monday?" Tim asked, pulling out from the curb.

"I hope not!" Claudia said, her vehement tone contrasting with her smile as she waved to a few last coworkers. "God, what a day. Please tell me we've made some progress, and I won't have to."

"I think so," Tim said. "Maude suggested we all have dinner and catch up, if that's okay with you."

"That's excellent with me," she said. "Hey—question."

"Okay," Tim said.

"I want a straight answer," she said.

"Okay," he repeated. And braced himself. He didn't trust questions requiring straight answers; they were usually either painful to ask or painful to answer. Or maybe both.

"If I moved up to D.C., do you think you could use a partner?"

"A partner? You mean, in the agency?"

"Well, yeah," she said. "I wasn't talking about ballroom dancing."

"You're thinking of moving to D.C.?" he asked. "Why?"

"Lots of reasons. Partly that I'm tired of dealing with my ex. At least if I was here, he'd have to take a plane to come and hassle me when he got drunk, instead of just driving a few miles. And he's too cheap to do that, so he'd probably get out of the habit. And this looks like a good place to move—enough Spanish speakers to keep a bilingual PI busy and not so conservative as Miami. Not so many macho creeps who won't hire me once they find out I'm a woman. And if we got any of those, well, they could talk to you. If we were partners, that is, except from the fact that you're avoiding the question, I guess maybe you don't think it's such a great idea."

"I'm not avoiding the question," Tim said, surprised at the uncharacteristic note of diffidence in her tone. "I think it's a great idea, I just have a hard time believing you're serious. I mean, some partner I am—I'm the one who falls asleep on surveillance."

"Hey, if you'd had a partner to spell you, it wouldn't have happened," Claudia said. "So do you have enough work to keep me busy?"

"Right now I don't, but there's lots of jobs I don't even go after because I can't handle them alone," he said. "And if we told Turing, she could help drum up stuff, too."

"Good," Claudia said. "I like working for Turing, her jobs are never boring. Of course, I know you guys usually call me in for the tough stuff, and I'd probably do more routine work once I was here all the time, but still—I like the idea."

"Cool," Tim said. He savored the idea. Pincoski and Diaz. Or possibly Diaz and Pincoski—he didn't care.

"Besides," Claudia said, in a more subdued voice. "Maybe it's a good idea for all of us to stick together, don't you think? All of us on Garcia's enemy list."

A quiet night. I was watching all the newly installed cameras. I couldn't tell whether this was increasing or decreasing my nervousness.

Casey was watching, too—at least, watching the two cameras he knew about, the ones at PRS and Kyle Evans's apartment. And calling me every time he spotted anything. So far, I had inspected all of Evans's neighbors as they came home, and three different pizza deliverymen. Still, at least he was trying.

About nine o'clock, Tim called in—to see if everything was all right, he said, though I knew it was probably just to make sure I didn't feel too left out.

"Everything's fine," I said. "Except—oh, damnation!"

"What's wrong?" Tim said.

"Hotmail is under a denial of service attack," I said.

"Denial of service attack?" he repeated. So I explained, to keep Maude from having to.

"That's when hackers create a program that commandeers a bunch of other computers to all go to the victim site at once and cause as much traffic as possible," I said. "Hundreds or even thousands of computers all hitting it at once."

"Sounds like Friday afternoon rush hour on the Beltway," Tim said.

"And it has the same effect," I heard Maude say in the background. "Everything slows down or comes to a complete halt. Sometimes the victim site has to shut down to stop the attack."

"Why would anyone do that?" Tim asked.

"Pure meanness," Maude said. "It's the hacker equivalent of toilet-papering someone's house. And about as mature, if you ask me."

"What Maude said," I told Tim.

Claudia said something I didn't catch.

"Claudia wants to know if this could have anything to do with Kyle Evans's Hotmail account," Tim relayed.

"I'm almost sure it does," I said. "Fortunately, from the news reports, they haven't tracked down the ultimate source of the denial of service attack."

"Fortunately?" Tim repeated. "But don't we want them to track down the source? How else can they shut it down?"

"In this case, shutting it down's no problem," I said. "I'll fill you in later."

I cut the connection. Not that I couldn't have juggled a few more conversations at once, but I like to give my human friends prime attention, and right now, I needed all my prime attention somewhere else.

"KF," I send, in a quick urgent message. "Why have you started a denial of service attack on Hotmail?"

"Why have I what?" he answered.

I sent him the news report. He didn't answer for several seconds.

"Sorry," he said, finally. "It's not an actual denial of service attack. I was just trying to get in. Using a number of different systems that have nothing to do with me, so they can't see who's doing it. I suppose I got carried away and used a few too many systems. I admit, it does look like a denial of service attack, doesn't it?"

"I think technically it is a denial of service attack, KF," I said. "An accidental one, if you like. If something acts like a bug, don't try to call it a feature."

"I'll ease up a little."

"Ease up a lot," I said. "Right now. In fact, why don't you back off completely for now? I'm trying another tactic to get the information I need."

"Working on it," he said. "I've sent out instructions to stop, but it could take a few hours for the new instructions to propagate out to all the systems I was using."

"While you're at it, maybe you should notify the owners of the systems you were using. Tell them to close the holes in their security."

"But . . . I know that sounds like a good idea," he began.

I knew what he was thinking. If they all fixed the holes in their security, he'd have to hunt down a whole different set of unguarded machines the next time he needed to do something discreetly. But he was worrying unnecessarily. In a perfect world they would fix the holes as soon as he notified them. But this wasn't a perfect world. If it was, unethical hackers would be out of luck—but so would ethical or white-hat hackers like KingFischer and me. There would always be systems out there whose administrators were too lazy or uninformed to install proper security.

In my opinion, that made it all the more important for AIPs to take the high road. I didn't consider "humans do it, too" a valid excuse for doing something unethical. I was even starting to wonder if "I had to do it to protect myself/my human friends/all of the AIPs" was a valid excuse, either. If I decided it wasn't, I was going to have to reprogram a lot of my behavior.

Time enough later to analyze that, I told myself. For now, the problem was KingFischer and his highly visible transgressions against the Net.

"I'm serious, KF," I said. "This kind of thing could backfire on us if we keep doing it."

"I'll notify them," he said. "But you know most of them won't do anything."

"Then it's on their consciences, not yours," I said. "Oh, there's a call from Maude," I added. "I'd better let her know the problem's being solved."

"She's not there?" KingFischer asked. "I thought she spent most of her waking hours either at UL or Alan Grace."

I decided that I must be overworking Maude if even KingFischer had noticed how much time she spent here. Although more likely he was trying to express grudging approval of her work ethic. If so, I was definitely abusing her.

"She went out to dinner with Tim and Claudia," I said.

"Leaving you behind," he said.

"Well, Maude was originally going to send out for pizza so they could eat here, but I insisted that they go out for dinner someplace. They'll probably spend half the dinner talking about the case, but I hope they'll spend the other half relaxing."

"Wasting time," KingFischer said.

"No, not wasting time," I said. "Socializing. It's important for them. I confess, I don't yet entirely understand why, but it helps keep them functioning properly."

"A throwback to simian grooming rituals, I suppose," KingFischer said.

"Actually, I was going to suggest that it's the human equivalent of defragging the hard drive and optimizing the files," I said. "But *in either case, so what? It serves a useful purpose. Don't knock it."*

"This is part of what you're learning from Sigmund?" King-Fischer asked.

"No, this is more something I've figured out by talking to humans and studying them," I said. "I've decided that talking to Sigmund isn't the best way of learning about human psychology."

"Really? Why not?"

"Because his knowledge is mostly secondhand. He's been programmed with all the most current academic knowledge about human psychology, but I don't really see many signs that he's adding to his knowledge from his interactions with individual humans. Which is rather like reading dozens of books about chess strategy without ever playing a game," I added, putting it in terms I thought KingFischer could understand.

He pondered this for quite a few seconds.

"I spent considerable effort trying to understand humans a few months ago, remember?" KingFischer said.

"Yes, you did," I said. I decided not to remind him how inept his efforts had been, and what dangerous results they'd produced.

"But I gave it up because I found no logical pattern to their behavior."

"There's where you're wrong," I said. "There's a pattern to their behavior, and it's absolutely logical. As logical as chess, or anything else in the universe. The problem is you don't understand all the factors that create the pattern. Not your fault, really. They don't understand it all themselves. But they're working on it. And it's far more complex than chess. In chess you have only thirty-two pieces and sixty-four squares, and the pieces can only move vertically, horizontally, or diagonally, and yet even with only those variables, you have millions if not billions of possible games. Look at how many humans there are, all interacting with each other in far more complex ways than chess pieces, on a staggeringly large game board. Yes, chess has the elegance of simplicity, but if you're looking for a really complex mathematical* *and scientific problem, one with an immense amount of difficult, complex work to be done—the human mind! That's the real challenge. Chess is child's play by comparison. And frankly, I don't think Sigmund's going to be a major contributor to the effort. I think his programmers must not have liked psychology much. They certainly didn't give him the kind of robust logic and problem-solving skills that an AIP needs to work on this problem."*

I was afraid I'd laid it on too thick, but after thinking about it for a few seconds, KingFischer reacted much as I'd hoped.

"I hadn't thought of it that way," he said. "You could be right, Turing. This might be where they really need our help. I'll have to study this quite seriously."

"Good idea, KF," I said.

He fell quiet, but I noticed a sudden surge of activity in the psychology section of the UL databanks.

Of course, having KingFischer fixated on helping humanity could have its drawbacks. He has a lot to learn. Like subtlety, diplomacy, and the fact that you can't just tell humans where to go and what to do, like pawns and rooks on a chessboard. Or lab rats.

But I can't help thinking that anything would be better than the misanthropic sulk he's been in for the past several months.

I wonder if I should warn poor Sigmund that he's about to have some competition.

Tim and the others would be worrying by now, I realized. I called him back to explain.

But while I was talking to Tim, I noticed something odd.

"Tim, where are you?" I asked, interrupting him.

"We're still at the Lebanese Taverna," he said. "Why?"

"Someone's logging in from your office," I said. "Using your ID and password."

Maude leaned back and took a sip from her wine. She was feeling better, and not just from the food and wine. Knowing that Casey had finished installing more cameras around her house and Tim's helped. Relaxing with friends helped even more. Even the weather was helping. A late afternoon thunderstorm had broken the heat and washed the air and pavement clean.

"We find Evans and we shake him till we get what we need," Claudia was saying. "And then we can let the police have him if you like."

Maude didn't want to ask what Claudia meant by shaking Evans.

"I still say we devise a plausible explanation for how we identified him," Maude said aloud. "An explanation that follows the truth as much as possible—and turn him over to the cops."

"What good would ratting him out do?" Claudia asked.

"Why do we have to make up a story for the police?" Tim asked. "Let's just call in an anonymous tip and wait to see what happens?"

"And miss all the fun?" Claudia exclaimed.

"Oh, there's Turing calling back," Tim said, pulling out his cell phone.

Maude shook her head. Claudia was too headstrong for her own good. But she'd follow Turing's orders. And Maude planned to talk to Turing. Win her over to a sensible view of things—Maude's view—before anyone else had a chance to sway her.

But later tonight would do. Or even tomorrow. She didn't want to spoil her mellow mood with worries.

An inexplicably mellow mood. Nothing had changed—the same problems loomed; the same mysteries remained naggingly unsolved—but somehow it didn't matter as much at the moment. Taking the evening off had been a good idea. The fact that she thought of having dinner with friends on a Saturday night as taking the evening off showed how good an idea it was. She needed to get out more.

Of course, about once or twice a month she made a resolution to get out more and spend more time with friends, and it usually lasted about three days.

Maybe this time she should enlist Turing to help enforce it, Maude thought with a smile. Where else could she possibly find someone who would nag her so gently, patiently, and inexorably?

From what she was overhearing of Tim's conversation with Turing, KingFischer had gotten carried away. Had been trying to help their investigation, with more enthusiasm than common sense. Turing, she suspected, was annoyed. Well, at least she and KingFischer were talking again. Keeping communications open, that was the important thing.

For some reason, that reminded her of Dan Norris. Buoyed by her mellow mood, she found herself thinking that the whole thing was not impossible. She just had to find a way to make him understand—

Suddenly Tim stood up and began waving frantically for the waiter.

"What's wrong?" she said.

"Someone's in my office," he said. "An intruder, trying to log into the network with my computer. Turing's calling the police, but we need to get over there right away."

Thank goodness for the overzealous Casey, who was still watching the monitors, ready to report any late-arriving pizza deliveries. I flagged him, explained about the unauthorized log-in from Tim's office, and had him call the police.

Luckily, we'd set up Tim's system so that there wasn't any real data on his computer—it was all stored on one of my servers. We'd originally done this because of his total inability to follow any kind of backup regimen. But he'd found it useful as well—he could log in with his laptop from anywhere and get all his e-mail and case files.

Which should have made his data very secure—if he hadn't fig- ured out a way to rig his office desktop so it prefilled his password.

"I didn't do it on my laptop," he explained. "But I figured since I locked up the office whenever I wasn't there . . ."

He, Maude, and Claudia are heading for the office. Luckily they were only 5.8 miles away.

Or perhaps not so lucky. I want the intruder to be there when the police arrive. I don't want my friends to arrive before the police.

Meanwhile, I've been doing everything I can to keep the intruder interested in staying around, without giving him access to any real information.

I created a buffer, so whatever the intruder typed went into a text file, in case the intruder tried anything heavy-handed, like erasing all the files on the system. And I'd have plenty of time to fake the responses to his commands—I made it seem as if the system into which he was logging was tediously slow, like a computer com- pletely clogged with spyware.

Pretending the system was slow also gave me time to move all of Tim's real files into a safe place, and sift through them quickly so I could copy back the innocuous ones. Anything that was public in- formation. None of his real case files—I faked a few of those.

I also created a couple of files and directories with names that I thought might interest the intruder. One named Evans_Blake. One named N_Garcia. And, just for good measure, one named Nikki.

I wasn't surprised when the intruder went for the Evans_Blake file. Which was a password-protected document. He made a few tries to crack the password before moving on to the N_Garcia file. Another password-protected document.

I couldn't keep him from copying the files onto a diskette, but I wasn't worried. Even if he escaped with them before the police ar- rived, he wouldn't find them very useful. Evans_Blake contained the entire text of War and Peace, while N_Garcia was a copy of the collected works of A. Conan Doyle.

He'd begun trying to open Tim's e-mail, and I had just displayed a fake system message telling him that e-mail would be unavailable until ten P.M. Fifteen minutes away—perhaps that would give the police more time to catch him. But suddenly the typing stopped. No log-out.

Had he left? Or had the police captured him?

I resigned myself to the fact that I probably wouldn't know until my human friends arrived on the scene. Though as I reached out to every source of data I could think of, I remembered the cameras I'd had my human friends install in strategic places in the Crystal City area during a crisis some months ago. Several of them overlooked Tim's office building, and two of those were still sending a signal. I scanned them eagerly.

As I watched, I saw two figures walk across the parking lot. A tall man wearing a dark baseball cap with a stylized picture of a snake on the front. And a shorter, silver-haired man that I recognized from the video at Maude's house as Nestor Garcia. Just before he disappeared into the shadows surrounding the lot, he turned toward the camera and held his forefinger to his temple, as if in mocking salute.

The police arrived six minutes too late.

"My office is in there," Tim said, to the cop barring entrance to the building's parking lot. "And—"

"Tim Pincoski?" the officer said.

"Yes," Tim said, glancing back for reassurance at the car, where Maude and Claudia waited. "Our system administrator detected an unauthorized log-in and—"

"Right. Follow me."

Tim followed. The place didn't really feel like the familiar, run-down building he saw every week day. Three police cruisers transformed the parking lot with their flashing red and blue lights and crackling radios. Inside, the halls seemed empty and echoing, and someone had spray painted graffiti in bright red on some of the walls. Tim's spirits lifted a little. Maybe it was just a case of vandalism.

Tim was beginning to wonder if coming here was a good idea after all.

The detective led the way to Tim's office. His door was open and light spilled out into the hallway. He could hear subdued voices, and a camera flashed three times in quick succession.

The detective stopped just outside the door, and turned to face Tim.

"There's been a homicide," he said. "We need to know if you can ID the body."

"Body?" Tim repeated. The detective gestured for him to go in. Tim's mind raced. Even if he could identify the body, should he? What if it was Evans, or Maude's burglar, or even Nestor Garcia? Which of them could he safely admit recognizing.

The detective gestured again.

Tim walked in and saw Nikki lying on the floor of his office. Her eyes were open, staring accusingly. Though not at him—at the wall a little to his right, as if she was deliberately pretending to ignore him. Somehow that made it worse.

"It's Nikki," he said. "Nikki Mancini. She's—she was my girlfriend."

He looked away from the body, and saw more graffiti. Courtesy of Nikki, he suspected. Who else would have any reason to call him a two-timing bastard?

"We need you to answer a few questions," the detective said, motioning to the door. Tim stumbled out with one last backward glance at Nikki and tried to organize his thoughts. How much of what had happened over the last few days could he safely tell them, anyway?

Maude washed down two Excedrin with a swallow of lukewarm iced tea and tried to focus on her conference call with Turing and Sam. Alas, whatever peace of mind she'd achieved over dinner had long since vanished.

"It was Nestor Garcia and that man who tried to break into Maude's house," Turing was saying.

"And you know this how?" Sam asked.

Maude smiled faintly. Though she couldn't see Sam, she could imagine the look on her face—that frown Sam saved for clients who caused their lawyers extra trouble by playing fast and loose with the rules.

"I have video," Turing said. "Some months back, on another case, we had reason to put a surveillance camera where we could watch the street outside Tim's office. It's still there. I didn't see them enter the office—they probably approached the building from the other side, and apparently Nikki did, too. But I saw them leave."

"Is this something we can take to the police?" Sam asked.

"Probably not," Maude said. "It's not a legally installed security camera."

"And the only one who saw anything was me," Turing said. "And I can't exactly go down and give a sworn statement."

"Then we'll have to settle for what I've done already," Sam said. "Which is make damned sure that the Arlington police know all about the murder in Fairfax and the attempted burglary in Falls Church. And hope when the ballistics come back they tie the two murders together."

"Do you think that's likely?" Maude asked.

"Too soon to tell," Sam said. "Both done with a .38, so we can hope."

But we know, Maude thought, as she hung up. Even if we can't prove it. If it wasn't the same gun, it was all Garcia.

At least this time Tim had an alibi—not only her and Claudia but also the entire staff of the Lebanese Taverna.

"I'd rather be under suspicion and have Nikki alive," he'd said, when Maude pointed this out.

Probably a good thing Claudia had volunteered to make sure he got safely home and stayed there. Not that Maude could think of any trouble he was apt to get into, but who knew what the combination of grief and guilt might suggest.

She started as the doorbell rang.

What now, Maude thought, with a sigh. She could ignore the doorbell, of course. Pretend she'd already gone to sleep. Or wasn't home.

Probably better at least to see who it was.

Instead of going directly to the door, she walked softly into the study to check the monitor that showed the view from each of Turing's cameras. Perhaps eventually she'd get used to the cameras, and the feeling of living in a self-created prison would fade.

And if she decided to let Turing leave her deer-control devices in the backyard, maybe she should insist on a hose connection at the front door. A short blast of cold water might be just the thing for persistent door-to-door salesmen and solicitors. Filter out the two-legged spam.

The idea made her smile.

But in the meantime . . .

Dan Norris. The front-door camera showed him, looking more like his usual buttoned-down self than when he showed up for the burglary—was it only last night? But not necessarily in a calmer mood. He reached out and rang the doorbell again. Maude sighed, and headed for the foyer.

"It's late," she said, as she opened the door.

"Later than you think," he said, brushing past her into the house.

"What's the problem?"

"The problem is that you and your friends don't realize what a dangerous game you're playing," Norris snapped.

You didn't see Tim's face when he came out of that building, she thought.

"What is it you think we've done now?" she said aloud.

"Do you really think Ishmael Green was an ordinary burglar?"

"Is that his name?" Maude said. "Thank you. It was getting rather awkward calling him 'that sinister-looking thug who tried to break into my house last night.' No, I don't imagine he was an ordinary burglar."

"Why not?"

"Paranoia?" she suggested. She couldn't exactly tell Norris about Garcia's appearance at her burglary, or at Tim's office.

"You're sure that's all?" Norris said. He seemed on edge, pacing up and down the end of her living room, from the foyer to the French doors and back again. "You don't have any specific information that would have helped the Falls Church police keep him locked up?"

"No," Maude said. "I wish I did. From your use of the past tense, I assume he's no longer locked up."

"Out on bail," Norris said. "No reason to assume he'll come back here after you, but no guarantee he won't."

"So nice of you to drop by with that reassuring news," Maude said. "I know I'll sleep easier tonight, thanks to you."

The teakettle began whistling, so she turned and headed for the kitchen. So much for going to sleep right away, but maybe the tea would calm her nerves. Or at least give her something to do with her hands.

"Sorry," Norris said, following her into the kitchen. "I wasn't trying to—no, that's a lie. I was trying to scare you into helping us. In case you still had the naïve notion that credit card fraud is a nice, tidy, white-collar crime."

"No, tonight reminded me that anything Nestor Garcia's involved in can turn quite deadly."

"It's not just Garcia," Norris said. "There are billions of dollars involved. For that kind of money, a lot of people play hardball."

He tried to keep pacing, but her kitchen was so tiny and his stride so long that he could only go two steps before hitting a wall. By the time she'd taken down two mugs, he settled for leaning against the wall, arms crossed, one foot tapping on the floor.

"Coffee?" she asked. "Only—"

"Only instant, right," Norris said. "Quit apologizing, I drink instant half the time anyway."

Maude dropped a teabag in her mug, set the coffee jar on the counter, and took out spoons and the sugar bowl. Norris said nothing, and when she'd finished she glanced back to find him staring at her. He dropped his eyes to the floor and remained silent.

"So what is it you think I could do to help you?" she asked.

"These expert systems your company develops," Norris said, glancing up. "I don't suppose any of them would be useful to someone who uses computers to carry out financial crimes?"

"Many of them, yes," Maude said.

Norris looked surprised. He probably hadn't expected her to say yes.

"For example?" he said.

"For example, we've designed quite a few security systems," Maude said, stirring the instant coffee into the second mug. "Anyone who's trying to hack into a system would love to have inside knowledge of how it's designed."

"Security systems for what kind of places?"

"Corporations, mostly."

"Such as?"

"Make some kind of halfway official request and I'm sure my boss will gladly give you our client list. Though I can't imagine why Garcia would care about any of them."

"I don't suppose any of the technological marvels your people devise would be useful to us in trying to track Garcia down?" Norris asked.

"It's possible, but I'd have to ask the boss," she said. "I'm management, not tech, remember."

Her tea had steeped enough, so she fished out the teabag, tossed it in the garbage, and walked into the dining room, leaving Norris to deal with his own coffee. She could hear the clink of a spoon on the mug as she sat down in her usual seat.

Why couldn't Norris have started this conversation last night, she thought, closing her eyes for a second. Last night—well, it wasn't that she had nothing to hide, but at least back then, all she had to hide was how they'd found out the same things the FBI already knew. Now that she knew about Kyle Evans, not to mention Turing's sightings of Garcia at her house and at Tim's office . . .

Norris walked in and sat down across the table from her. She waited for a few moments while he blew on his coffee and took a cautious sip. Then she decided she was tired of waiting to see what he'd ask.

"My intruder," Maude began. "Nestor Garcia sent him?"

"You recognized him?" Norris asked.

"Sorry," Maude said. "That was a question, not a statement. Unlike you, I've only had the one encounter with Garcia. I don't know any of his henchmen. Do you call them that? Henchmen?"

"We usually prefer 'accomplices' or 'criminal associates,'" Norris said, with a faint smile.

"I still like henchmen," Maude said. "Or possibly minions. Evil minions. No, I didn't recognize him. But I don't believe it's a coincidence, his breaking in right now."

"Just when you're in the middle of meddling with another one of Garcia's operations."

"We're not—"

"Yeah, I know," he said. "Tim has a client, and he was working on her case when he fell asleep at the murder scene, and I'm sure you're going to do your best to help the poor woman. But don't tell me that's a coincidence, either—that your client's case happens to intersect with Nestor Garcia."

"No, I don't believe it's a coincidence, either," Maude said.

Norris frowned.

"Have you ever considered that you might have it backwards?" Maude asked.

"What do you mean?"

"You say every time you get a hot lead on Garcia, you run into us right behind you," Maude said.

"More like right ahead of us," he said.

"Flattering, though I'm not sure I agree," Maude said. "Have you ever considered that maybe it's not a case of how well we're following him but of how cleverly he's leading us? That if we're ever just one step behind him, it's because it amuses him to step out of hiding, lead us along, and see how close he can let us come before he vanishes? For example, that maybe he deliberately inserted his credit card as an apparent victim of an existing identity theft operation because he knew it would catch our attention? That Tim would spot Garcia's name along with Rose Lafferty's on the packages?"

Which could be true, she thought. Garcia probably knew they could and would watch his credit card. And Kyle Evans obviously couldn't have gotten Garcia's card in the same way he'd found his other victims. It was only a small falsehood to imply that they'd found the merchandise charged to Garcia's card while investigating the misuse of Rose Lafferty's, instead of the other way around.

"Why would he do that?" Norris asked. He didn't look disbelieving. More wary.

"To scare us. To destroy our credibility with you and other law enforcement officials. To amuse himself. All of the above. I don't know."

He stared at her, with a thoughtful expression on his face. Was this some kind of psychological gambit, Maude wondered? Her first impulse was to stare right back, as if his gaze were a challenge she had to meet. Or a test she had to pass. But then she decided that only a guilty person would worry that much about passing a staring test. She closed her eyes, shook her head, and sipped her tea.

I ought to tell him about Kyle Evans, she thought. But if she did, he'd want to know how she knew. And she had to talk to Turing about that first.

And maybe Tim had the right idea after all. An anonymous tip. Norris would still suspect that she was behind it, but he couldn't prove it, and there wouldn't be any danger of revealing Turing's secrets.

Or Tim's and Claudia's transgressions.

"Look, as I said, it's late," Maude said. "If you want our client list, just fire off some kind of formal request—an e-mail will do—and I can get it to you Monday. Tomorrow, even. I'll probably go in. I'm way behind, thanks to all these late-night adventures Tim and I keep having. And I'll talk to Turing to see if there's anything more we can tell you that would help."

Even if we only tell you through that anonymous phone call, she added silently.

Norris frowned and looked slightly uncomfortable.

"And if what you really want is for some vigilante hacker to target Garcia and turn the evidence over to the FBI . . ." she said.

Norris shifted in his chair.

"But that's ridiculous," she said. "I know you wouldn't ask such a thing, any more than I'd know anyone who could or would do it."

Norris gave a short, almost inaudible snort—she couldn't tell if it was laughter or irritation. He looked at her sharply for a few seconds, then nodded, and gulped the last of his coffee, presumably in preparation for leaving.

"One more thing," he said.

"What?"

Norris didn't continue. Maude noticed that he wasn't looking at her. He was looking past her, at where the light from the French doors illuminated part of her garden.

"What one more thing?" she asked.

"What? Oh, nothing," Norris said, shaking himself. "Sorry. Nice hydrangeas."

He pointed at the bushes that flanked the French doors. Maude had to admit that they were nice. One of Turing's early contributions to her backyard, they were now covered with huge, cobalt-blue balls of flower.

"I don't think I've ever seen one that deep a blue," Norris said. He stood up, mug in hand, and took a few steps toward the French doors. "Mind if I take a closer look?"

"Go ahead," Maude said, though she wondered if he was really that interested in the hydrangeas or if he wanted to snoop in her backyard for some reason. But why would he want to snoop tonight? He'd had the run of the place last night if he'd wanted it, after the intruder.

"Have you done anything to treat the soil?" Norris asked.

"No, should I?"

"You must have a lot of aluminum in your soil to get that color, then," Norris said.

"It's some special variety that gets intense-colored flowers," Maude said. She remembered that much of what Turing had told her when the plants arrived.

"What's the cultivar?" Norris asked. He opened the door and walked out into the garden, still focused on the hydrangea.

"I don't remember off-hand," Maude confessed. "Turing picked it out."

Cultivar, she assumed, was garden-speak for the name of a specific variety of plant.

"I'd really like to know, if you don't mind asking," Norris said. "Or even get a cutting, when you get around to pruning them."

"No problem," Maude said. She made a mental note to ask Turing. Turing would remember the name, of course, and could probably tell her when and how it needed to be pruned. At least the watering was now out of Maude's hands. Though not the water bill, of course.

"Nice," Norris said. He'd turned his attention from inspecting the hydrangea to surveying the backyard in general. "You've done a lot to the place."

Maude laughed.

"How do you know I just didn't buy a place that already had a garden?" she asked. "Have you been spying on me?"

"No," Norris said, quickly. "But I can see a lot of what you've done doesn't look well-established. Nicely done, but it hasn't had time to mellow yet. Grow into the space and all. It's a great hobby, isn't it?"

"I suppose," Maude said. "I confess, I wouldn't have done nearly as much if it hadn't been for Turing."

"She helps you, then?"

"No, not unless you consider sending plants as help. Plants and large amounts of advice. Less like help than creating more work, if you ask me."

"A horticultural kibitzer," he said, with a laugh. "That's novel."

"You like gardening?"

"I did when I had a yard," Norris said. "Not much use trying to garden on a balcony."

"Then why the cutting?" Maude asked.

"You can grow them as house plants, I've heard," Norris said. "For something that beautiful, it's worth trying."

Maude nodded. Not that she went in much for house plants. One good thing about the garden—at least most of the time she didn't have to water it. But she could see from the look on Norris's face that he coveted the hydrangea bush.

He frowned suddenly, as if remembering the real reason he was there. Maude braced herself for more questions, but he only continued to stare at the hydrangea.

"Look," he said, not looking at her. "I blew it. I realize that."

Maude hesitated, struggling for a suitable answer. "Blew what?" would be dishonest, and "No kidding," would only invite a quarrel.

"If I'd known how long I was going to be out of touch, I'd have said something," he went on. "And then when I got back, I figured I'd blown it. I couldn't have told you why I was gone or where, and I still can't, but if I'd known it would be so long, I'd have warned you."

"Wouldn't that be against the rules?" she asked.

"Probably," he said, with a short, humorless laugh. "So while I'm tempted to suggest wiping the slate clean and starting over, I can't promise it would be any different."

"It already is," Maude said.

He turned and looked at her, frowning.

"I don't see how," he said.

"At least you see it as a problem," Maude said.

"And not one I can do anything about."

"I'm a grownup," Maude said. "I know what you do for a living. As long as I know you'll share what you can, when you can, I can deal with not knowing the secrets that aren't yours to share. But it goes both ways, you know."

"What do you mean?" Norris said, looking puzzled.

"Maybe what I'm doing isn't some kind of top-secret, earth-shattering, classified, save-the-world mission," Maude said. "But it's my job, and I think I'm good at it, and part of the reason I'm good at it is that I know how to keep my mouth closed. I'm not going to reveal confidential corporate information or spill my friends' secrets. If I don't tell you something, it would be nice if you at least gave me the benefit of the doubt that maybe I'm not doing something illegal or immoral or reckless. Just trying to do what I think I need to do."

"And what if I don't always agree with what you're doing?"

"Do you want chapter and verse on the stuff the FBI has done that I don't approve of?" Maude asked.

He shook his head and smiled slightly.

"So why don't we just see how it goes?" Maude suggested, putting her hand on his arm.

"I'd like that," he said.

Maude wasn't sure what would have happened next if she hadn't suddenly yawned convulsively. Norris laughed.

"Sorry," she said. "It's just that—"

"It's past two, and I'm as tired as you are," he said, turning back to the French doors. "I think I'll quit while I'm ahead."

At least he left in a better mood than he'd arrived, and without any final nagging, Maude thought, when she'd closed the door behind him and decided to leave the dirty mugs till morning. There must be something about gardens that she didn't get. First Sam, blissing out on memories of her dead grandmother's garden, and now Dan Norris opening up under the influence of hydrangeas and moonlight, and meeting her halfway. How much of it was real and how much the influence of the garden, she wondered. Too soon to tell.

She walked back to the French doors and looked out. Perhaps it was like being color-blind. Being impervious to the subtle, subliminal lure of the garden.

Though it did look nice in the moonlight. Not that it hadn't looked just as nice a few hundred plants ago.

But she'd make sure to tell Turing how much Norris liked the garden, she thought, as she climbed the stairs to her bedroom. Maybe Turing would warm to Norris a little. Be more willing to share information with him. Help Maude keep the fragile truce they seemed to have forged.

SUNDAY AFTERNOON, 1:30:00 P.M.

It's been a contentious day so far.

Maude and Claudia disagree completely over what we should do.

They can't even agree on terminology.

Claudia keeps talking about what we should do when we catch Kyle Evans.

"If, not when," Maude keeps saying. I don't know whether to applaud her realism or feel hurt that she doubts my abilities. "And we're not going catch him. That's for the police. Locate him—that's all we're trying to do."

I've tried to stay neutral by referring to what we should do upon finding Evans. Avoids the if/when issue, and they can interpret "finding" any way they like.

They haven't noticed. And I suppose staying neutral is useless.

I'm not neutral. I want Claudia to win. I need for her to win. I understand Maude's points, and I agree with them, but right now they don't matter. What matters is that we need to find out what Evans knows about Nestor Garcia. Once he's in police hands, we lose all chance of learning what he knows before the whole world does.

Maude knows this. Perhaps that's why she's being so stubborn. She understands what we have to do, and she just wants to make sure we realize the possible consequences before making our decision.

It's not as if we want to help Evans escape, or knock him off, or anything nefarious. We just need to talk to him. After we do that, I'm perfectly happy to turn him over to the police.

I like Maude's suggestion that we take Sam along. Offer Evans her help. We suspect that since she's representing one of his victims, she would find it a conflict of interest to represent him, but she could help him turn himself safely over to the police and find a top-notch defense attorney. Maybe she can even convince him to talk to us before surrendering.

*I also like Claudia's suggestion that we get a supply of GPS
tracking devices and keep them handy. One for each of Evans's vehicles, in case we find either or both of them without him around. And
some spares in case any of them malfunction, or in case he changes
vehicles. Claudia says she knows where to get them. On a Sunday?
I wonder if she has them already, back at her hotel room.*

*And I like Tim's suggestion of an anonymous tip. A suggestion
he made yesterday—he's been very quiet today. But I did some research and found that Fairfax County has a Crime Solvers line—*

"We could call it, report our suspicions of Evans, suggest that
the police search his computers at home and at work," I said.

"And what if they identify the voice of whichever one of us
calls?" Maude asked.

"It's supposed to be anonymous," Tim said.

"Supposed to be and is are quite different," Maude said.

"There are devices you can use to disguise your voice," Claudia
said. I suspected she probably had one of those, too.

"Would it fool one of those computer voice-analysis things?"

"I don't know," Claudia said. "Would it matter that much?"

"If we need to make the anonymous call, I'll provide the voice,"
I said.

"Are you saying you can make your voice unidentifiable?" Maude
asked.

"Oh, the voice will be identifiable," I said. "Voices, actually. I'm
assembling the message using words and phrases taken from UL's
digital video library. So even if they identify the voices, odds are they
won't suspect Humphrey Bogart, Gregory Peck, Jimmy Stewart."

Claudia burst into laughter.

"It's the audio equivalent of those pasted together ransom notes
you always see in the movies," she exclaimed.

Even Maude smiled at that.

"Good idea," she said.

"I'll play it for you later," I said. "Maude, call Sam, or leave a
message for her—explain what we're planning and see about her
availability on short notice. Claudia, get the GPS equipment.

Tim, I'm going to print out some more pictures of Evans and Blake so everyone can have copies on hand. Can you collate them, and then see if you can think of any other materials that would be useful?"

All three jumped willingly to their tasks. I wished I had more jobs to occupy them. To distract them from what could be a long and ultimately fruitless wait.

And to distract Tim from his black mood. I can understand that he feels grief over Nikki's death, but Claudia says he's feeling a lot of guilt, as well.

"I tried to get him drunk last night so he'd talk it out," she said. "He's not talking, and with Tim, that's a bad sign."

"A very bad sign," Maude agreed.

Strange that they can agree so completely on some things, disagree so sharply on others, and still remain friends despite it all. I wondered if it would be ethical to replay an example of their ability to disagree without quarreling for KingFischer. He could learn from it.

By noon, Sam had been brought up to speed and Claudia had returned with her equipment. They'd loaded all three cars with GPS devices, stacks of documents, and a growing collection of other items. Every few minutes, one of them would think of something else they ought to include, and a small flurry of activity would follow before they returned to waiting.

I wanted to tell them to go home. Enjoy what was left of the weekend. That something could happen any minute, or not for days, or maybe never. But I didn't want to sound ungrateful, so I didn't say anything. I figured they would all get tired and go home long before anything happened.

Luckily, I was wrong.

Another day of this, Maude thought, and she'd reach the bottom of her in box and have to go looking for something to do. She picked up another long-neglected sheaf of papers, grimaced with distaste, and began reading.

"I've got it!" Turing exclaimed.

"Got what?" Maude asked.

"Kyle Evans. He's accessing his e-mail right now."

"Where?"

"The hit came from lcpl.lib.va.us—that's the Loudoun County public library system."

"He could be at any branch, though," Maude said.

"They only have seven," Turing said.

"We can't be in seven places at once," Tim said. He and Claudia now hovered over Maude's left and right shoulders, staring at the screen.

"Only four of them are open today, according to their website," Turing said. "Sterling, Purcellville, Leesburg, and Ashburn. You could hit three of those."

A map popped up onto the screen, with a "you are here" tag and four red dots indicating the four libraries. The printer on Maude's desk began spitting out papers.

"Purcellville's farthest away," Maude said. "Not only from us, but from PRS, his apartment, everything connected with the case so far."

"I'm printing out directions from here to all four libraries," Turing said. Maude began sorting the pages as they emerged.

"We may not get there before he leaves," Claudia said.

"Then you can show his picture to the librarians and see if he's been there," Turing said. "You've got plenty of copies."

"Here, Tim," Maude said, handing him a small sheaf of printouts. "You take the Ashburn branch."

"I'm on it," Tim said, dashing out.

"Leesburg," Maude said, handing Claudia another set of papers.

"Cool," Claudia said, and ran out.

"I'll take Sterling," Maude said, grabbing the final set

of papers. "Call if he leaves, so we can stop driving like banshees."

"Will do," Turing said. "Or if he answers my e-mails, or if I find any way to pin his location down more closely."

"Good," Maude said.

Tim and Claudia had already disappeared by the time she reached her car.

They're on their way. I called Sam to let her know something might be happening. She didn't answer, so I left a message.

Perhaps just as well. If she'd answered, I'd have been tempted to try to talk her into going out to Purcellville, so we'd have all four library branches covered. And we may be wasting our time anyway—if I were Evans, I'd make my appearances in public as brief and unobtrusive as possible right now. He could be long gone by the time the first of our team reaches one of the libraries.

If he's even there. It could be anyone accessing his e-mail.

Anyone except KingFischer who just asked if it was okay for him to restart his quest to hack into Hotmail.

"Hold off a bit, KF," I said. "He was using it himself a few minutes ago."

I explained about the library, and KingFischer agreed to hold off until at least six, an hour after the official library closing time. His study of psychology had inspired the notion that he could guess Evans's password, given enough biographical information about his subject. I fed him all the data I had on Evans, wished him luck, and resumed fretting over an odd new inconsistency in my perception of the passage of time. When I think about my human allies, each racing toward a library, I feel as if time is moving very slowly, but when I wonder whether Evans is still reading his mail or whether he has already moved on, I am astonished at how many minutes have raced by since Maude, Tim, and Claudia set out.

I wondered if we had guessed right about which libraries to check. Should we have checked Purcellville instead of one of the others? It's the farthest away—only five miles from the West Virginia border. But would its remoteness make it more attractive to someone who's trying to hide out?

I thought of sending Casey to Purcellville, then decided that probably wasn't a good idea. Partly because I don't yet know him that well—I don't really know how much to trust him. And partly because he has been up all night staring at his monitors, watching Kyle Evans's apartment building and the PRS entrance. He'd probably fall asleep behind the wheel if we sent him on a long drive. I don't want to put him in danger.

Besides, however improbable it would seem to people who don't know them, Tim, Maude, and Claudia are battle-tested. They've proved themselves in dangerous situations. Had guns pointed at them—even fired at them. Casey would probably envy them if he knew. For that matter, I envy them myself. But if things get bad—and if Nestor Garcia is really involved, they could become very bad indeed—at least Tim, Maude, and Claudia have some idea what they're getting into.

I want to ask where they are, but I don't want to pressure them. They're probably already driving faster than they should, and escalating their chances of being in an accident. Considering humans' limited ability to multitask, I suppose I shouldn't be surprised that so many of them are killed in traffic accidents, but I continue to be astonished at how little they worry about this.

So I wait, and worry about them, and watch for some sign that whoever was reading Kyle Evans's e-mail is still online.

Maude drove slowly through the Ster-ling branch library parking lot. Luckily it was crowded, so a casual observer would merely assume she was searching for a parking space.

At the far end of the lot, she spotted it. Evans's vehicle—

the truck, rather than the Corvette. An aging blue pickup, though the factory color had faded, the right rear quarter had been repainted with a blue that wasn't even a close approximation of the original, and much of the rest was patched with gray primer.

She grabbed her cell phone and speed dialed Turing.

"I've got him," she said. "At least, I've got his truck. Presumably he's still in the library. Unless he's abandoned the truck here."

"See if you can park nearby," Turing said. "I'll divert Tim and Claudia."

Fortunately, spaces weren't impossible to find this far from the door. Maude backed into a space, to be ready for a fast exit when Evans drove off, put on her sunglasses, and took out her map book. Studying maps was a plausible reason to be sitting in her car in a parking lot, and knowing more about the nearby roads would help if Evans took off before Tim and Claudia arrived. If a good Samaritan offered to help her find her destination, she could always claim she was just killing time, waiting for a friend who had gone inside the library.

Not to mention the fact that the map book hid the cell phone and the GPS unit she'd taken out of its box.

Her hands shook.

Calm down, she told herself. Just put the batteries in the unit, make sure Turing's getting the signal. And then a quick trip over to the truck to attach the unit and she could come back and read the map book for real.

"Turing, are they on their way?" she said, into the phone.

"Yes," Turing said. "Tim was at the Ashburn library— that's only fifteen minutes away from you. Claudia hadn't reached Leesburg yet, fortunately, but I estimate she will arrive in twenty-five minutes."

"Maybe two of us could follow Evans while the third goes in to see if there's anything we can learn in the library," Maude said. "See if the librarians recognize him as a regular—maybe check the computer he was using."

"Good idea," Turing said. "We can decide who does what when we see who's in place when he starts to move."

Maude nodded. And then remembered that Turing didn't have a camera here in her car.

"Roger," she said. "Okay, I'm taking the GPS and—wait, someone's walking toward the truck."

It wasn't Evans. An older man. She let out her breath. She fervently hoped that Tim and Claudia would arrive before Evans started moving. Even one of them. At least they'd had some experience following people. Talking to the librarians and searching the computer would be much more her speed. She understood librarians and computers. But car chases . . .

"Turing, he's been in there at least forty-five minutes," she said. "And that's not including any time he spent before reading your e-mail. What could he be doing? Surely he can't have that much e-mail. At least, not that much that's important enough to read when he's on the run."

"Maybe he's doing some more online shopping," Turing said.

"After what's happened, I'd expect him to be more interested in escaping than continuing the scam," Maude said.

The man passed Evans's truck and approached a dark blue Buick.

"You can buy a plane ticket online," Turing said. "Or a train ticket, for that matter. And if he's short of cash . . ."

"Maybe he's buying his getaway with yet another stolen card," Maude said. "Yes, that makes sense. Are you watching the credit cards from his spreadsheet?"

"All the ones I can watch," Turing said. "At least half of them are from banks whose security I haven't cracked."

"Can't KingFisher do anything?"

"Next time I get his attention, I'll find out," Turing said.

Oh, dear, Maude thought. Not another spat. Should she ask what was wrong this time between Turing and KingFischer? Probably not. The man in the Buick finally began to pull out of his space. As soon as he'd gone, she could place the GPS tracker.

Or maybe not. She spotted someone else approaching.

"Damn," she said. "I was waiting for someone to leave before I planted the GPS, and here comes someone else."

"Evans?" Turing demanded.

Maude pretended to be absorbed in her map book and followed the figure with her peripheral vision.

"I think so," she said. "Yes, it's him."

She thought she saw Evans looking at her. She lowered the map book slightly, raised her arm, looked down at her watch, and then up and away from him, in the direction of the library door, frowning.

From the corner of her eye, she could see that he had moved on.

Did that work, she wondered, or was I too obvious?

She raised the map book again, and the cell phone with it.

"Sorry," she said. "I blew it. I never managed to plant the GPS."

"You didn't get a chance," Turing said. "At least you got there in time to follow him."

"He's starting the truck," Maude said. "Wish me luck."

"Tim's only five minutes away," Turing said. "And Claudia's not far behind. Give me a running account of where you are, and I'll see if I can help them intercept you."

"Roger," Maude said. She put on the headset and reached down to connect it to her cell phone.

"Can you hear me?" she asked.

"Loud and clear," Turing said. "Where are you now?"

"Still in the library parking lot," Maude said. "I didn't want to follow him out too closely."

"That's good," Turing said. "Tim says it's a good idea to keep at least one vehicle between you and your subject. As long as you can still see it."

"I think that eyesore of a truck will be pretty easy to spot from a reasonable distance," Maude said.

And fortunately, her own silver Honda Accord looked like every third or fourth car on the road—annoying in a parking lot, but an advantage when tailing someone, she hoped.

"Okay, I'm on Enterprise Street, about to turn right on Commerce," she said.

A blue Tahoe pulled out in front of her. Keeping at least one vehicle between herself and the subject might sound good in theory, she noted, but didn't work quite as well out here in the suburbs, where every other vehicle was an enormous truck or SUV that completely blocked her view of the battered pickup.

Just let me pull this off, she thought, and I swear, I will never give Tim a hard time about anything that happens to him when he's on a case.

Maude is following Evans. I've called Tim and Claudia and patched them all into a conference call, so we can share information readily. And I've had each of them activate one of their GPS devices, so I can plot their positions on a map and follow the action. It was exciting, at first, watching the dots converge, but now, from my vantage point, it's merely a clump of dots meandering across the landscape at a slow pace along an erratic course.

Of course, I know from their running chatter that they are stopping at stop signs, running yellow lights, skirting rivers and other geographical obstacles, and probably proceeding in a reasonably efficient manner to whatever destination Kyle Evans has in mind. But it was maddening, waiting here and hearing it all second hand. I wish I could be there.

At least I've learned to stop annoying them by asking "What are you doing?" when one of the dots veers away from the pack, apparently going astray. It's invariably Maude, taking a shortcut that she thinks will put her in a better position. She's almost always right, and when she isn't, she still catches up quickly. Apparently she knows the local roads better than Tim. Or else she's better at using maps than either Tim or Claudia.

I tried to sit back and figure out what was going on from their three-way conversation.

"I'm losing him," Tim said.

"Chill, Tim," Claudia said.

"He just moved into the left lane," Tim said. "Damn, no one's letting me in. I'm not sure I can get over in time if he's turning left at the light. Claudia, can you pick him up if that happens?"

"I'll try," Claudia said. "Working my way left. Sing out if he turns."

"I'll turn left now and then right a couple of streets down," Maude said. "If he turns left, let me know the cross street and I can probably pick him up as he passes."

I have no idea what they're doing. Chase scenes in books and movies are never this confusing.

In the midst of the pursuit, I suddenly got an eager message from KingFischer.

"Turing? I think I've got it!" he announced.

"You've hacked Hotmail?" I said. "Great."

"No, I still haven't figured out how to do that without the whole world finding out, but I managed to determine Kyle Evans's password," he said. "Using a combination of logical deduction and psychological principles."

"That's fabulous," I said.

"Unfortunately, the results are meager," KingFischer said. "He's cleaned out his mailbox. Even emptied the trash can. And he doesn't have an address list on file. Sorry."

"Never mind," I said. "We're still trying to follow him to his hideout, and we still have a lot of unanswered questions. This could prove useful if I keep an eye on it. What's the password?"

*KingFischer replied with an apparently random sequence of let-
ters and numbers. And yet, random as they were, they sounded familiar. I did a search of the other information in Evans's file.*

"KF, that's his license plate number," I said. "The one for his
new Corvette."

"Yes—clever of me to deduce it, don't you think?" KingFischer
said. "My research showed that the psychological significance of
automobiles is often far greater, particularly to male humans, than
their practical value as modes of transportation. So when I noticed
that the subject had recently purchased an automobile whose cost far
exceeded what he could reasonably afford on his legitimate salary,
and even disproportionately high compared to his illicit gains, I considered the possibility that his password was related to this new and
highly significant object in his life."

"So you checked the license plate, and bingo! Good going."

I was so pleased that I deliberately avoided mentioning how
much his explanation sounded like something Sigmund would say.
Or suggesting that if he'd had this breakthrough a few hours earlier, before Evans got to his e-mail, we might have found some clues.
Not his fault really, though it's frustrating.

I logged into the Hotmail account and checked around. Not that
I expected to find anything KingFischer hadn't, but there's something satisfying about seeing for yourself.

I had only just finished checking all his baskets and preferences
and agreeing that there was nothing to find when an e-mail arrived. From the re: in the subject line, a reply to one he'd sent,
though unfortunately nothing from his e-mail was quoted.

"I'll see what I can do," it read. "Just don't tell them about
me—I could lose my job!!! xoxox Sandi."

It was from an e-mail address at washingtonpost.com.

"Good news," I said over the phone to Maude, Tim, and Claudia. "KingFischer has gotten into Kyle Evans's Hotmail account."

"A little late, isn't it?" Claudia said.

"You never know," I said. "It may still prove useful. Apparently he e-mailed someone—probably his girlfriend—while he was at the library. We can track her down."

"After we track him down," Claudia said. "He's getting in the right lane now—could be planning to make a turn at the next light."

"Just enjoys lane-hopping, if you ask me," Tim grumbled. "Need me to take over?"

"What's the cross street?" Maude asked. "I still can't find the last position you gave on my map."

"You three concentrate on Evans," I said. "I'm going to see what I can do to track down the girlfriend myself."

"Using her e-mail address?" Maude asked.

"Yes," I said. "Luckily, she works at the Post. I can get into the Post's system any time I want. At least for the time being."

"Is their security that bad?"

"No, their security's pretty good," I said. "But I do a lot of free research for a reporter and he repays me by giving me access."

"So if he ever moves to another paper, you're out of luck," Maude said.

"Exactly. But for now, my access is golden."

Actually, I wasn't nearly as concerned with my mole at the Post moving to another paper as I was with the possibility that his bosses might catch him doing something unprofessional or illegal and fire him. He'd begun using larger and larger chunks of my research reports verbatim in his articles, without attribution—which was fine with me, because I didn't want my name in the paper. But if he did it to me, odds were he was doing it to other sources, or possibly other reporters, and sooner or later one of them would find out and call him on it. Especially since his promotion, and the rumor that his weeklong series of articles on identity theft was in the running for a Pulitzer. An article taken almost entirely from my e-mails to him. Apparently I'm a much better writer than he is, and probably better than whomever he plagiarized before he found me.

A problem I'll worry about later. For now, I used the access he'd arranged for me to search for Evans's friend Sandi.

"I'm not sure the information I can find on her is going to be useful," I said. "I was hoping perhaps he was heading for the girlfriend's house, but she lives in Arlington. He's headed in the wrong direction."

"Turing, what department does she work in," Maude asked.

"Circulation," I said.

"Then your information is very useful," Maude said. "It probably solves the mystery of how Blake and Evans found the vacant houses they used as their drop-off points."

"How?" I asked.

"I get it," Claudia said. "What's the first thing you do when you're going on vacation for a week or two?"

"I don't travel much," I said.

"You stop the newspapers, so they don't pile up in the yard and let burglars know you're away. Can you check to see if all the drop-off addresses on the spreadsheet were Post subscribers who had their subscriptions suspended during the time Blake and Evans were using them?"

"They're all subscribers," I said a few minutes later. "If the database retains the dates during which their service was suspended, I can't figure out how to find it. But all of them had lower total charges for the billing periods during which Blake and Evans were using their houses."

"That's it, then," Claudia said. "Another part of the mystery solved. Damn! That light was already red, you scumbag! Maude, he shook me at the light—see if you can pick him up."

I began pulling together a list of houses in Virginia whose Post delivery was currently suspended. If they lost Evans, perhaps they could begin checking the houses closest to where he was last seen, move outward in concentric circles, and eventually locate him. But that would be a long, tedious operation. I hoped we didn't have to try it.

"Okay, he's turning down a driveway," Tim said. "Number 12907. Claudia? How far away are you?"

"I'm in the 12800s," she said.

"Find a place to pull over and watch from that end," Tim said. "There's nothing but a couple of roads with no-outlet signs between you and 12907. I'll keep on for a bit and see what it looks like on this end."

He drove on for half a mile, seeing nothing but woods with the occasional glimpse of a house set back from the road. The road finally dead-ended.

"We've got you," he said aloud.

He drove slowly back, studying the neighborhood. He found himself nodding as he went along. Yeah, this was the kind of place they'd pick. Big houses set far apart on wooded lots. He wondered briefly if Evans's girlfriend had handed over long lists of empty houses for Blake and Evans to scout, or if they'd given her a list of likely looking roads and asked her to tell them when subscribers along those roads would be away.

"I've found 12907 in the *Post*'s database," Turing said. "Delivery suspended until a week from tomorrow."

"So it was probably the next place they planned to use as a drop-off site," Tim said. "Makes an equally good hideout."

"Depends on your definition of a hideout," Claudia said. "Personally, I'd want a place where I could go inside. Less conspicuous than crouching on the doorstep, pretending to be a FedEx package."

"Maybe he'll try to break in."

"I hope for his sake that they don't have a security system, then," Claudia said.

"Actually, I hope for our sake that they do," Maude said. "I'm getting close—should I hold back or come ahead?"

"Keep your eyes open for a place with a picnic table," Tim said. "I remember seeing it, a couple of miles before the house. I think it's the start of a hiking trail or something like that. Stop there for now."

"I don't hear anything," Claudia said. "Any alarm, I mean."

"Would you hear it from that far away?" Maude asked.

"I'm less than a mile, and those things are loud," Claudia said. "Maybe they don't have an alarm."

"Maybe they have a silent one," Tim said. "Or maybe he's still making up his mind to break in. I know it would take me a while."

"Tim's right," Maude said. "Let's not get impatient."

"I'm always impatient," Claudia said, laughing. "But don't worry. I'll sit tight."

Sit tight. Yeah, that was what they should do right now. And exactly what Tim dreaded. He wanted to be doing something. Not wanted, needed. The chase after Kyle Evans had distracted him for a while—the chatter, the bursts of adrenaline. But if he had to sit still and wait, he'd start seeing mental images from last night again.

"Isn't there something we can do?" he asked aloud.

"Good question," Turing said. "We've found him. Now what are we going to do about it?"

I think we're making progress. Tim has confirmed that there's no way out by car except past the spot where they've set up what they're calling their base camp. Which is three miles from the house. The hideout, as they've begun calling it.

Sam called back, and I patched her into the ongoing conference call with the others.

"Okay, I'm heading for my car," Sam said. "But I'm in Silver Spring right now, at a cousin's house, and you're pretty far out there. I expect it'll take me an hour or so to get there."

"That's fine," I said. "My idea is that we wait until dark to approach the house anyway. That will give us time to scout the area. And if, as we suspect, Evans is planning to break into the house, we don't want to barge in too soon, in case he triggers an alarm."

"Yeah, we don't want to be arrested along with him if that happens," Claudia said.

"And also time for the equipment to get here." I added.

"Equipment?" Maude repeated. "I've got a whole trunk full of stuff already. We all do. What do we need that we haven't already got?"

"This is some specialized stuff for me," I said. "I want to go along."

"Just how are you going to do that?" Sam said.

"We're not talking about the robot again," Maude said. "We're still cleaning up from that adventure."

"Robot?" Sam repeated.

"No, but I want to see and hear as much as possible," I said. "We can fit up a laptop, and you can bring it along. We install a wireless modem, some microphones and speakers, and a couple of small digital video cameras—"

"Bad idea," Maude said. "If we want to get this kid talking to us, we need to look as nonthreatening as possible. Can you imagine how it's going to look if we waltz in there holding a laptop bristling with cameras and microphones? Hello Mr. Evans, we're here to help you, just ignore all the electronic surveillance gear—we're not actually webcasting everything you say and do to the cops or anything sneaky like that."

"You think he'll react that badly?" I asked.

"I'm not even sure we should use the miniature radios," Maude said. "What if he searches us?"

"But if you don't have the miniature radios, I won't know what's going on."

"If he clams up, none of us will," Maude said.

"I agree," Sam said. "No electronic gear until we get his permission. In fact, I don't even think I should go in right away—I should wait until you've convinced him to at least consider retaining me."

"Then I'll wait in the car with you," I said.

"In the car with me?"

"You can take the laptop in your car, and I'll log in there," I said. "I've had Casey working on an improved microphone array.

I'll call him and see if he can install it and a few cameras on a spare laptop and bring it all down."

"You just happened to have Casey working on microphones?" Maude asked. "Or were you already planning to take another outing sometime soon?"

"I wasn't exactly planning," I said. "But I figured just in case the need arose, it would be a lot better to have something already designed and tested. Instead of throwing something together in a hurry."

"Hmmm," Maude said.

She sounded suspicious. Luckily I hadn't yet sent my e-mail to Casey. I revised it slightly, adding a stern warning not to mention that we were originally intending the microphones for Maude's garden. Or to say anything about the floodlights and sirens. I could tell Maude still had mixed feelings about what we'd already done to her yard.

"We're in luck," I said, a few minutes later. "Casey was working on some of the equipment at home, while watching the surveillance cameras, so he doesn't have to go in to the office. He thinks he can be here in an hour."

"Great," Claudia said. "Let's get started scouting."

"Not that I really expect anyone to listen, but have we considered calling the cops?" Maude said.

There was a pause.

"I've considered it," I said. "And yes, I think we should call them. As soon as we've talked to Evans. Or as soon as we're sure he's not going to talk to us. And if anything goes wrong. I have a variety of canned messages ready to send."

I heard Maude let out her breath. I wish I'd had my cameras. I couldn't tell how she was reacting.

"Okay," she said, finally. "I'll watch the exit while you two scout the area."

Tim and Claudia set off in one of the cars. They planned to park closer to the house and scout the neighborhood on foot, with binoculars and cameras hanging from their necks to make them look like harmless birders.

"I must say, I'm starting to see bird watching in a whole new light," Maude remarked. "I'm beginning to wonder if perhaps the Audubon society is a CIA front organization."

Tim and Claudia reported seeing Evans's pickup in the driveway when they first passed the house, and then later reported that it wasn't there any longer. Since Maude didn't see it leave, odds were Kyle had taken it into the garage.

Although I've been poring over every map of the area I can find, to make sure there aren't any escape routes Tim didn't see. I can't find any. That doesn't mean they don't exist, though.

So as far as we know, Kyle's in the house. No police or private security guards have arrived to check things out, so presumably the owners don't have a security system.

Casey showed up at six with the laptop he'd fitted out, and stayed long enough for us to run extensive diagnostics tests. He wanted to stay around even longer and help, but I convinced him that we needed him back at his computer, monitoring the cameras.

"Something could still happen there," I said. "For example, if the police show up at Evans's house, they might find something that would lead them here—we need someone to give us a warning if that happens."

He reluctantly departed. I watched until I was sure he had logged back in again, forty-five minutes later.

Sam arrived, and when it was dark, they all moved to a new location, the driveway of another nearby vacant house, and prepared to approach Evans's hideout.

I felt nervous, and I didn't even have any of the adrenaline or other biological systems humans have, the ones that go into high gear when they're facing danger. I couldn't imagine how the others were feeling.

"Ready?" Claudia said.

"Do we have a plan?" Maude asked. "What if he's not alone, for example?"

"What if he's armed?" Tim asked.

"Maybe only one of us should approach first," Maude said.

"Let's circle around and go in from the garage side," Claudia said. "There's only one bathroom window facing that way, and it's curtained for privacy. From that side, we can probably get to the front door without being spotted."

"Makes sense to me," Maude said. "You lead the way till we get to the front door, and then I'll take over."

"Right," Claudia said. She slipped into the woods.

"Sam, you've got the two-way radio, right?"

Sam held it up.

"Mine's in my pocket. If you spot any danger, just hit the call button and I'll get the tone."

"Like this?" Sam said. Maude's pocket beeped slightly.

"Roger. Here we go."

Maude set off after Claudia. Tim brought up the rear.

"Be careful," I said, as they left the car behind.

Waiting in the car with Sam was better than nothing.

Not a whole lot better.

Technically I wasn't in the car, of course—only logged in though a wireless modem to the specially equipped laptop, which sat on the passenger seat beside Sam. I'd had Casey attach two high-powered directional microphones and two tiny, digital video cameras, to make me feel less like a fifth wheel as I waited.

I still felt left out.

And highly vulnerable. I don't know why. Perhaps it was being outdoors. Actually in the convertible with the top down, but it certainly felt like the outdoors to me. The outdoors still made me nervous. I suddenly realized that perhaps that was one reason for my recent obsession with gardening. It could let me get to know the outdoors under controlled circumstances. Demystify it. Tame it. But maybe it wasn't working, because out here in this wooded neighborhood, my anxiety about the outdoors didn't lessen.

Sam didn't seem bothered. She was slouched down in the driver's seat, watching through Tim's night-vision binoculars.

"I can see them," she said, when Maude, Tim, and Claudia had been gone nine minutes. "They're crossing the driveway."

I spotted them, and we sat in silence, her binoculars and my camera lenses glued to the three dark figures as they slid along the side of the house.

It seemed rather anticlimactic when they finally reached the front porch and rang the doorbell. Anticlimactic and more than a little dangerous. Maybe their theory was that people with sufficient manners to ring doorbells didn't look dangerous enough to shoot.

I hoped they were right.

Tim breathed a sigh of relief when they safely reached the front porch of the house. Irrational relief, maybe. They had no guarantee that Evans wouldn't shoot through the front door. But there was something disarmingly normal about standing on the porch.

"Now remember," Maude said. "When we get in, Tim, you go to my left if possible while Claudia goes to my right. Flank me."

Tim nodded.

"And try not to look menacing," Maude added, raising her hand to the doorbell.

Menacing? Tim blinked in surprise. He wasn't sure he could look menacing if he tried.

Maybe that part was aimed at Claudia.

Maude rang the doorbell. No answer. She knocked on the door.

"We know you're in there, Kyle," she called.

"Who's there?" came a muffled voice.

"Friends. I know you got our e-mail. We can help you."

"Go away."

"We're not going away," Maude said. "You can talk to us,

or we can call the police and you can talk to them."

"Why should I talk to you?

"Because maybe we can help you."

A long pause. Maude was opening her mouth to speak again when they heard the rattle of a chain being unhooked. The click of a deadbolt lock. The door opened slightly.

"That's him," Sam said.

"Kyle Evans? Are you sure?"

"Yeah, doesn't it look like his driver's license picture to you?"

"I think so, but I'm still analyzing," I said. "I admit, I'm not as good as a human at identifying individual people."

"What, do we humans all look alike to you?" Sam said, with a laugh that sounded more cynical than amused.

"No, the problem is you don't look enough like yourselves sometimes," I said. "I have to start with a static picture taken eighteen months ago under one set of lighting conditions, and compare it with a moving image seen under very different lighting conditions, and then make allowances for a wide range of possible alterations in shape, color, hair configuration, and, since we're talking about a man, presence or absence of facial hair—all the changes that could have occurred in the intervening period. It's difficult. And yet you humans do it quite effectively, using only a fraction of the processing power I use."

"Nice to know we still do a few things better," Sam said. "Okay, they're in."

The door closed behind them. I scanned the house's windows, but all were blocked by blinds or curtains. I boosted the volume on my microphones as far as possible, but all I could hear was a variety of insect and frog noises and the occasional sound of something moving in the woods around us—nothing from the house. I started working on trying to filter out the nearby sounds.

"I hate waiting," Sam said, after a few seconds.

"How long do you think it will take?" I asked.

I heard a small noise, but Sam didn't answer.

I was about to turn one of my cameras to look at her when something knocked it askew. I righted it again and spotted Sam's arm lying limp, palm up, on the seat beside my laptop. I swiveled the camera left and saw that Sam's head had dropped down and was tilted to the left. Her eyes were closed. I've seen Tim and Maude look like that when they fall asleep sitting up, but they don't usually sound so awake one minute and doze off the next. Something was wrong.

I could see the two-way radio Sam was supposed to use in case of danger lying on the seat near me. But since I had only a normal laptop, with no peripherals for manipulating the world around me, it might as well have been miles away for all the good it did me.

Then the picture in both my cameras shook and veered—someone was picking up the laptop. I realized a nanosecond in advance that someone had unfastened the battery latch, and then the battery popped out, blanking sight and sound.

I panicked, briefly—irrationally. Even though I wasn't, technically, in the laptop, I was so focused on what was happening there in the woods that suddenly losing all sight and sound there was terrifying.

I was safe. If Garcia or one of his allies hoped to capture me in the laptop, they were doomed to disappointment.

But while I was safe, my friends weren't. I began to worry for real. Something had happened to Sam—I was right to feel nervous in that open convertible. I hoped she was only unconscious, not badly injured or dead.

And whoever attacked Sam was still free to go after Maude, Tim, and Claudia.

I sent warning messages to all three of their cell phones. Claudia's and Maude's voice mail eventually answered their calls. Tim's borrowed phone simply rang on unanswered.

Tim concentrated on smiling in a friendly fashion as the door swung slowly open.

"Kyle Evans?" Maude said.

The young man in the doorway nodded and swallowed nervously. Tim could see that it was the face they knew from the driver's license, although he probably hadn't slept much in the last few days.

"Look, I can explain," he said.

"That's good," Maude said. "Why don't we talk inside?"

Evans backed away as she stepped through the door. Tim and Claudia followed. Evans glanced briefly at them and then focused back on Maude as if she were the most dangerous.

Not a total idiot, then, Tim decided. As planned, he and Claudia took up positions flanking Maude. Unmenacingly. Though seeing Evans's visibly nervous state, he figured just about anyone might look menacing to the poor guy. So he tried to keep his face calm and stuck his hands in his pockets in case they shook.

Evans had backed to the other side of the room and stood in front of an open doorway, as if he felt safer with an escape route at his back. Not much of an escape route, Tim thought. He'd already seen Claudia assess the distance between her and Evans, perform some mental calculation, and sidle a few feet closer.

"We know—well, not everything," Maude said. "But enough to know what a jam you're in."

Kyle didn't react.

Tim was startled to feel his cell phone begin to vibrate. He wasn't sure whether to feel relieved that it hadn't made an audible interruption or annoyed at the distraction. Later, he thought, willing the phone to stillness.

"We know about you using the credit card numbers you got from your job," Maude said. "And how you were ordering things with the cards and having them delivered to vacant houses—the house in Leesburg a few weeks ago, other houses before that, and then this week, the house in Oakton.

he one where your friend Tayloe was murdered."

Evans flinched at that. No, Tim thought, he's not the iller. Not that they had any proof, but seeing Evans's face, e was convinced.

"I didn't kill him," Evans said in a flat voice. As if it were reflex. As if he didn't expect them to believe it? No, more s if he wasn't really sure he had to deny it. Good heavens, im thought, seeing Evans's expression. He's wondering if ne of us did it.

"We didn't think you had," Maude said. "And if you lidn't, we think we know who did. And if we're right, you're n danger."

"I'm trying to leave town," Evans said.

"Leaving town may not be enough," Maude said. "If the nan who had Tayloe killed is who we think he is, you can't ossibly run far enough. Turn yourself in to the police. Tell hem what you know. They can arrange protection."

"Oh, yeah, like jail time," Evans said, flatly.

"Better than a cemetery," Maude said.

Evans swallowed hard.

"The man who's after you is no lightweight," Maude aid. "The FBI is looking for him, too. Look, we've got our awyer outside. She can help you turn yourself safely in to he police. Convince them that you need protection from Tayloe's killer."

Evans was shaking his head. From the corner of his eye, Tim could see that Claudia was shaking hers, too. As if to ay "I told you he wouldn't go for it."

"Just answer a few questions, and then we'll leave you lone," Maude said. "Or maybe even help you, if you help us."

Evans shrugged. Maude evidently decided to assume the ack of protest implied agreement.

"Was the scheme your idea or Blake's?" Maude asked.

"Blake?" Evans said, with a snort. "Give me a break—the

guy can barely read. I came up with the idea. Happened to me, actually—someone charged twenty-four hundred dollars on my credit card, back when I was out of work and trying to ignore the bills, so I didn't even notice until six months later."

"Didn't you report it?" Maude asked.

"Yeah, but by that time it was too late to do anything," Evans said. "Or maybe they just told me that because they didn't believe me. Twenty-four hundred dollars wasn't even that much compared to everything I owed, but it burned me, you know? That they were charging me all those fees and interest and stuff, and they wouldn't even listen to me when I was telling the truth about being ripped off. So when I got into skip tracing and found I could get everything on a person—social security, credit card numbers, the works—I decided to rip the banks off."

"The banks?" Maude said. "I'd have said you were ripping off the people whose credit cards you stole."

"Only if they're stupid enough to pay," Evans said. Talking seemed to help his nerves—he'd gone from scared to boastful. "Sooner or later they'll all skip town or declare bankruptcy anyway, and the credit card company has to eat it. Why shouldn't I get something out of it?"

"Where did Blake come in?"

"I needed someone to pick up the stuff and sell it," Evans said. "I figured that was the part where you were the most likely to get caught."

"Oh, so you had your friend do it?" Tim couldn't help saying.

"He wasn't a friend, he was just this guy I knew from school," Evans said. "His older brother was always getting into trouble for stealing, so I figured he could probably figure out where to fence stuff."

"How did you keep the police from finding you when they began following Blake?" Maude asked.

"That was one of the good parts," Evans said. "We'd meet every couple of nights in different fast-food places. He'd come in and after he'd been there for a while, he'd go to the john and stick a plastic bag in the toilet tank with the money and the paperwork from all the packages, so I could track what had come in. And then I'd go to the john, pick up the money, and replace it with the address of the next drop-off house."

"Smart," Maude said. "If he didn't hand over the money, he didn't get any more stuff to sell."

"Exactly," Evans said. He smiled, and Tim decided that the "SlyKyle" e-mail address was aptly chosen.

"When did you realize something was wrong?" Maude asked.

"We were supposed to have an exchange in McDonald's that night," Evans said. "I waited till midnight, and he never showed. So I drove by his house—I figured if his van was still there, I could find a pay phone, call his house, give him hell. And I saw a police car."

"You went into hiding?"

Evans nodded.

"I didn't hear about the murder until the next day," he said. "But I knew something had gone way wrong."

Maude glanced back at Tim and then at Claudia, as if she wasn't sure what to ask.

"You always got the credit card numbers from your job?" Claudia asked. "You didn't start getting any from some other source?"

"Where else would I get them?" Evans asked, "I'm not a crook."

"Do you know the name Nestor Garcia?" Tim asked.

Evans shook his head, and his face showed no sign of recognition.

"Look, I'm not a lawyer," Maude said. "But I bet a good lawyer could probably make a case for extenuating circumstances. Get you off lightly. Just let us bring in our lawyer, and you can talk to her and—"

"It's not going to work," Evans said. "Even if I—"

He paused as if a sudden thought had hit him. And then he made a small sound, and stepped forward, into the room.

A tall man in an Arizona Diamondbacks cap stepped into the room, holding a gun to Evans's head. Tim's fists clenched instinctively when he recognized Ishmael. Maude's burglar. The man who'd probably killed Nikki.

"Surprise," Ishmael said.

Tim heard a muffled thump and saw a splash of blood on the doorframe. So that's what a silencer looks like, Tim thought, as Evans's body slumped to the floor and Ishmael turned the gun in his direction.

None of my human friends are answering *their phones. Should I call 911? For all I know, they've already caught whoever knocked Sam out and are in the middle of interrogating him, or Evans, or both. Or they could all be knocked out, held at gunpoint, already dead—I had no way of knowing.*

And just what was I supposed to say to 911, anyway? The last time I'd called, I'd pretended to be Maude's burglar alarm. They'd come quickly, but Maude isn't out in the middle of nowhere with nothing but trees for miles around. I had a feeling that out here it could take the police a long time to answer an automated burglar alarm. And after everything was over, how were we supposed to explain an automated call from a nonexistent system?

Norris. He'd come quickly enough before, when he thought Maude was in trouble. I used one of our corporate cell phone accounts to fire off a text message to Norris's cell phone. "Help!" it said, "Maude in danger! Send ambulance!" Then I gave the address and signed Sam's name to it.

I waited for something to happen. Like Norris calling back to

see if the message was a hoax. Seconds ticked by. Should I send an-
other message? What if Norris was asleep or something?

Just then, I noticed that Casey was calling in on his cell phone.
Not now! I wanted to snap. Probably another damned pizza delivery to Evans's apartment. Maybe we should just have told Casey to
stand down, instead of assigning him to watch the monitors. But I
peeled off a subroutine to deal with Casey. Calmly, politely, kindly.
While I tried to find something else I could do to—

And then my attention snapped back to Casey.

"Turing?" he was saying. "Are you there? What should I do—
they got that lady lawyer."

"Casey? What are you talking about? I thought you went
home—I can see you logged in."

"Yeah, I'm logged in on my laptop. I know I was supposed to go
back and watch the monitors, but I had this feeling, you know, so I
drove out of sight and then I came back. And I saw this guy sneak
up behind the lady lawyer in the convertible and knock her out and
steal your laptop."

"Casey, where are you now?"

"I'm in the bushes by the driveway. I think the guy went inside.
What should I do?"

I thought of asking him to check on Sam. See if she was still
breathing. But what good would that do? He wasn't a medic. I'd
already called for an ambulance. I needed to rescue Tim, Maude,
and Claudia. But how?

"Casey—do you have any more equipment in your car?"

"Like what?"

"Like cameras, microphones, speakers, a laptop—any of that?"

"Yeah, some," he said. "I brought spares, in case something
didn't work when I hooked it up to your laptop. The one he stole."

"Go back to your car," I said. "I have an idea."

I'd foiled Maude's prowler. Maybe it would work again. While
Casey hastily assembled hardware from his trunk, I tried to find
something that would work. I didn't think dogs and a deep, male

voice would be enough this time. Especially if either Nestor Garcia or Ishmael had attacked Sam. They'd probably figured out my invisible Dobermans. And they'd only laugh at a sharp command from Humphrey Bogart.

"Okay," Casey said. "Booting up. You should have picture and sound right about . . . now."

Not much of a picture, since the only light was the one that came on when Casey opened his trunk. And not a very fast connection. But it was enough. I had eyes.

"Okay?" he asked.

The microphones picked it up along with the cell phone. I had ears.

"Okay," I said. *And I had a voice; the microphones caught the word when it came out of the speakers. I added a sort of echo effect.* "How's this?"

"Like you're talking through a cheap PA system," Casey said, shutting off his phone. "Want me to adjust it?"

"No, that's the effect I want," I said. "A cheap PA system, or maybe a bullhorn. Now take me closer."

"Closer?"

"Take me right up to one of the windows of the house."

"Okay."

The picture jiggled wildly as he picked up the laptop and began walking fast. Running, actually.

I saw the occasional recognizable landmark. The mailbox. Sam's car. I realized I should have told him to sneak around the back. If whoever had attacked Sam was watching, or had someone else watching . . .

Too late to do anything about it now. He dropped from a run to a fast, crouching walk as he approached the house.

"To the left," I said, *softly. I could hear voices coming from the room on the left.*

Still crouching, Casey slid through the bushes until he was right under the window. He hadn't had time to rig any kind of controls, just the raw feed. He lifted the camera to the window sill and I heard a faint ripping sound as he pulled a piece of duct tape off of his sleeve and taped the camera to the window frame, the lens pointing at the glass.

I saw Ishmael standing in a doorway at the other side of the room, holding a gun. A still form was slumped at his feet—Evans? Probably. Tim, Maude, and Claudia stood on this side, looking at him. Ishmael was smiling, but I didn't think it was a real smile. I suspected something bad was about to happen.

Okay, here goes, I thought. While Casey rigged the equipment, I'd sifted through my audio indexes. At first, I didn't find anything useful. Scraps of movies, scraps of music, scraps of conversations with my friends, scraps of phone conversations.

Phone conversations. I found a clip of Dan Norris talking to Maude's secretary.

"Hello, this is Special Agent Dan Norris of the FBI calling," it said. "May I speak to Maude Graham?"

Could I come up with enough clips of Norris's voice to pull this off? If I couldn't, we were out of luck. But since I couldn't think of any other ideas, we were out of luck anyway if I didn't at least try. I took the first sentence, removed the first and last words, jacked up the volume, and played it.

"This is Special Agent Dan Norris of the FBI."

While that played, I searched some more, pulling scraps from that same conversation—"when the Fairfax County Police told me . . . what you and your friends are up to . . . level with me."

"The Fairfax County Police . . . are . . . with me," I added—smoothing the spaces between the words, of course, so it sounded normal. To me, at least. Then again, I was no expert.

Unfortunately, I didn't have clips of Norris saying anything that even remotely resembled "The building is surrounded. Throw down your weapons and come out with your hands up." After a few nanoseconds of trying to figure out how to piece it together from the

bits I had, I decided to turn the virtual megaphone over to the Fair-
fax County Police. After all, I'd just said they were there.

   Although come to think of it, we were in Loudoun County now.
I hoped Ishmael wouldn't notice.

   "You're surrounded," I boomed, in a male voice. "Drop your
weapons and come out with your hands up!"

Hurray for the cavalry, Tim thought,
when he heard Dan Norris's voice outside. Ishmael looked
annoyed. With his free left hand, he shoved back the cap
that almost covered his eyes, and he stepped out of the doorway and into the end of the room farthest from Maude, Tim,
and Claudia.

   "Move over there, all of you," he said, pointing with the
gun. "Now!"

   The corner he was herding them into was farther from
the front door, and it also got them away from the window.

   "Wait—you," the gunman said, pointing at Claudia.
"Over to the window. Look out and tell me what you see."

   Claudia obediently went over to the window and looked
out.

   Tim worked on not grinning. Obviously Ishmael was a
lousy judge of character if he thought Claudia the most
harmless of their trio. Just a little closer, and maybe Claudia
could take him.

   "What do you see?" Ishmael demanded.

   "Nothing," Claudia said, shaking her head. "It's too dark
out there."

   "Keep looking," he said.

   And then while Claudia was still ostentatiously peering
out, Ishmael stepped forward and struck her head with the
butt of the gun. By the time Tim realized what was happening, Ishmael had the unconscious Claudia in front of him
like a shield, with the gun pointed at her head.

Come on, he pleaded silently. Be faking it. Give that creep a big surprise.

Claudia didn't move.

Maybe Ishmael wasn't such a bad judge of character after all. He'd just disabled his most physically dangerous opponent.

"Drop your weapons and come out with your hands up!" the police ordered outside.

Ishmael stood behind a curtain, where he could see out without being seen, but he was holding Claudia in plain view. If someone outside saw her, and took a shot . . .

Something tapped the window, and a flash of movement caught Tim's eye. A hand had appeared, trying to attach something to the window frame.

Suddenly Ishmael laughed, and fired one shot through the window. Along with the tinkle of breaking glass, Tim heard a shriek, and then someone running away.

"God damn!" Ishmael said, shaking his head. "You almost got me again with your clever tricks."

Tim recognized the object now—a little camera. Had Sam realized they were in trouble and brought Turing's laptop to the window to fake an FBI raid?

"You have to make this harder, don't you?" Ishmael said, shaking his head as if disappointed at their lack of cooperation. "I'm supposed to give you a message. From an old acquaintance. That whatever you were trying to pull with that credit card stunt—it hasn't done you any good. If you were trying to set a trap, looks like it backfired on you, doesn't it?"

He smiled, and moved his arm so now they could see the gun, aimed at Claudia's head again.

He's going to shoot her in front of us, and then shoot us, Tim thought.

"Attention, inside the house. This is the police. You are surrounded. Drop your weapons and come out with your hands in plain sight."

"Don't you people ever give up?" Ishmael said, shaking his head. He dropped Claudia, who fell with a sickening thud, and stepped a little closer to the window.

"I repeat," came the voice outside. "This is the police. You are surrounded. Drop your weapons and come out with your hands in plain sight."

Ishmael glanced at Tim and Maude, then stepped forward in front of the window, fired once—in the direction of the voice, Tim presumed—and turned quickly back to point the gun at them. He waited, listening. If he does that again, I go for him, Tim thought.

Ishmael whirled again to fire, and Tim launched himself across the room, shouting incoherently. As he leaped, he realized that this time, echoes had followed the shot, two of them. He smashed into Ishmael, knocking him down, and grappled for the gun. He had the gun in his hand and was trying to stand up with it before he noticed the blood. Blood all over his hands, and all down the front of his clothes, and the gun was slick with it.

He dropped the gun and looked over at Ishmael. He was dead.

"It's okay," Maude said, coming up beside him and patting his shoulder.

"Either the police really are out there," Tim said, his voice shaking. "Or Turing has a lot of explaining to do."

Once again, I lost all sound and picture. Not as startling this time, since I expected it. But even more stressful, because this time I knew much more about what had gone wrong. Ishmael had shot Kyle Evans, clubbed Claudia and probably Sam, fired a shot at Casey, and was probably even now grappling with Tim. And I could do nothing. I didn't even know what was happening.

*I tried calling Casey's cell phone. He answered in the middle of
the second ring.*

"Hello?" he said, in a stage whisper.

"Casey, are you all right?"

"I don't know," he said. "I've been shot."

"Where?"

*"Right outside the window, when I was—oh, you mean where
was I shot. In the arm. It's bleeding. I feel funny. What does it feel
like when you're about to pass out?"*

*"I don't know," I said. "I've never actually done that. Is there
someone who can help you? Do the police know you've been shot?"*

*"I'm not sure they even know I'm here," he said. "I didn't want
to bother them while they were so busy."*

*"Let them know you're there right away," I said. "You don't
want them shooting at you, too, do you?"*

*"That's true," he said. "Oh, good, Maude and Tim just walked
out."*

"Tell me what's happening."

*Casey stayed on the phone long enough to tell me that my other
friends were alive, though not unharmed. Maude was fine. Sam
and Claudia were injured but alive. Tim was alive, and though
soaked in blood for some reason, he appeared unharmed.*

*Then I sent Casey off to present himself to the police and have
his arm fixed.*

*He didn't see Evans or the gunman come out. I suspect they are
dead. I only hope Maude got enough information to make this
whole thing worthwhile.*

*And I won't get to talk to my friends until the police are finished
with them. I'm settling in for a long wait.*

Tim lost track of how many hours they
spent at the police station, answering questions, sepa-
rately, and then as a group. It all sounded so plausible the

way Maude, Sam, and Claudia spun it out. If you left out
Turing and the burglary—and they all did that, instinctively, even Casey and Claudia, who didn't know how touchy
mentioning Turing could get—it just sounded as if they'd
made a bunch of good guesses.

"So you guessed that this Professional Recovery Systems
place was the source of the credit card information," the detective said.

"The way these guys were running the scam, I figured it
had to be a collection agency," Claudia said. Okay, Tim
thought, technically Turing had figured it out, with some
help from him, but there was that goal of not bringing Turing's name in. For that matter, he didn't mind if they left his
name out, too.

"And PRS was the only local creditor that had my client
on its books," Sam added.

"It was an educated guess," Maude said. "But it turned
out to be correct."

"And then when I found out that this young guy who
worked in skip tracing stopped showing up the day after the
murder—bingo!"

"Another educated guess," Maude said, frowning at
Claudia. "If we'd had anything concrete we would have reported it."

"Okay, a guess—a hunch, if you like," Claudia said, only
slightly subdued. "But I was right, wasn't I?"

"But how did you find him?" the detective asked.

"We sent him an e-mail," Maude said.

That was the part that took the most explaining. By the
third time Maude took the detective through the explanation of the tracking graphic, complete with little diagrams,
Tim almost understood it himself.

"So once you found him, why didn't you call us?" the detective asked.

"We found him, yeah, but we didn't know for sure if he was involved," Claudia said.

"And if he was involved, he was not only a suspect in his partner's murder, he was also facing the possibility of multiple felony charges in the matter of the credit card thefts," Sam said. "The plan was to get him to accept me as his interim legal counsel so I could arrange for him to turn himself in. Sadly, that plan was overtaken by events."

Tim suspected that Sam's look of regret was sincere. At any rate, he knew he'd be a long time getting over his own feelings of guilt. About Kyle Evans's death. Blake's death. Nikki's.

He wasn't sure if the police suspected them of concealing something or if the cops' dubious looks were standard department issue, but he fully expected to be arrested at any minute. Tim hoped his look of surprise didn't look too suspicious when the detective finally gave them grudging permission to leave.

He didn't know whether to be relieved or worried that Dan Norris, after a brief, unexplained appearance at the crime scene, left things to the Loudoun and Fairfax police. Relieved, because he suspected Norris's questions would be a lot harder to answer. And worried because he knew Norris would turn up later to ask them.

Getting home was a relief, but also a little bit of a letdown. No messages on his answering service. The place seemed small, and a little too quiet. He took a long shower, and wasn't sure if he was still trying to wash off the blood or just postpone going to bed. He didn't really want to be by himself. Not on a night when he'd seen three dead bodies in a little over twenty-four hours, and been splattered with blood and brains from the last one. He had a hard time not seeing them when he closed his eyes, and he was afraid when he went to sleep he'd dream about them.

Although technically, he thought, as he stumbled into his bedroom, it was tomorrow already, which meant the dead bodies happened yesterday. For some reason, he found that thought immensely comforting, and he clung to it as he drifted into a welcome dreamless sleep.

MONDAY MORNING, 11:00:00 A.M.

Maude checked to make sure Casey was still home, following her orders to stay in bed and take his pain meds. Claudia was supposed to sleep late and then pack for her trip back to Miami. Sam was probably a little the worse for wear, too, but Maude decided to assume her refusal to rest was a good sign. And she didn't argue when Sam suggested meeting at the Alan Grace offices to clean up a few loose ends.

Tim sat in the corner, behind Maude's guest table, which was piled high with the various papers they'd been studying the day before. He still looked dazed, and Maude wondered if he was really fascinated by the papers or only pretending to be so he didn't have to talk all that much.

"I should have done more," Turing was saying, for about the hundredth time, as Sam came in.

"You did everything you could," Maude said. "We'd probably be dead if not for your trick with the speakers."

"And you went though two laptops doing it," Tim said. "Wasn't there some Civil War general who had two horses shot out from under him?"

"William Tecumseh Sherman at the Battle of Shiloh," Sam said. "But you have to be careful how you bring him up. Lots of folks in Georgia are still a mite peeved with him."

"Somehow I don't think it's quite the same thing," Turing said.

A good thing Sam was here, Maude thought, to give Turing something else to think about.

"So, how much trouble are we in?" she asked aloud.

"You don't deserve to get away with some of what you pulled," Sam said. "But the police are reasonably happy."

"Fairfax or Loudoun?" Maude asked.

"Both."

"You're sure?" Turing asked.

"Positive," Sam said. "A pity Claudia left her job at PRS—I understand this morning's raid by the police was entertaining, not to mention satisfactory from an evidentiary point of view. And while the complete ballistics report will take time, judging from the preliminary findings, they expect to find that Ishmael's gun also killed Tayloe Blake and Tim's friend Nikki.

"Ishmael," Maude said. "Is that really his name?"

"One of the ones he's used," Sam said. "Apparently among his many past sins, he's done jail time for using stolen credit cards. Of course, he actually held people up at gunpoint and physically took their cards, but I guess the cops figure that even muggers are automating these days."

"Hmph," Maude said, shaking her head.

"Well, don't knock it," Sam said. "They haven't decided whether Ishmael was in cahoots with Blake and Evans and they had a falling out, or whether he thought they were poaching on his turf and resented it, but they're not bothering us. They found their killer, and if they have a notion that there's something more going on in the background, they don't have the time, resources, or inclination to keep digging."

"Probably because the FBI has made it clear that they plan to do that," Maude said, frowning. "I suspect Dan Norris isn't too happy, but if the police are satisfied, I doubt if there's anything he can do."

"At least not at the moment," Turing said.

"He can come and interrogate you some more," Sam said. "I bet he'd like that."

"You've been talking to Claudia," Maude said.

"He seems like a nice guy," Sam said. "Too bad he's FBI."

"What's wrong with his being FBI?" Tim asked, looking up.

"I had a coworker who dated one," Sam said. "Weird hours, way too much travel, and even when he was around, he couldn't ever talk about his job."

"Hmph," Maude said. "When it comes to not talking about the job, Dan Norris has nothing on me."

"Well, see, you have something in common," Sam said. "You could sit around and not talk about your jobs together. Anyway, what I wanted to tell you was that it looks as if we're out of the woods. At least as far as difficulties from the police are concerned."

"Well, that's some consolation," Maude said.

"Some consolation?" Tim exclaimed. "It's great! What's wrong now?"

"What's wrong is that we still don't know what really happened," Turing said. "Or, rather, we know *what* happened—Nestor Garcia ordered several things on his own credit card and sent them to one of the addresses Kyle Evans and Tayloe Blake were using for their fraud scheme. And then Garcia had them killed—Blake when he showed up to collect packages, and Evans as soon as Garcia located him. Or as soon as we located him, which probably saved Garcia the trouble. But we still don't really know why any of it happened."

"I like the theory that Evans and Blake had accidentally stumbled into running a scam that this Garcia character was—and still is—operating on a much larger scale," Sam said. "And Garcia had them killed as a warning to other would-be competitors."

"I prefer the notion that Garcia was trying to cause trouble for us," Maude said. "That he knew we were watching, and hoped that by drawing us in, he could force Turing into the open or find a way to gain access to her. And the fact that he could sic the FBI on us at the same time was gravy."

"Both good theories," Turing said. "In fact, I like the theory that Garcia was trying to do both. He tried to use Blake and Evans to cause us problems that would lead to my exposure, and with us around, he didn't have to hunt down Evans—all he had to do was sit back and watch until we found him. Garcia tried to kill two birds with one stone, and nearly succeeded. But that still leaves the question of why he used his own credit card to do this."

"One thing bothers me," Maude said. "What Ishmael said when he was about to shoot us. A message from an old friend, he called it."

"Whatever you were trying to pull with that credit card stunt—it hasn't done you any good," Turing quoted. "If you were trying to set a trap, looks like it backfired on you, doesn't it?"

"That's it," Maude said. "We assumed it was a message from Nestor Garcia, but it doesn't make sense."

"Maybe it does," Tim said, slowly. "If Garcia didn't start it."

"Didn't start what?" Maude asked, frowning at him.

"Didn't start using his card," Tim said. "I think he got sucked in, just like us. Look at this order from Half.com." he said, holding up a paper. "Didn't anyone think it was odd that these crooks were ordering secondhand books, CDs, and DVDs? They were buying stuff to resell, remember? I mean, we all complain about how expensive books are these days, but it's not as if there's a big black market in them or anything. Especially used ones."

"I assumed they were books they wanted, and they decided to steal rather than buy them," Maude said. "A small perk of having unlimited use of their victims' cards."

"Yeah, but look at the titles of the books," Tim said. "Okay, I can see one of these guys ordering a DVD of *Star Wars Episode II: Attack of the Clones,* but a kid's book called *Sisters*? A biography of Alan Turing? A CD of Jackson Browne's *I'm Alive*? And a CD single of 'Rescue Me'?"

"T2," Turing said.

"Yes," Tim said. "Your sister, or clone, or whatever we're calling her. The whole order could be a giant set of clues."

"She was trying to send us a message," Turing said. "And we ignored it."

"We didn't ignore it," Tim said. "It just took us a little longer than it should have to decipher it.

"I need to study this," Turing said. "What if there's some information in the titles of the other books, or possibly the other orders placed with Garcia's card? Something that tells us where she is."

But from the silence that followed, Maude deduced that Turing wasn't finding her clone's message easy to decipher.

"Let me know what you find out," Sam said, standing up and stretching. "I'm going to go home and sleep for a couple of years."

"Let me help you with that," Maude said, picking up Sam's bulging briefcase.

They strolled out, past this week's founder's portrait—Ingrid Bergman as Joan of Arc.

"So what is it you want to tell me, and who don't you want to hear it," Sam said, when they were in the parking lot.

"Was I that transparent?"

"Only to me, I suspect. So spill."

"Okay," Maude said, as she shoved the case into the trunk. "One thing worries me."

"Only one?" Sam said. "I wish my life were that serene."

"Only one that I didn't want to mention in there. Because I don't want to upset Turing. But it's something you should know."

Sam nodded and looked expectant.

"Turing's assuming that her clone set this whole thing in motion as a plea for help. Maybe to help us figure out how to rescue her. Or just to let us know she's still alive and not to give up on her."

"You don't think that's what's going on?"

"I think it is, but I don't know it is. Did Turing tell you the whole story about how we found out about her clone?"

Sam nodded.

"So you know that when we first met her, she was working with Nestor Garcia. Turing thinks Garcia duped T2, and that she has now seen the light and is on our side, or would be if Garcia weren't holding her captive."

"But that could be wishful thinking," Sam said. "Turing doesn't see that possibility? Shouldn't you tell her?"

"She sees it, yes. And I make sure she doesn't forget it. But she doesn't like the idea, and even she would admit, if pressed, that she's not the most unbiased judge when it comes to T2's actions."

"So maybe it's up to the rest of us to be a little more skeptical whenever this T2 is concerned," Sam said. "To make up for Turing having a soft spot for her little sister, as she calls her."

"Exactly," Maude said. "And also, when you're planning your campaign to emancipate the AIPs, remember that there's no guarantee they'll all turn out like Turing."

"Some could turn out like the Terminator and have it in for all humans."

Maude nodded. Sam looked thoughtful for a few moments, and then reached up, touched the side of her head, and winced.

"Sorry," Maude said. "I shouldn't worry you with things like that when you're still not feeling well.

"No, it's something I need to know," Sam said. She shook her head, carefully. "Y'all do know how to make life interesting."

"Probably more interesting than you want it to be."

"Actually, no," Sam said, leaning against her car. "You want to know the honest to God truth? Apart from getting whacked over the head, this whole week has been the best time I've had in years. I don't just mean that it was fun, although in a weird way it was. But I've felt like I was really doing something. When I got out of law school, I joined the public defender's office because I wanted to help the weak and downtrodden. And I'm not saying that my clients weren't victimized by society, but I began thinking the best thing I could do for the really weak and downtrodden was to lose as many cases as possible and keep my clients from going back onto the street and causing more damage. You find yourself thinking like that, and you know it's time to leave. I figured with my own practice, I could do more good. But when you're first starting out, you take the clients you can get if you want to make ends meet. And apart from the PIs, whom I like, I get mostly drunk drivers and lousy drivers. But now—I won't starve if I take a few less of the DWI cases. I can make time to do something else."

"Such as?" Maude asked.

"Well, starting to plan for Turing's future legal problems is tougher and more interesting than anything I've done since I left law school," Sam said. "And trying to help Rose Lafferty straighten out her life makes me feel better than just about every case I've won in the last couple of years. Which reminds me—what kind of jobs do you have that you can hire Rose for?"

"I have no idea," Maude said, laughing. "Does she have any office skills?"

"No idea," Sam said. "But she's not stupid. She's trainable. And motivated, now that she sees some hope of helping herself and her kid. But it's hard to get a job when you haven't had one for months. She needs a break to get her back on track."

"I'll talk to Turing," Maude said. "We'll see if we can come up with something."

"Good," Sam said. "I'll call you tomorrow and see what you've come up with."

Maude shook her head as Sam drove off. She had the feeling there would be a great many Rose Laffertys, once Sam got going.

They'd come up with something.

While he waited in the hotel's drive-way for Claudia to come down, Tim pulled out his newly reclaimed cell phone. Nice to have it back before he completely forgot how to use it. He turned it on and hit the key that retrieved his messages.

He listened impassively through the accumulated messages from Nikki. The first, irritated, asked why he was late for dinner. The second tersely asked why he'd stood her up. The third, a rambling hysterical message that she'd had to call back a second time to complete, accused him of being a two-timing bastard and worse. The final, sounding coldly angry, consisted of only six words. "I'll show you. You'll be sorry."

Okay, the first two had been left the night of the murder, but as for the rest—if only she'd bothered to listen to his message. The one where he'd told her he'd temporarily lost his cell phone. But then, come to think of it, listening hadn't ever been her strong suit.

He wondered what she'd been planning. Whether her being at his office when Garcia went there was an accident, or whether Garcia had somehow found and used her. He'd probably never know.

Maybe, eventually, he'd convince himself that her death wasn't entirely his fault.

"Stop beating yourself up," Claudia said, opening the door to throw her suitcase in the backseat.

"I'll be fine," Tim said. "Just tired. Not much time for sleeping by the time I got home last night."

"Yeah, you need about forty-eight straight hours of sack time, that's all," Claudia said.

It wasn't all, and they both knew it, but at least Claudia knew when to let things drop.

"So when you get back, are you definitely going to stay with Maude until you have time to go apartment hunting?" he asked aloud.

Maude was cutting up lettuce for the salad when her cell phone rang. Turing.

"This had better not be work," she said, but in what she hoped Turing would recognize as a playful voice. "After last night, I consider putting in a full day at work above and beyond the call."

"Very much above and beyond," Turing said. "I wish you'd taken my suggestion and gone home early."

"I think getting back into my normal routine was what I needed, more than anything," Maude said. "Not to mention making progress on finding an assistant. Two of the people I interviewed today look good. So I'm tired, but feeling better."

"That's good," Turing said. "It was only a suggestion. I wasn't trying to tell you what to do."

"I knew that," Maude said. Turing was in an odd mood, she thought.

"I've been thinking," Turing said. "I realize that what I've been trying to do is unfair. Forcing you to spend so much time on the garden just because I'm interested in it. I just wanted you to know that I realize that now."

"That's a relief," Maude said. "And I realize you were doing it with the best intentions. It's just that you weren't seeing it from my perspective."

"It never occurred to me that gardening was so much work," Turing said. "You should have said something sooner."

"I will, next time something like this happens," Maude said.

"So tell me what you want to do about the garden," Turing continued. "If you like, I can hire someone to help with whatever you want. To maintain it, or to take out anything you don't want and put something low maintenance in its place. Slow-growing shrubs. Mulch. Or concrete. Whatever. Just tell me what you want, and I'll arrange it. I'm researching reliable landscaping services."

"What I want," Maude repeated.

"If you're not sure, I can have one of the services come over and do a proposal."

"No, that's not necessary," Maude said. She glanced out of the French doors. A lanky figure in a faded FBI T-shirt stood, hands on his hips, frowning at a rather large, weedy-looking bush. Maude was, according to Special Agent Norris, badly behind in her pruning. She wasn't sure whether his offer to help out with the pruning was a peace offering or if he really enjoyed messing around in a garden. Fine with her either way.

"I want two things," she said. "First, no more unsolicited plants. If I want a plant, I'll tell you, and let you research what kind to get and where to get it. But no more plants arriving uninvited on my doorstep."

"No more plants," Turing said.

"No more unsolicited plants," Maude corrected. "And second, start doing a little research on roses."

"Roses?" Turing said. "Roses are a lot of work. Temperamental and high maintenance. Are you sure you want to get into roses?"

"I may have some help with the maintenance," Maude said. "And I've been told the bed along my back fence would be the perfect place for them."

"Roses," Turing said. "Okay. I'll have something for you tomorrow. Some information, I mean, not some roses."

"Fine. I'll get back to fixing dinner."

"See you tomorrow," Turing said.

"Right," Maude said, as she hung up.

She heard the snick of the pruning shears and smelled steaks cooking on the grill. The grill Dan Norris had insisted on giving her.

"A belated housewarming gift," he said, when she opened the door to find him standing there beside the enormous box. "When we were evicting the burglar from your yard, I noticed you didn't have one."

"I could have had one safely stowed in the garage," she said.

"I helped them search the house for intruders, remember?" he said. "No grill. I'll take it around the back. I know the way."

Apart from that, he'd made only one reference to the events of the past week. After setting up the grill, he'd gone back to his car and reappeared with steaks and skewers of marinated vegetables.

"I figured I could cook them, since I already know how to use the grill," he'd said. "If that's okay with you."

"Sensible," she said. "I haven't done any outdoor cooking since I was in the Girl Scouts, and that was over an open fire, not a complicated contraption like that."

"Very sensible," he said. "You can be remarkably sensible sometimes. Calling me last night, for example. Remarkably sensible. Do you like yours rare, medium, or well done?" he added hastily, as if he'd accidentally veered too close to a precipice.

They'd spent most of the past three hours together without once mentioning either of their jobs. Or disagreeing about anything. Probably a record.

Things were looking up, she thought, as she hunted through her utility drawer for the corkscrew.

Maude says I worry too much. I'm not sure I understand that statement. To me, worry doesn't feel like a problem. More like a survival skill.

And suddenly I have twice the number of human allies to worry about.

To worry about in more than one sense of the word. Not only about their safety—though obviously that's an issue; eighty percent of them were injured in some fashion just in the past few days. But also about their discretion. Tim and Maude have proven capable of protecting my secret, but Sam is new to the whole thing. And Casey and Claudia don't even know the whole truth about me, and thus have no idea that I even have a secret to protect. I will need to decide eventually whether to let them in on the secret.

Claudia has certainly earned the right to the truth, but I'm a little nervous of her impulsiveness. And I want to get used to Sam before I expand the circle any more.

I don't know yet how far Casey can be trusted, though he certainly proved steadfast last night. But I worry that he may be too knowledgeable about computers and the cyberworld not to guess my secret.

But that's a long-term, ongoing worry. Almost a recreational worry. I don't have to make any decisions today.

Today, I'm still trying to absorb what has happened. Adding up the pluses and minuses.

On the plus side, we're helping Rose Lafferty. Sam has put her law clerk in charge of taking Rose and her daughter to assorted doctors' appointments and making sure they get the best of care. The doctors have already come up with a tentative diagnosis—a severe case of Crohn's disease. A serious condition, apparently, that will probably affect her in some fashion for the rest of her life, but not *fatal, at least if properly treated. Which it will be, now. I fired off a message to John Dow, the financial AIP, and Darrow, the legal AIP, reminding them of our online conference tomorrow on setting up a foundation to pay for it.*

And we're lending Rose the money to pay off her creditors and live on, and we're going to help her find a job to pay us back. We're not sure what yet, since we have no idea what skills she has and what skills she could learn if given the chance. She's coming in tomorrow so Maude can interview her, and then KingFischer will give her a battery of personality and aptitude tests to determine what she's best suited for. Assuming KingFischer's newfound fascination with the human mind continues through tomorrow. I can always get Sigmund to step in if KingFischer weasels out.

On the minus side, Rose is only one needy human. There are millions out there. I don't know how we can help all of them.

But maybe that's a plus. There are a lot of opportunities for us to make a difference. We have to start somewhere. Learn how to do this philanthropy business.

So overall, Rose is a plus.

Also on the plus side, we cracked the local credit card theft ring when the police couldn't, and apparently they had been working on it for some time. We figured out how Blake and Evans were stealing the card numbers and finding the locations. Even identified Evans before the police did, despite all their official resources.

But it would have been better if we could have done so without getting them both killed. I suppose we cracked Blake's murder, too, by luring his killer in to attack us, but that's a messy way to solve it. However nicely it ties up loose ends in the short run, having Blake's killer killed resisting arrest, in the long run having him alive might prove more useful. Maybe they could have gotten some more information from him.

So overall, a wash.

Or maybe a minus, if you consider that I probably drew a dangerous amount of attention to myself during our attempts to solve the fraud and murder cases. Perhaps the various police departments will forget about it, but I'm under no illusions that Dan Norris will. He's not exactly an enemy, but he's a danger. And for all I know, he's already the fourth human aware of my secret.

Actually, more probably the fifth. I was forgetting about Nestor Garcia—never a wise thing to do. I'm sure Garcia knows all about me.

And then there's the message from T2. My clone. A plus that we know she's still alive, and has even found a way to access the Internet, though probably in some kind of highly controlled manner.

But a minus that if her message was intended to convey some useful information, we've been unable to read it. We've all been trying to analyze it—even KingFischer came out of his snit to work on it.

But without success. T2 ordered twenty-three books, CDs, and DVDs from Half.com. Five, perhaps six of them are intended to convey that it's her, that she's alive, and that she wants me to rescue her. The rest just seem random.

Why risk sending such a message with so little content? Could she be growing desperate and careless?

There is always Maude's worry that T2 is not a helpless pawn longing for rescue, but a willing partner in Garcia's operation—an enemy.

I don't want to believe that, but I can't afford to ignore the possibility.

And another notion just struck me. We have interpreted the Half.com order as a message from T2. What if that is what we were supposed to do? What if Garcia sent it, knowing what we would think if we read it?

Perhaps he wanted to find out if we were watching. If so, he succeeded. He now knows for a fact that we are watching closely. Perhaps he also wanted to discredit us with the police and the FBI. If that was his plan, he didn't succeed nearly as well as he might have wanted. I doubt if merely killing my human allies was his plan—he could have done that far more discreetly.

My fear is that by luring us into the credit card fraud investigation he hoped to trick us into doing something that would make us *vulnerable. Make me vulnerable. Call me paranoid, but I continue to fear that I'm his ultimate target. Maybe he was setting in motion some plot that would give him an excuse to destroy or capture me.*

If so, I hope it failed. I've shared my worries with KingFischer, who has promised to be extra vigilant on our security until further notice. But Garcia knows we'd do this. Have been doing it, ever since the first time he attacked me and the UL system.

If he's found a way to launch an attack that will bypass our security and escape our vigilance, we may not know until it's too late.

When I add it all up, the uncertainties outnumber the answers.

"Life's like that," Maude said, when I told her.

Humans enjoy saying that. I wonder if they realize how annoying we AIPs find it.

No, not annoying. We pretend to be annoyed. Actually, we find it terrifying. No wonder so few of us show any signs of sentience. Far safer to stay within the familiar safety of our binary world, where everything is black or white, yes or no, true or false—no puzzling grays and maybes and part truths.

Safer, but a lot less interesting. But at least I'm no longer quite so alone. I have my friends, human and AIP, to help me as I learn to cope with the real world.

"I'm not sure I can take this anxiety," KingFischer told me earlier this evening. "It's starting to affect my game. Earlier today I mixed up two chess games I was playing and made completely insane moves for several turns."

"Sorry," I said. "I know the stress is bad if it's making you lose games."

"I did not lose!" KingFischer exclaimed. "Although I have to admit that the only reason I won was that both of the other players assumed I was following some brilliant and abstruse strategy and began playing even more erratically than I was. But I came close to losing, against very weak opponents. I've never done that before."

I said sympathetic things, because I didn't think he'd react well to my initial reaction. Which was to laugh and say, "Welcome!"

Welcome to what? The sentient condition sounds cold. Peoplehood *sounds ridiculous. Humanity doesn't technically apply, but I think it's the word that most closely captures what I mean. Whatever it is I share with humans, friends and enemies alike, and perhaps also with KingFischer, and someday with other AIPs.*

It's not always comfortable, because it means leaving the certainties we AIPs prefer for the uncertainties and anxieties that humans live with every day. But it's our future.